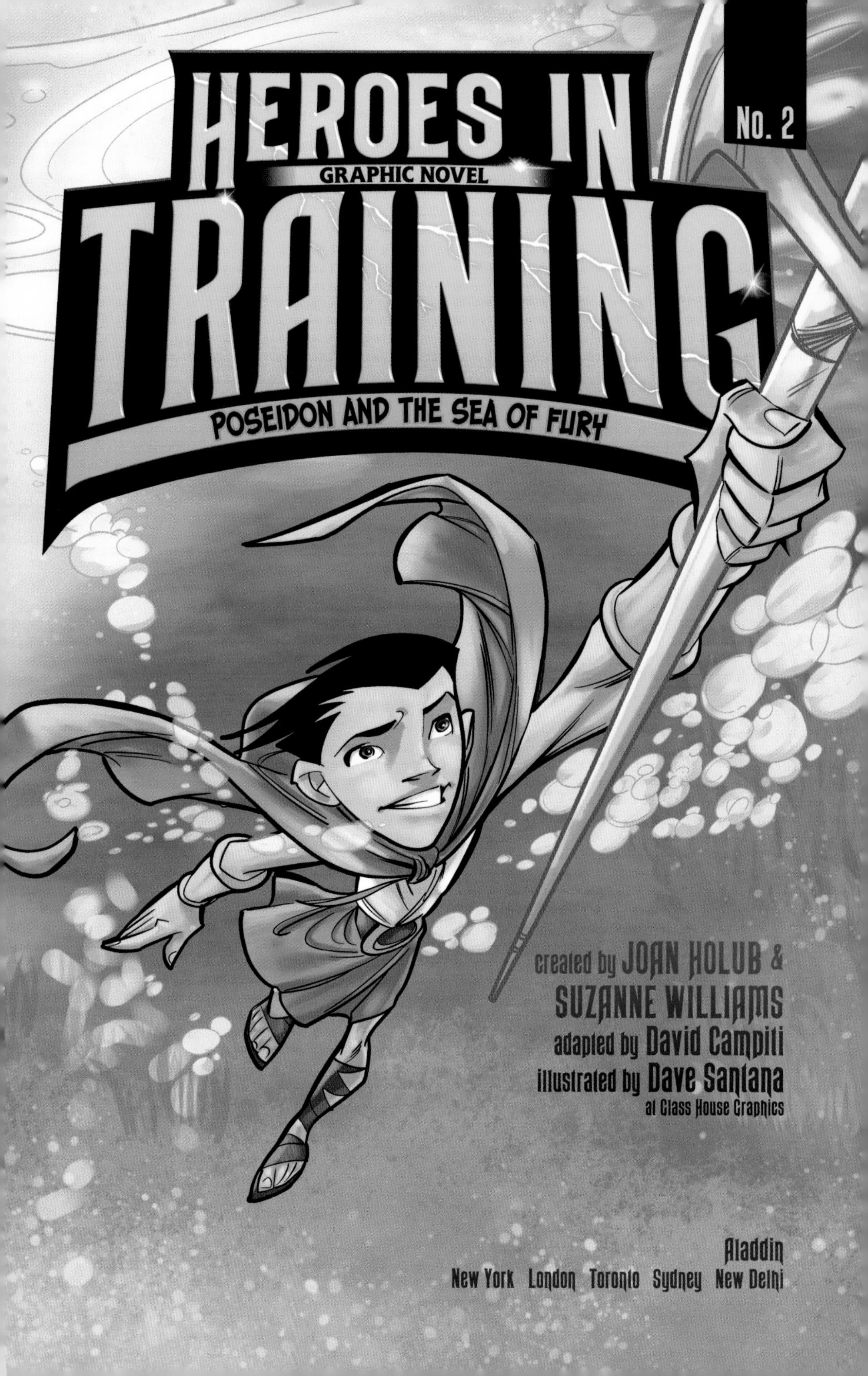
HEROES IN TRAINING
GRAPHIC NOVEL
No. 2
POSEIDON AND THE SEA OF FURY
created by JOAN HOLUB & SUZANNE WILLIAMS
adapted by David Campiti
illustrated by Dave Santana
at Glass House Graphics
Aladdin
New York London Toronto Sydney New Delhi

ALADDIN
An imprint of Simon & Schuster Children's Publishing Division
1230 Avenue of the Americas, New York, New York 10020
First Aladdin edition February 2022
Text copyright © 2022 by Joan Holub and Suzanne Williams
Illustrations copyright © 2022 by Glass House Graphics
Art by Dave Santana. Inks by Flávio Soares with João Zod and Juan Araujo. Colors by Felipe Felix and João Zod. Lettering by Marcos Inoue. Art services by Glass House Graphics.
For information about special discounts for bulk purchases, please contact Simon & Schuster Special Sales at 1-866-506-1949 or business@simonandschuster.com.
The Simon & Schuster Speakers Bureau can bring authors to your live event. For more information or to book an event contact the Simon & Schuster Speakers Bureau at 1-866-248-3049 or visit our website at www.simonspeakers.com.
Designed by Nicholas Sciacca
The text of this book was set in CCMonologus.
Manufactured in China 1121 SCP
10 9 8 7 6 5 4 3 2 1
Library of Congress Cataloging-in-Publication Data
Names: Holub, Joan, author. • Williams, Suzanne, 1953- author. • Campiti, David, contributor. • Glass House Graphics, illustrator. • Title: Poseidon and the sea of fury / created by Joan Holub and Suzanne Williams ; adapted by David Campiti ; illustrated by Dave Santana at Glass House Graphics. • Description: First Aladdin hardcover edition. • New York : Aladdin, 2022. • Series: Heroes in training graphic novel ; book 2 • Audience: Ages 8 to 12 • Summary: Young Poseidon must overcome his fear of the sea and its creatures to save a fellow Olympian. • Identifiers: LCCN 2021015452 (print) • LCCN 2021015453 (ebook) • ISBN 9781534481183 (hardcover) • ISBN 9781534481176 (paperback) • ISBN 9781534481190 (ebook) • Subjects: LCSH: Poseidon (Greek deity)—Comic books, strips, etc. • Poseidon (Greek deity)—Juvenile Fiction. • Gods, Greek—Comic books, strips, etc. • Gods, Greek—Juvenile Fiction. • Mythology, Greek—Comic books, strips, etc. • Mythology, Greek—Juvenile Fiction. • Adventure stories. • Graphic novels. • CYAC: Graphic novels. • Poseidon (Greek deity)—Fiction. • Gods, Greek—Fiction. • Mythology, Greek—Fiction. • Adventure and adventurers—Fiction. • Holub, Joan. Poseidon and the sea of fury—Adaptations. • LCGFT: Graphic novels. • Action and adventure fiction. • Classification: LCC PZ7.7.H656 Po 2022 (print) • LCC PZ7.7.H656 (ebook)
DDC 741.5/973—dc23
LC record available at https://lccn.loc.gov/2021015452
LC ebook record available at https://lccn.loc.gov/2021015453

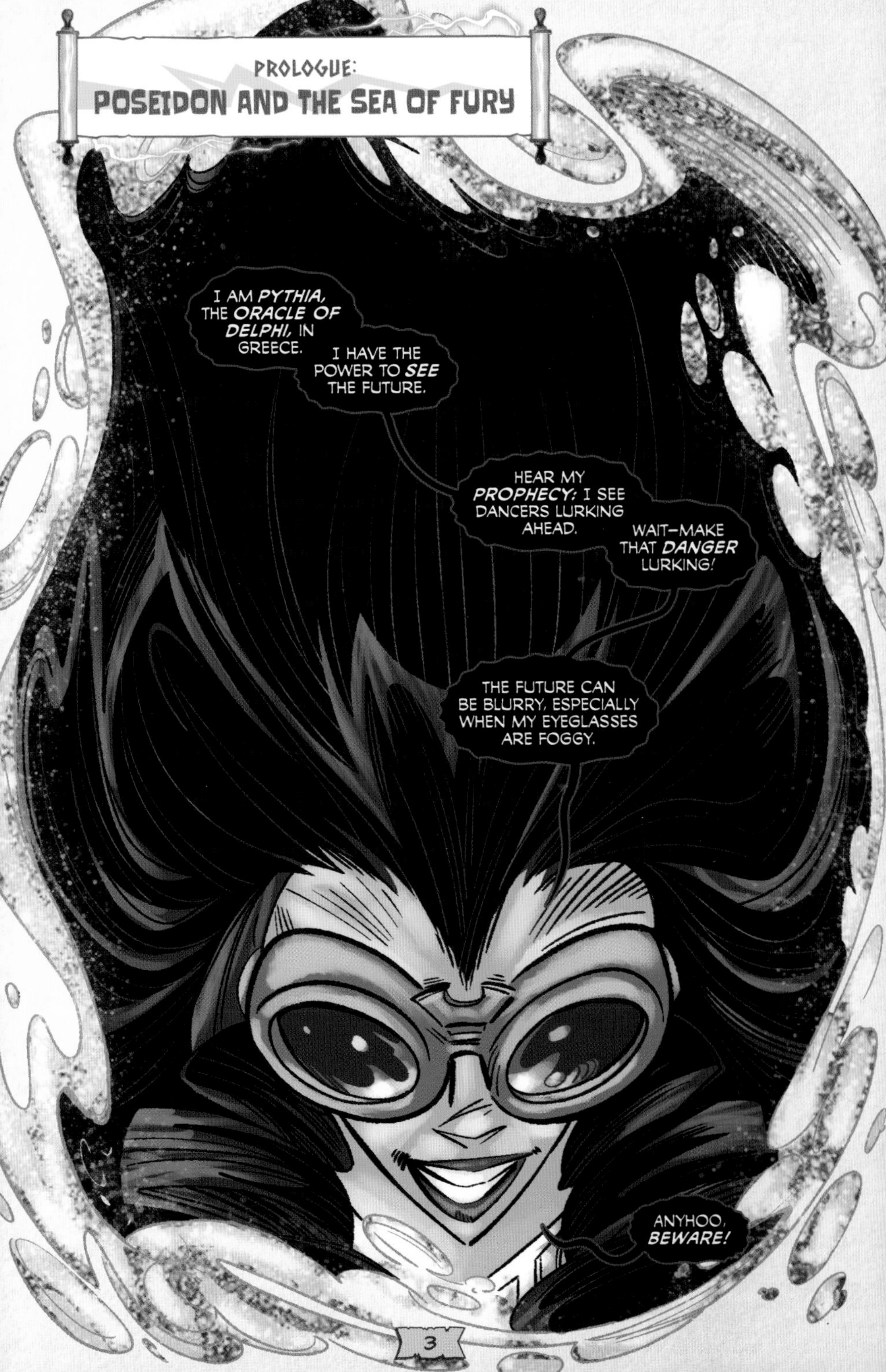
PROLOGUE:
POSEIDON AND THE SEA OF FURY
I AM PYTHIA, THE ORACLE OF DELPHI, IN GREECE.
I HAVE THE POWER TO SEE THE FUTURE.
HEAR MY PROPHECY: I SEE DANCERS LURKING AHEAD.
WAIT—MAKE THAT DANGER LURKING!
THE FUTURE CAN BE BLURRY, ESPECIALLY WHEN MY EYEGLASSES ARE FOGGY.
ANYHOO, BEWARE!

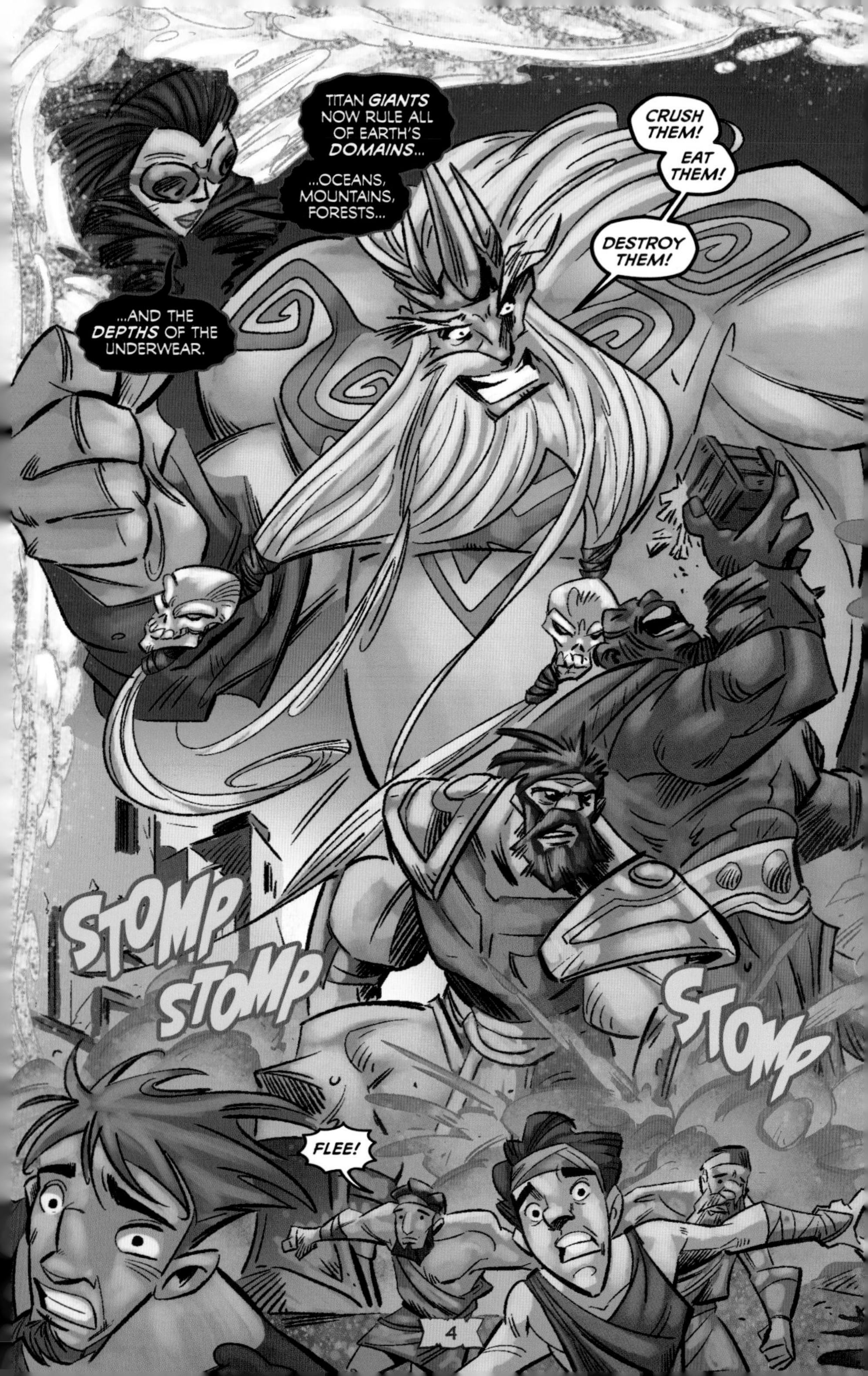
TITAN GIANTS NOW RULE ALL OF EARTH'S DOMAINS...
...OCEANS, MOUNTAINS, FORESTS...
...AND THE DEPTHS OF THE UNDERWEAR.
CRUSH THEM!
EAT THEM!
DESTROY THEM!
STOMP
STOMP
STOMP
FLEE!

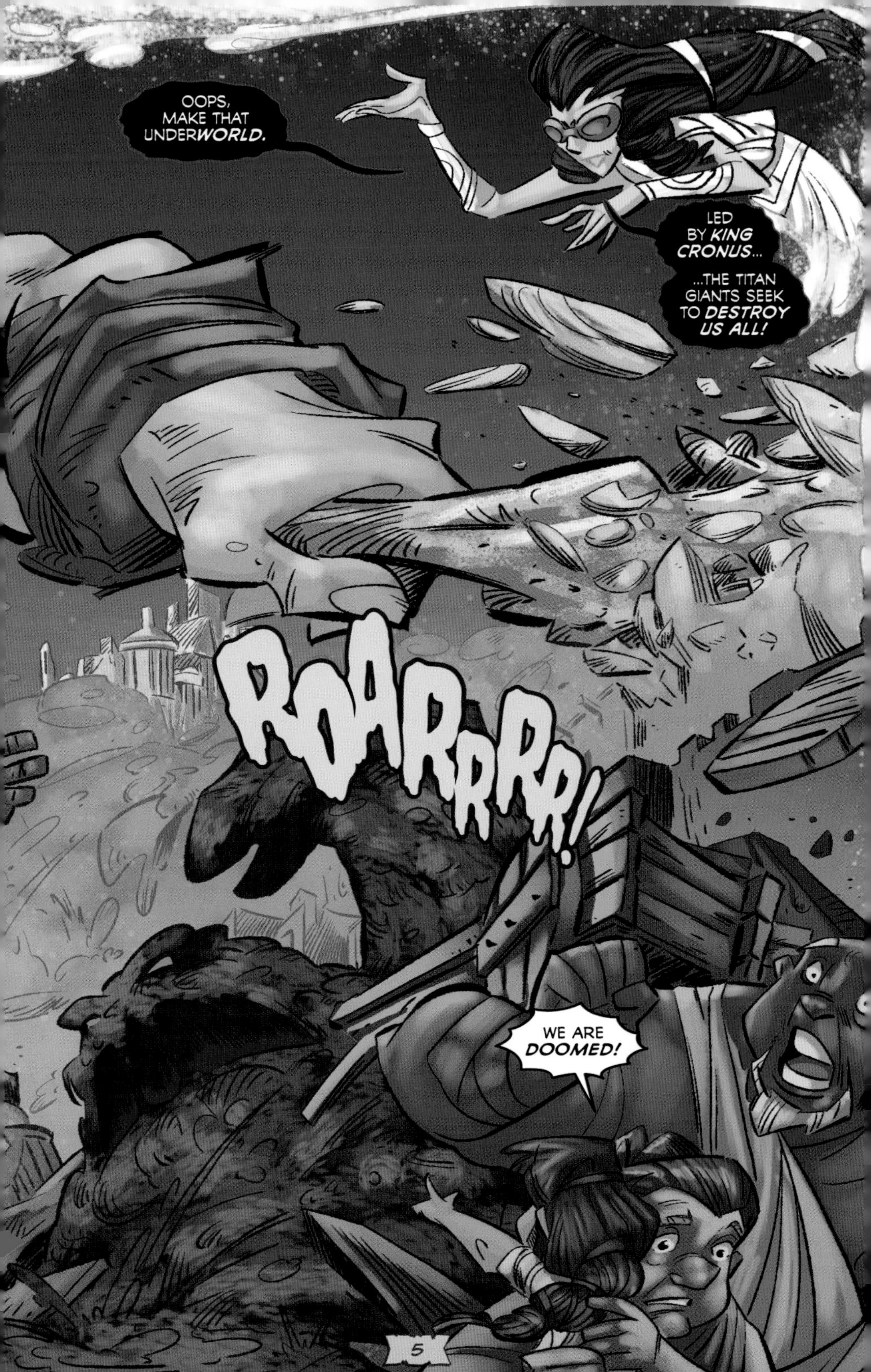
OOPS, MAKE THAT UNDERWORLD.
LED BY KING CRONUS...
...THE TITAN GIANTS SEEK TO DESTROY US ALL!
ROARRRR!
WE ARE DOOMED!

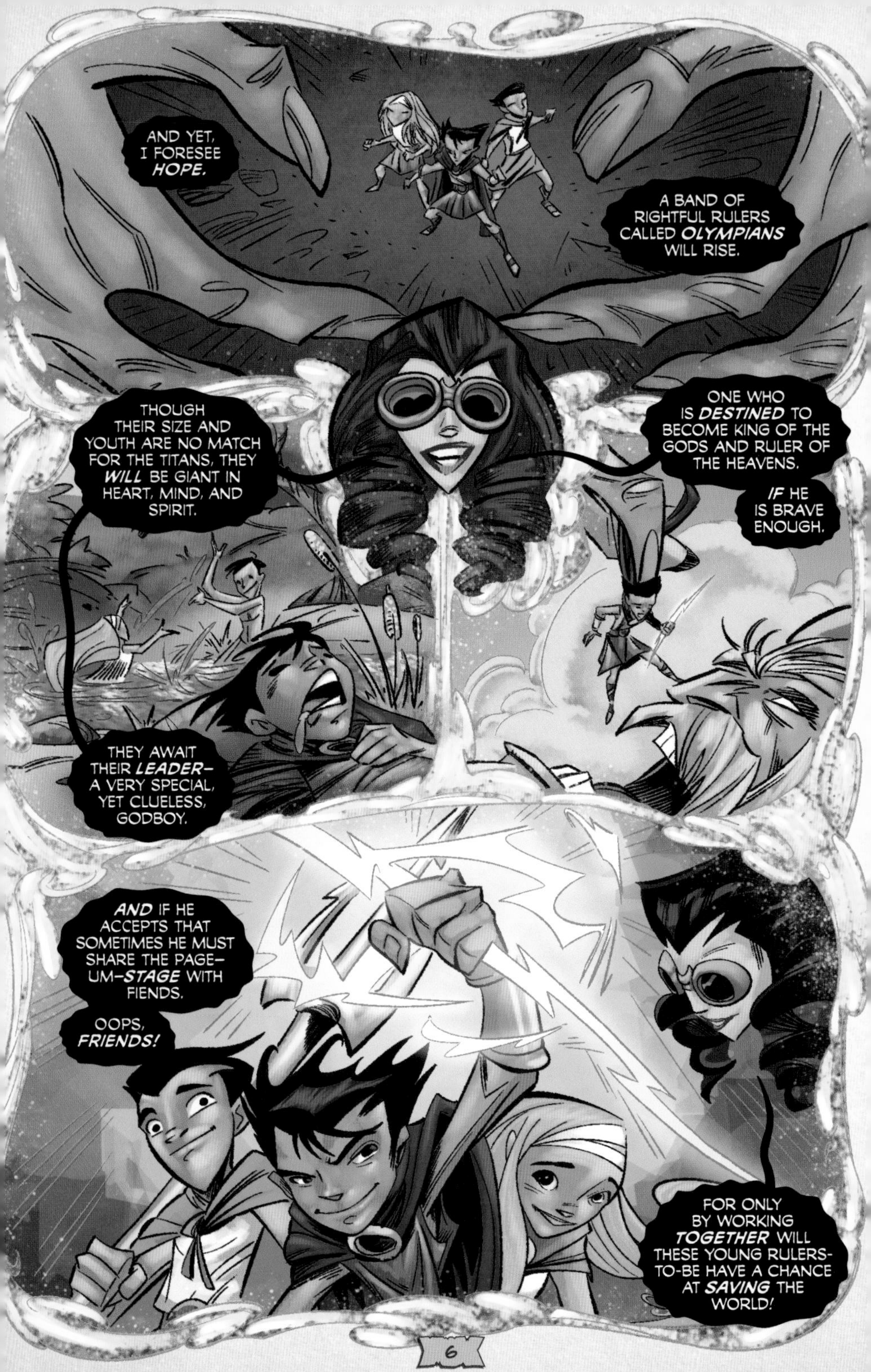
AND YET, I FORESEE HOPE.
A BAND OF RIGHTFUL RULERS CALLED OLYMPIANS WILL RISE.
THOUGH THEIR SIZE AND YOUTH ARE NO MATCH FOR THE TITANS, THEY WILL BE GIANT IN HEART, MIND, AND SPIRIT.
ONE WHO IS DESTINED TO BECOME KING OF THE GODS AND RULER OF THE HEAVENS.
IF HE IS BRAVE ENOUGH.
THEY AWAIT THEIR LEADER— A VERY SPECIAL, YET CLUELESS, GODBOY.
AND IF HE ACCEPTS THAT SOMETIMES HE MUST SHARE THE PAGE— UM—STAGE WITH FIENDS.
OOPS, FRIENDS!
FOR ONLY BY WORKING TOGETHER WILL THESE YOUNG RULERS-TO-BE HAVE A CHANCE AT SAVING THE WORLD!

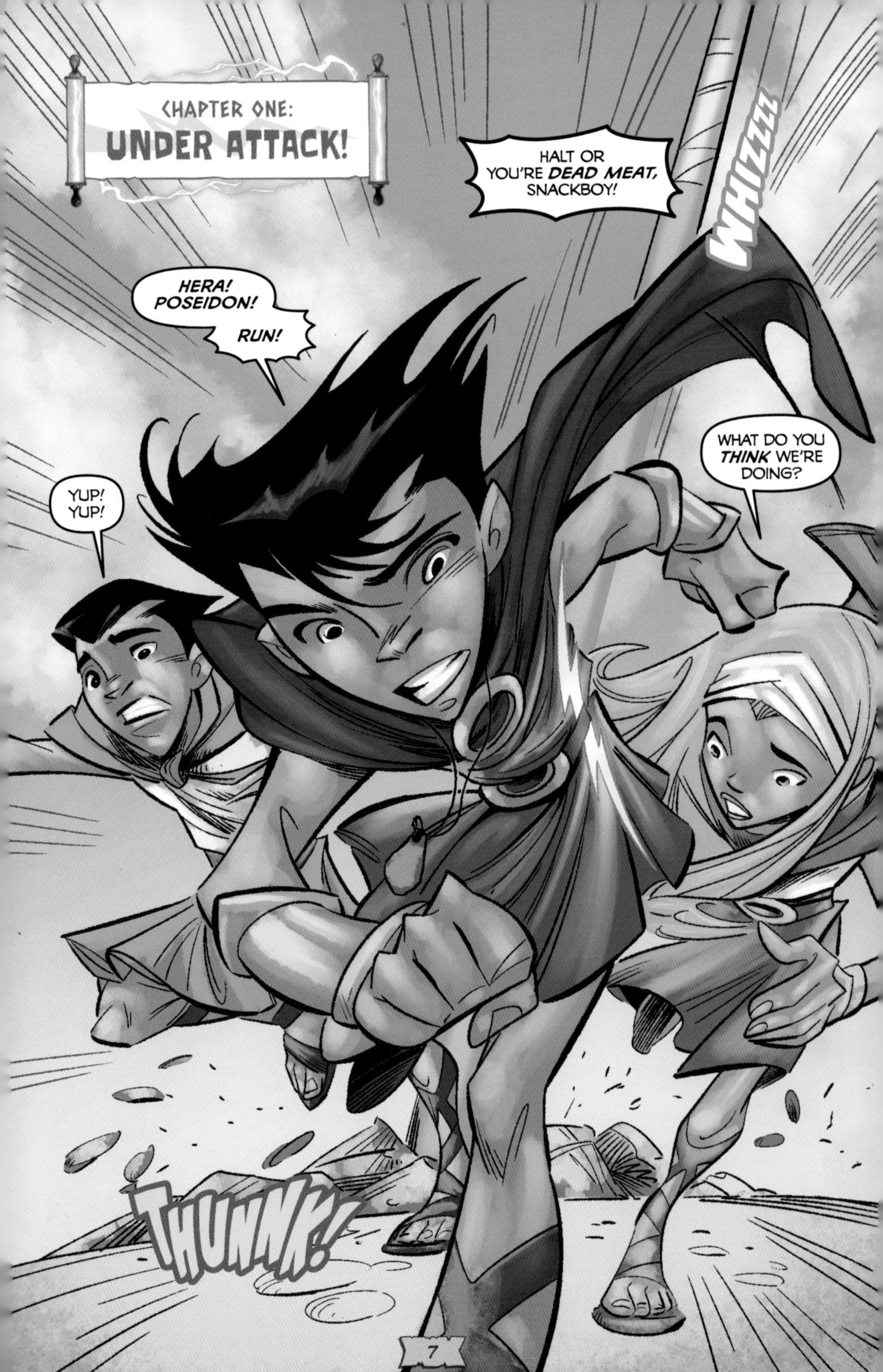
CHAPTER ONE:
UNDER ATTACK!
HALT OR YOU'RE DEAD MEAT, SNACKBOY!
WHIZZZZ
HERA! POSEIDON!
RUN!
WHAT DO YOU THINK WE'RE DOING?
YUP! YUP!
THUNNK!

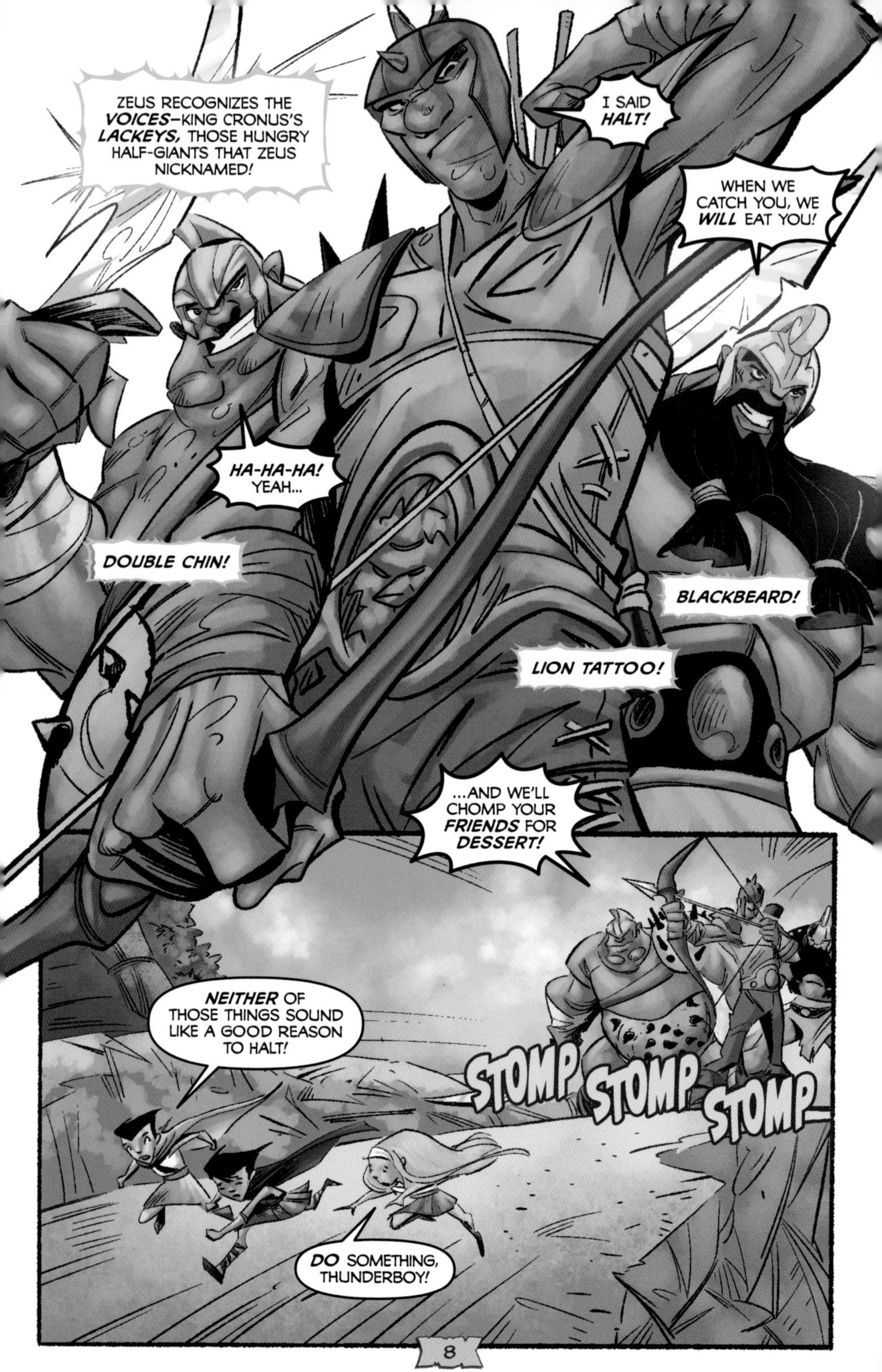
ZEUS RECOGNIZES THE VOICES—KING CRONUS'S LACKEYS, THOSE HUNGRY HALF-GIANTS THAT ZEUS NICKNAMED!
I SAID HALT!
WHEN WE CATCH YOU, WE WILL EAT YOU!
HA-HA-HA! YEAH...
DOUBLE CHIN!
BLACKBEARD!
LION TATTOO!
...AND WE'LL CHOMP YOUR FRIENDS FOR DESSERT!
NEITHER OF THOSE THINGS SOUND LIKE A GOOD REASON TO HALT!
STOMP STOMP STOMP
DO SOMETHING, THUNDERBOY!

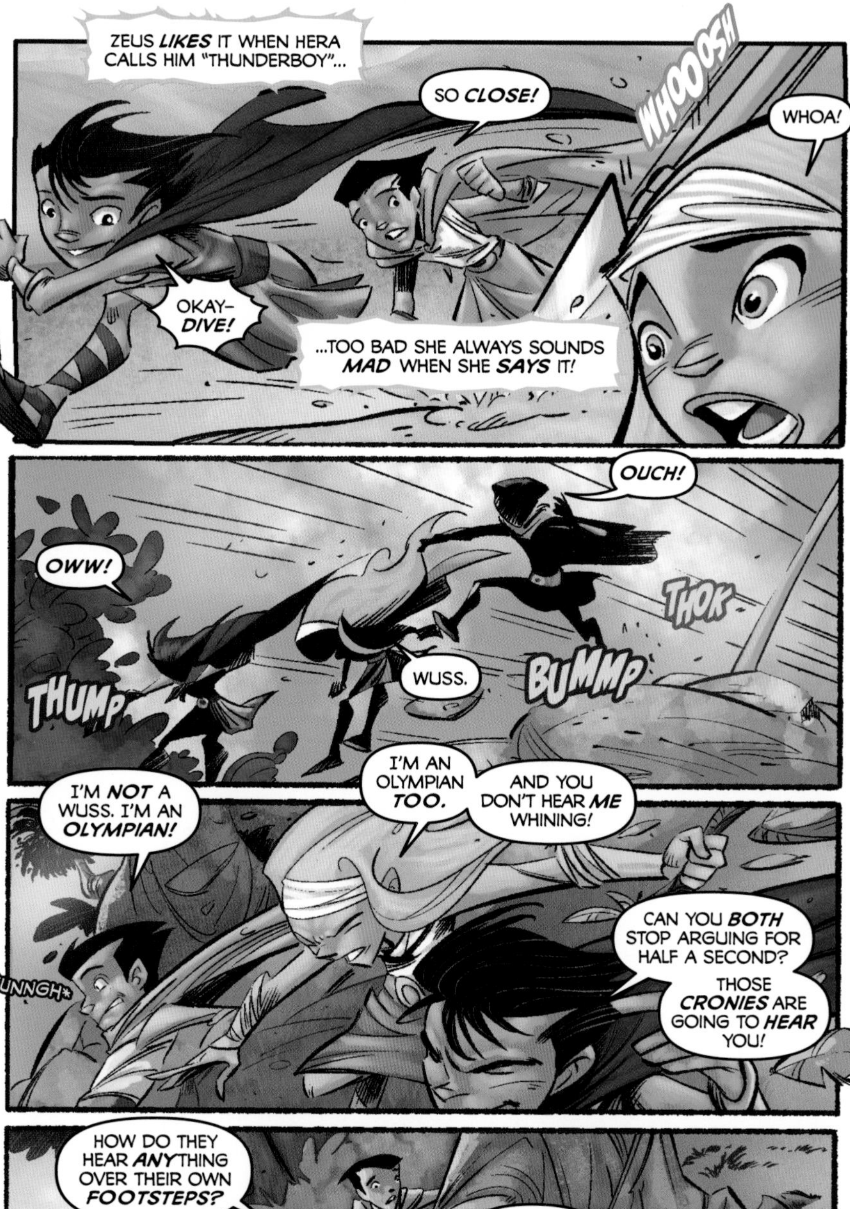
ZEUS LIKES IT WHEN HERA CALLS HIM "THUNDERBOY"...
SO CLOSE!
WHOOOSH
WHOA!
OKAY– DIVE!
...TOO BAD SHE ALWAYS SOUNDS MAD WHEN SHE SAYS IT!
OUCH!
OWW!
THOK
THUMP
WUSS.
BUMMP
I'M NOT A WUSS. I'M AN OLYMPIAN!
I'M AN OLYMPIAN TOO.
AND YOU DON'T HEAR ME WHINING!
UNNGH
CAN YOU BOTH STOP ARGUING FOR HALF A SECOND?
THOSE CRONIES ARE GOING TO HEAR YOU!
HOW DO THEY HEAR ANYTHING OVER THEIR OWN FOOTSTEPS?
DO YOU REALLY THINK THEY'LL EAT US?
THEY'LL MORE LIKELY DRAG US BACK FOR KING CRONUS TO SWALLOW US WHOLE!
NOW BE QUIET!

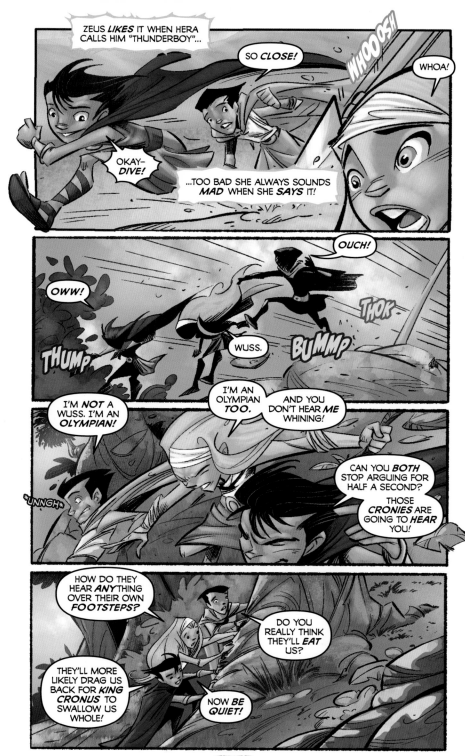

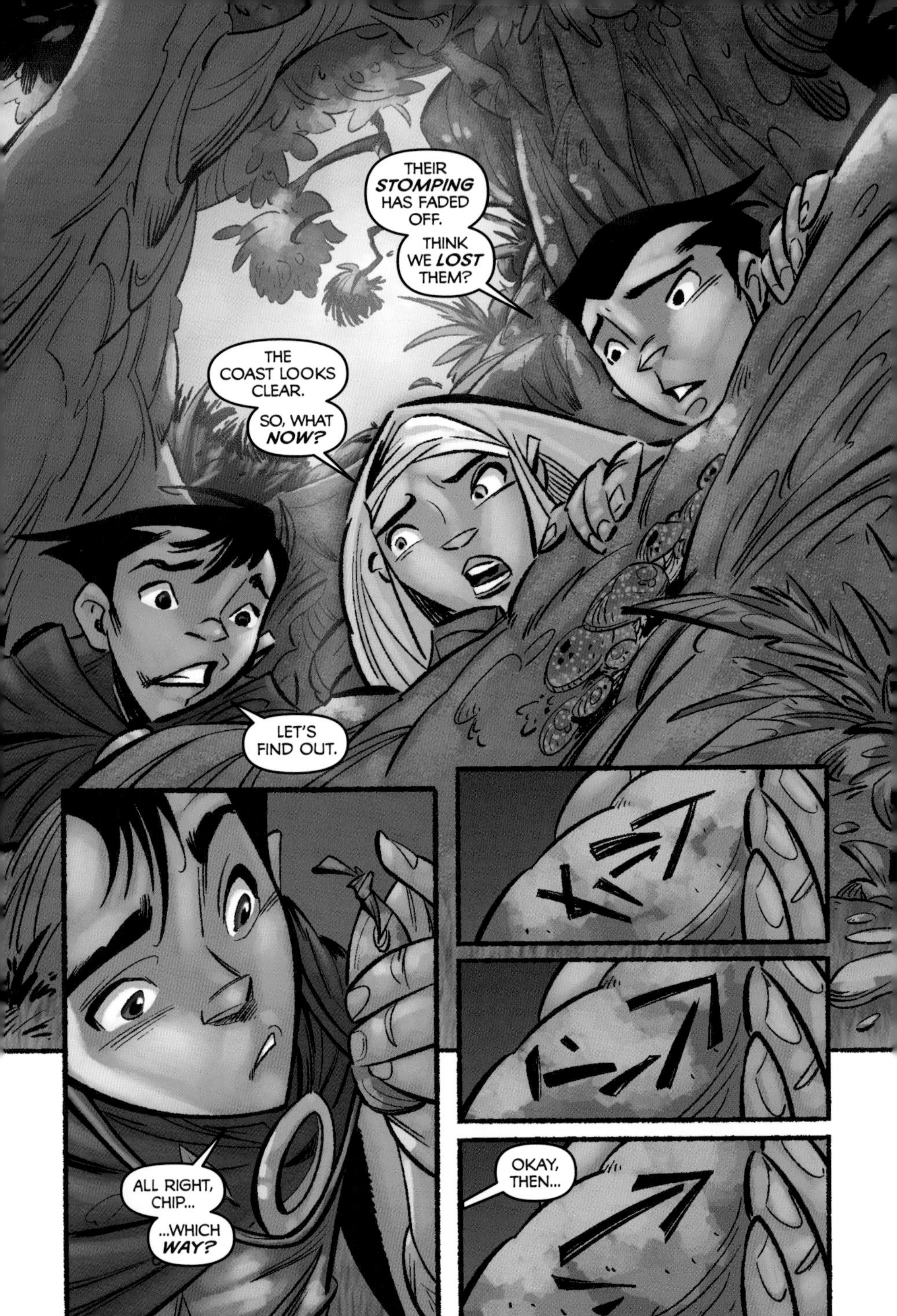
THEIR STOMPING HAS FADED OFF.
THINK WE LOST THEM?
THE COAST LOOKS CLEAR.
SO, WHAT NOW?
LET'S FIND OUT.
ALL RIGHT, CHIP...
...WHICH WAY?
OKAY, THEN...

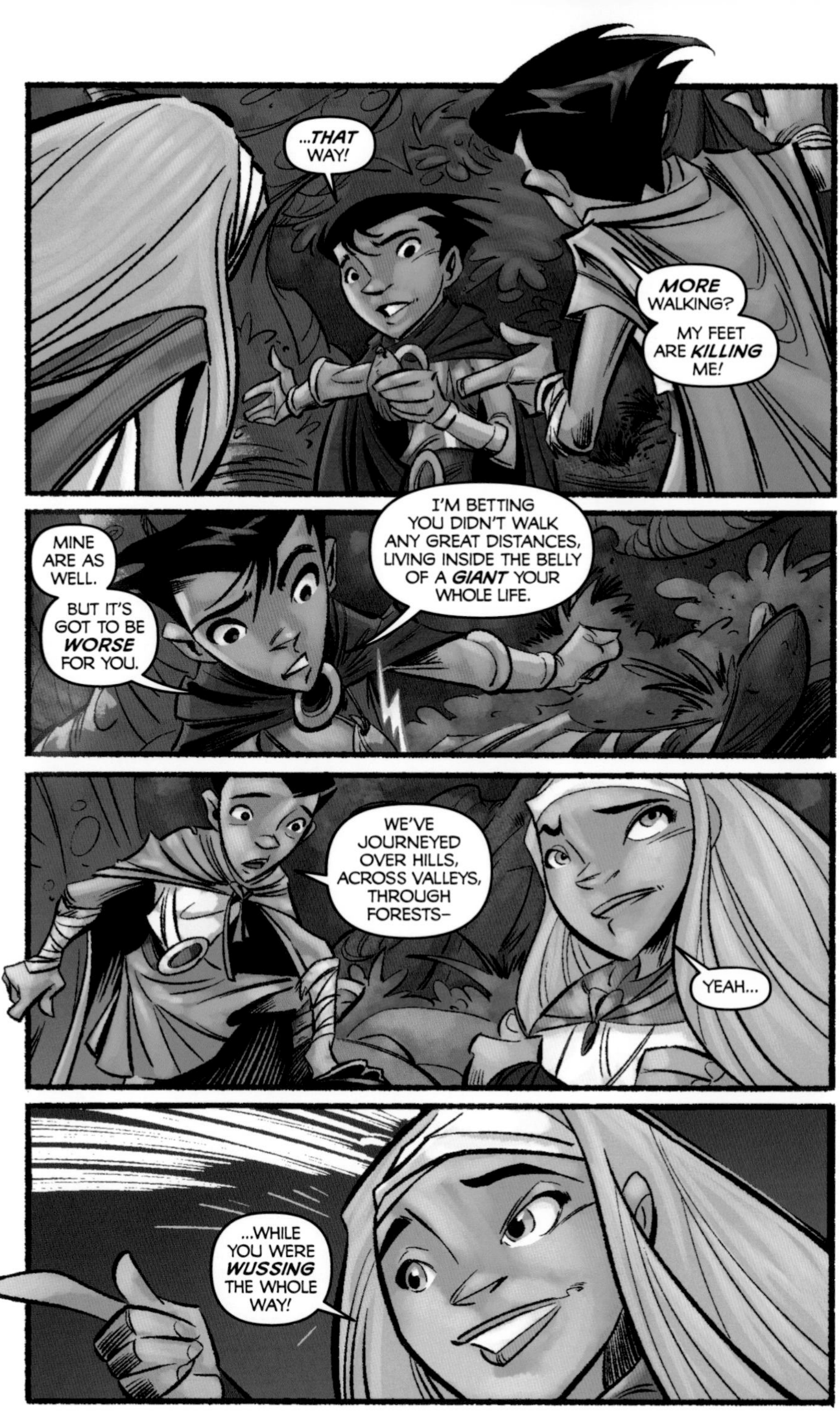
...THAT WAY!
MORE WALKING?
MY FEET ARE KILLING ME!
MINE ARE AS WELL.
BUT IT'S GOT TO BE WORSE FOR YOU.
I'M BETTING YOU DIDN'T WALK ANY GREAT DISTANCES, LIVING INSIDE THE BELLY OF A GIANT YOUR WHOLE LIFE.
WE'VE JOURNEYED OVER HILLS, ACROSS VALLEYS, THROUGH FORESTS–
YEAH...
...WHILE YOU WERE WUSSING THE WHOLE WAY!

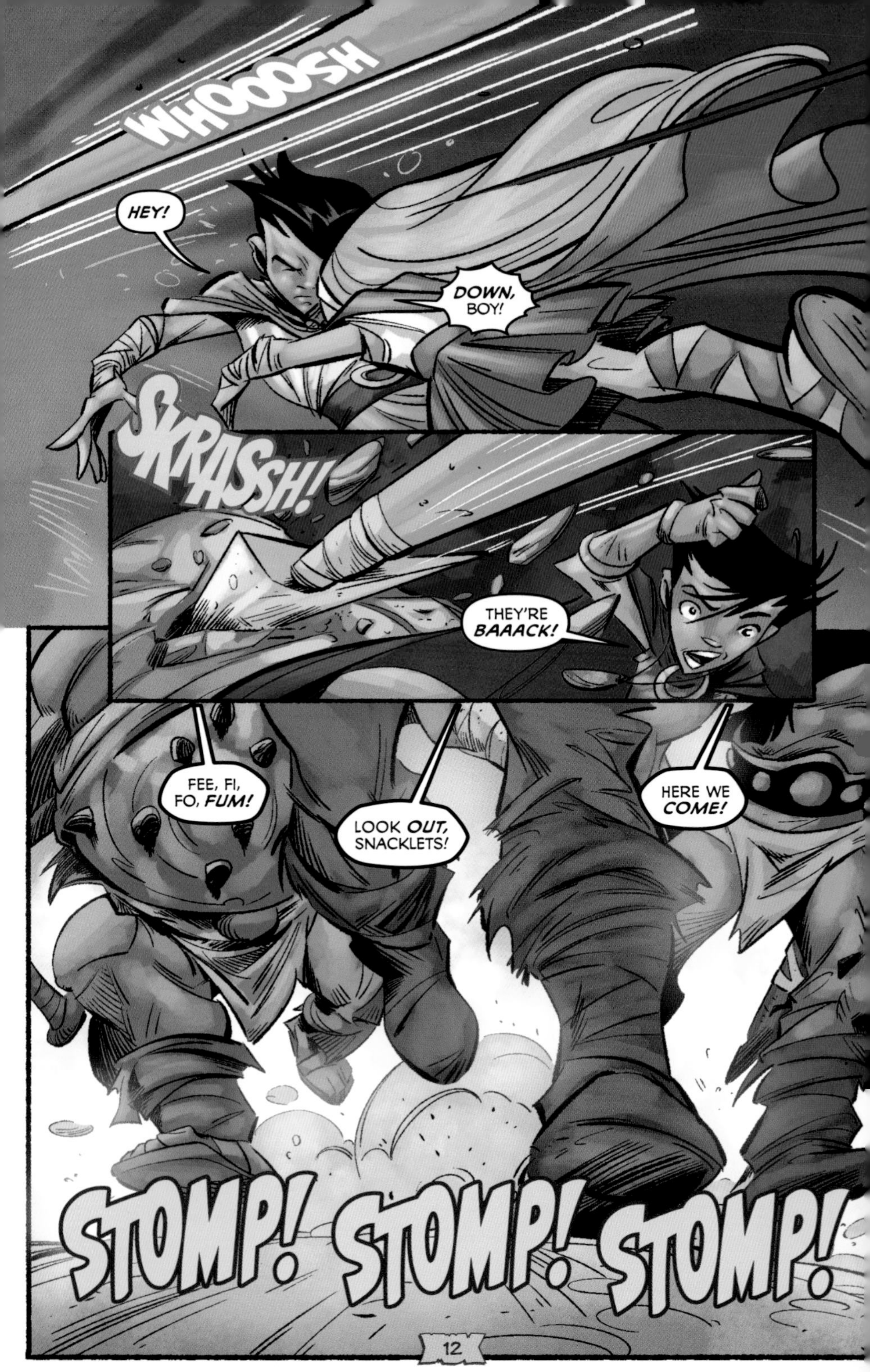
WHOOOSH
HEY!
DOWN, BOY!
SKRASSH!
THEY'RE BAAACK!
FEE, FI, FO, FUM!
LOOK OUT, SNACKLETS!
HERE WE COME!
STOMP! STOMP! STOMP!

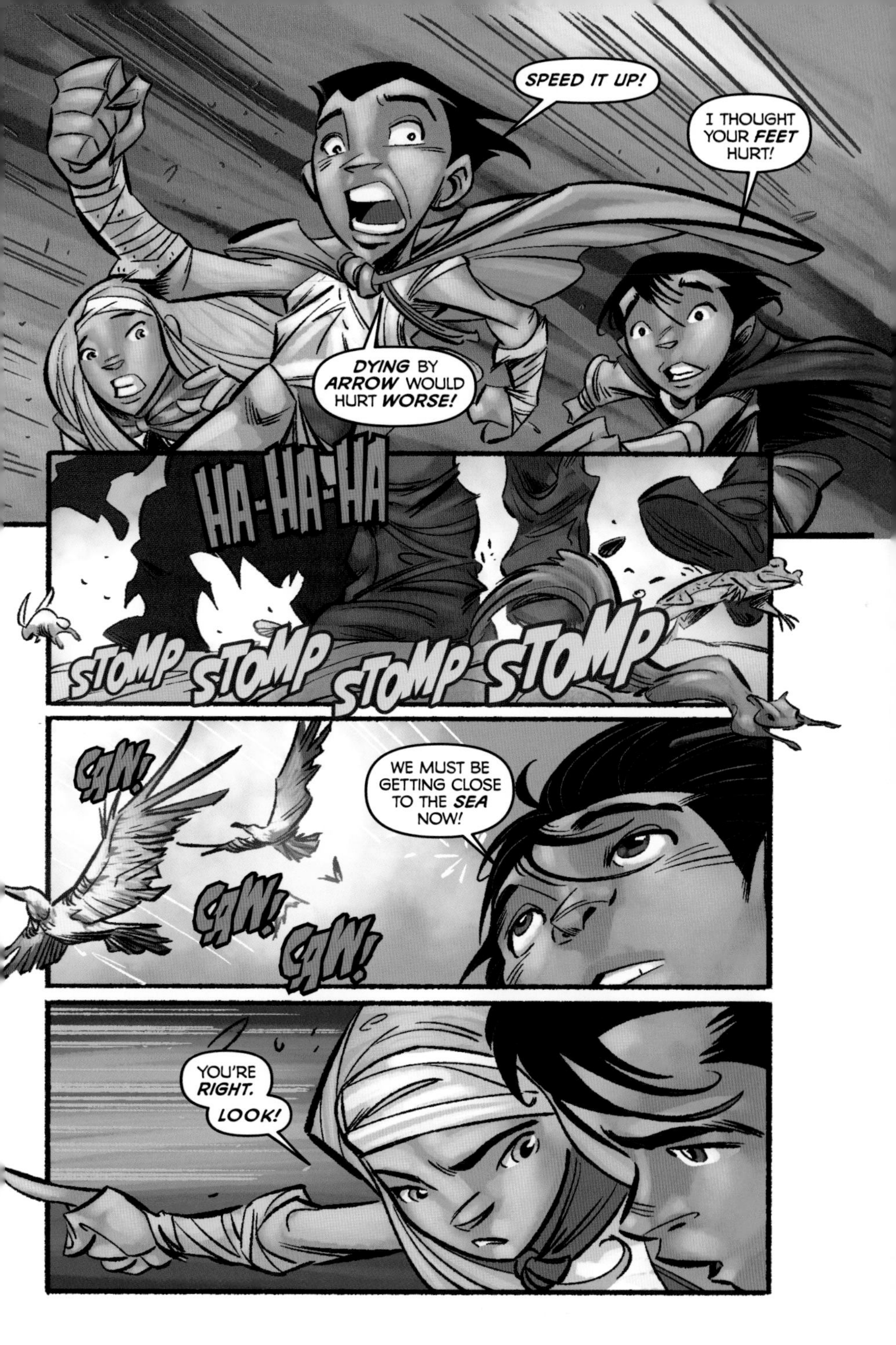
SPEED IT UP!
I THOUGHT YOUR FEET HURT!
DYING BY ARROW WOULD HURT WORSE!
HA-HA-HA
STOMP STOMP STOMP STOMP
CAW! CAW! CAW!
WE MUST BE GETTING CLOSE TO THE SEA NOW!
YOU'RE RIGHT.
LOOK!

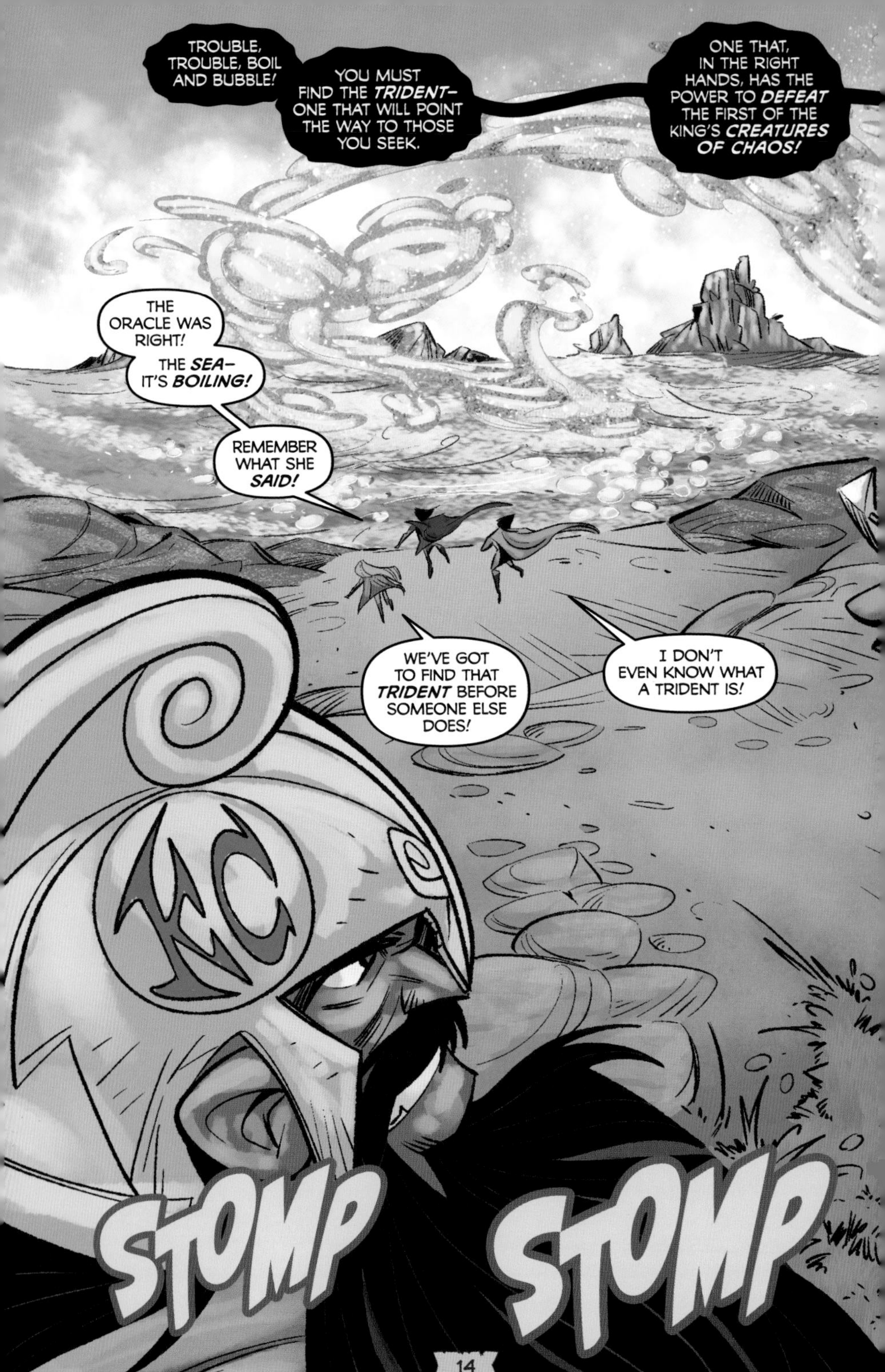
TROUBLE, TROUBLE, BOIL AND BUBBLE!
YOU MUST FIND THE TRIDENT— ONE THAT WILL POINT THE WAY TO THOSE YOU SEEK.
ONE THAT, IN THE RIGHT HANDS, HAS THE POWER TO DEFEAT THE FIRST OF THE KING'S CREATURES OF CHAOS!
THE ORACLE WAS RIGHT!
THE SEA— IT'S BOILING!
REMEMBER WHAT SHE SAID!
WE'VE GOT TO FIND THAT TRIDENT BEFORE SOMEONE ELSE DOES!
I DON'T EVEN KNOW WHAT A TRIDENT IS!
STOMP
STOMP

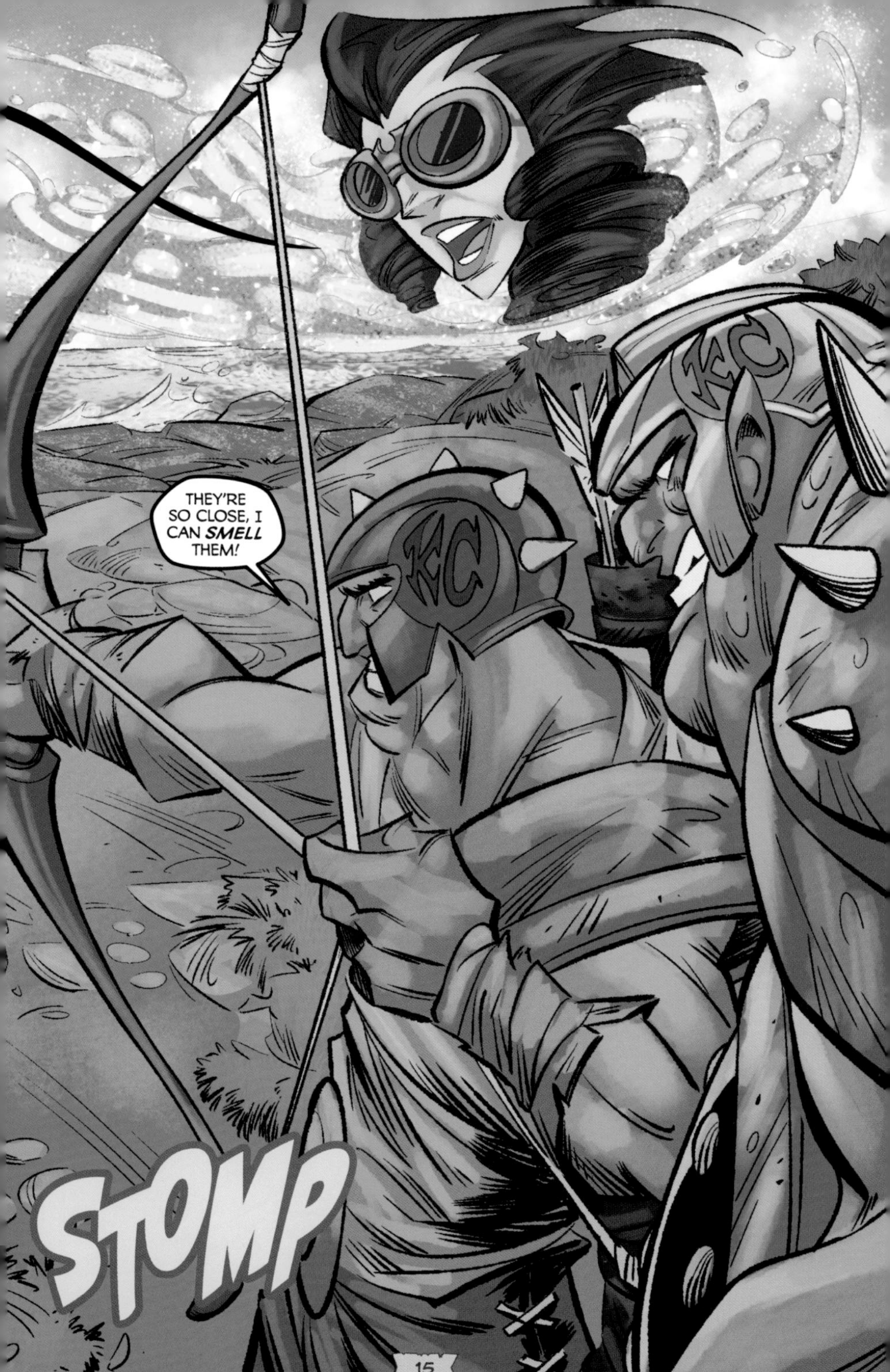
THEY'RE SO CLOSE, I CAN *SMELL* THEM!
STOMP

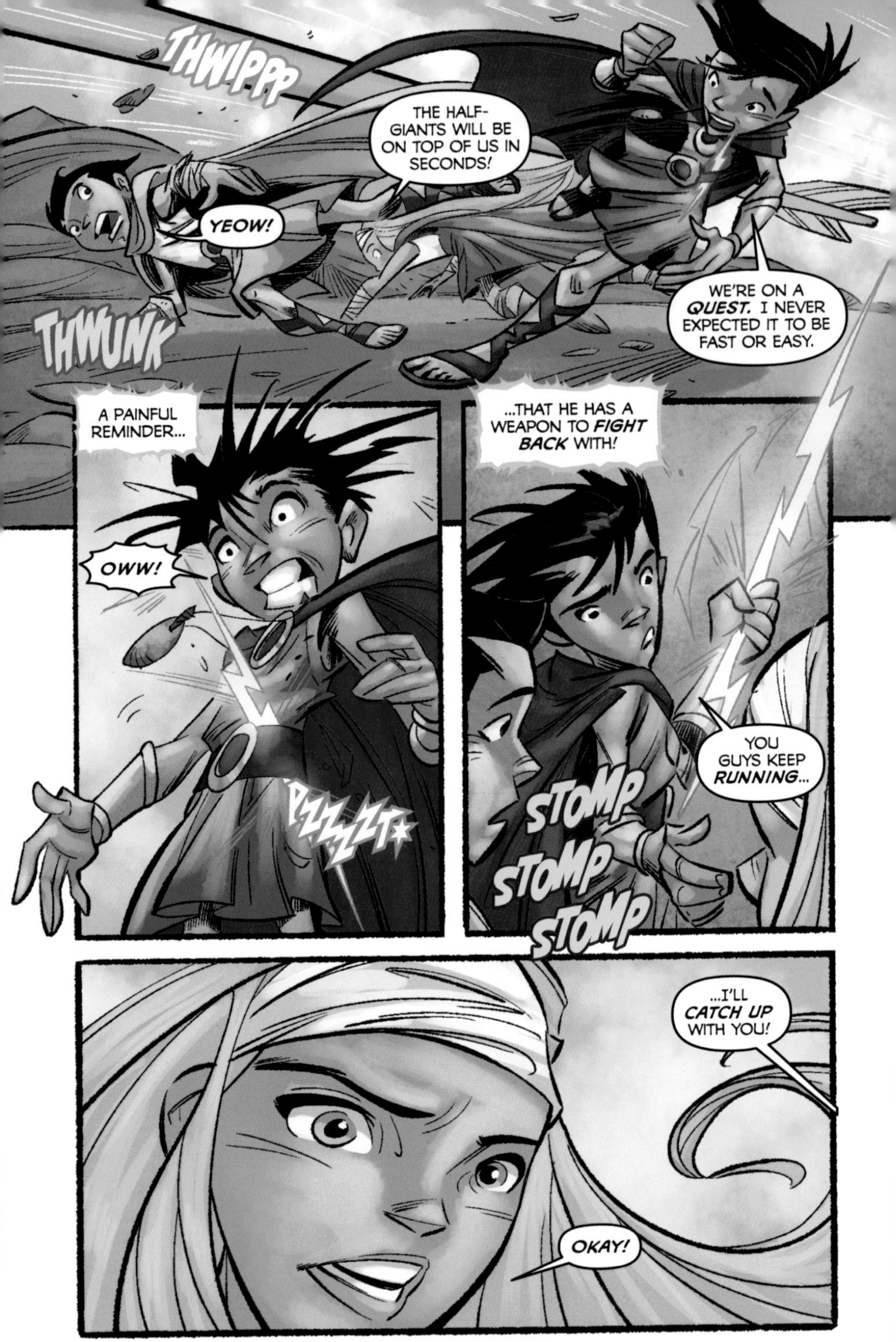
THWIPPP
THE HALF-GIANTS WILL BE ON TOP OF US IN SECONDS!
YEOW!
THWUNK
WE'RE ON A *QUEST.* I NEVER EXPECTED IT TO BE FAST OR EASY.
A PAINFUL REMINDER...
OWW!
PZZZZZT
...THAT HE HAS A WEAPON TO *FIGHT BACK* WITH!
YOU GUYS KEEP *RUNNING*...
STOMP
STOMP
STOMP
...I'LL *CATCH UP* WITH YOU!
OKAY!

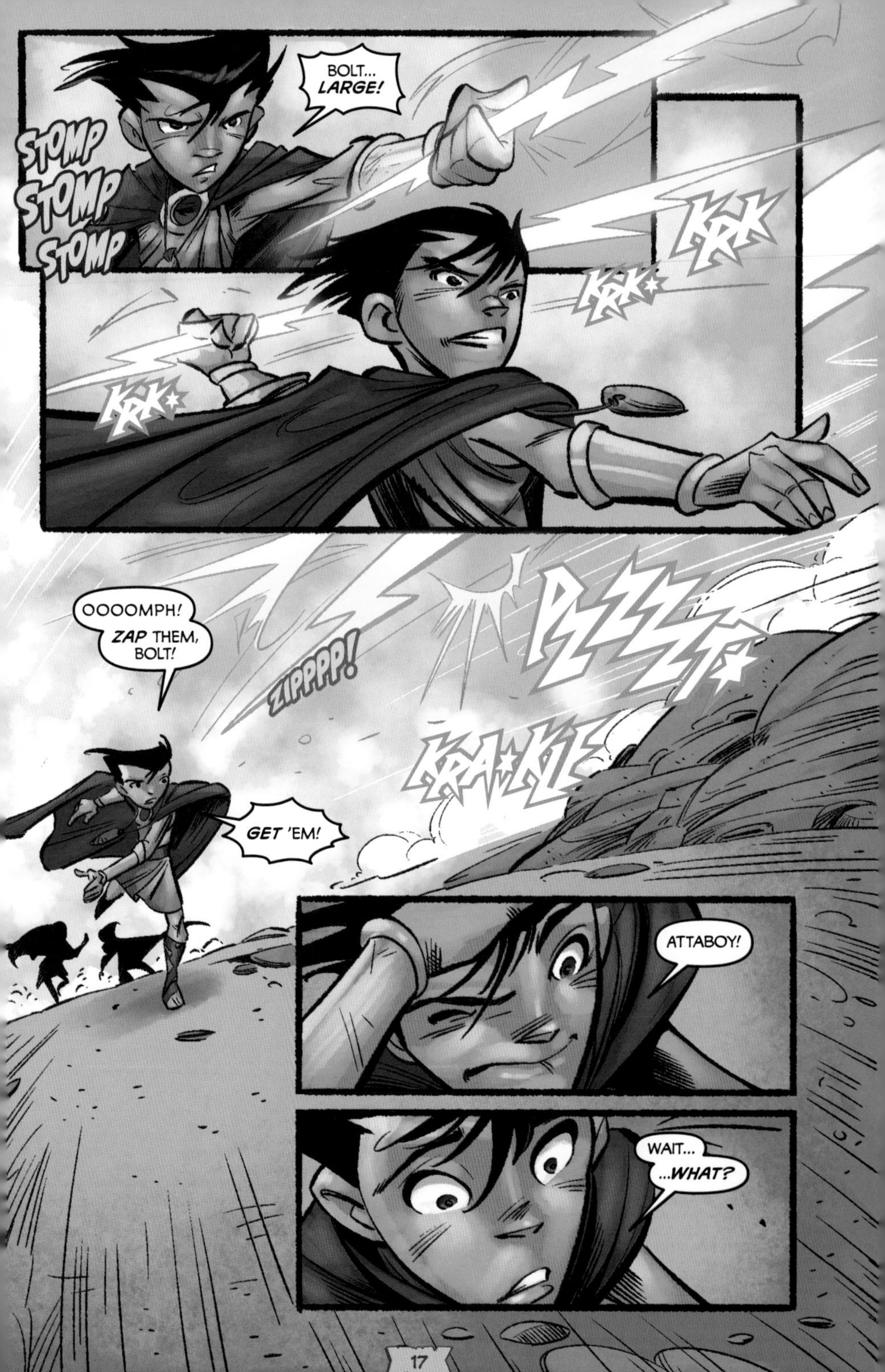
BOLT... LARGE!
STOMP
STOMP
STOMP
KRK
KRK
KRK
OOOOMPH! ZAP THEM, BOLT!
ZIPPPP!
PZZZT
KRA-KLE
GET 'EM!
ATTABOY!
WAIT... ...WHAT?

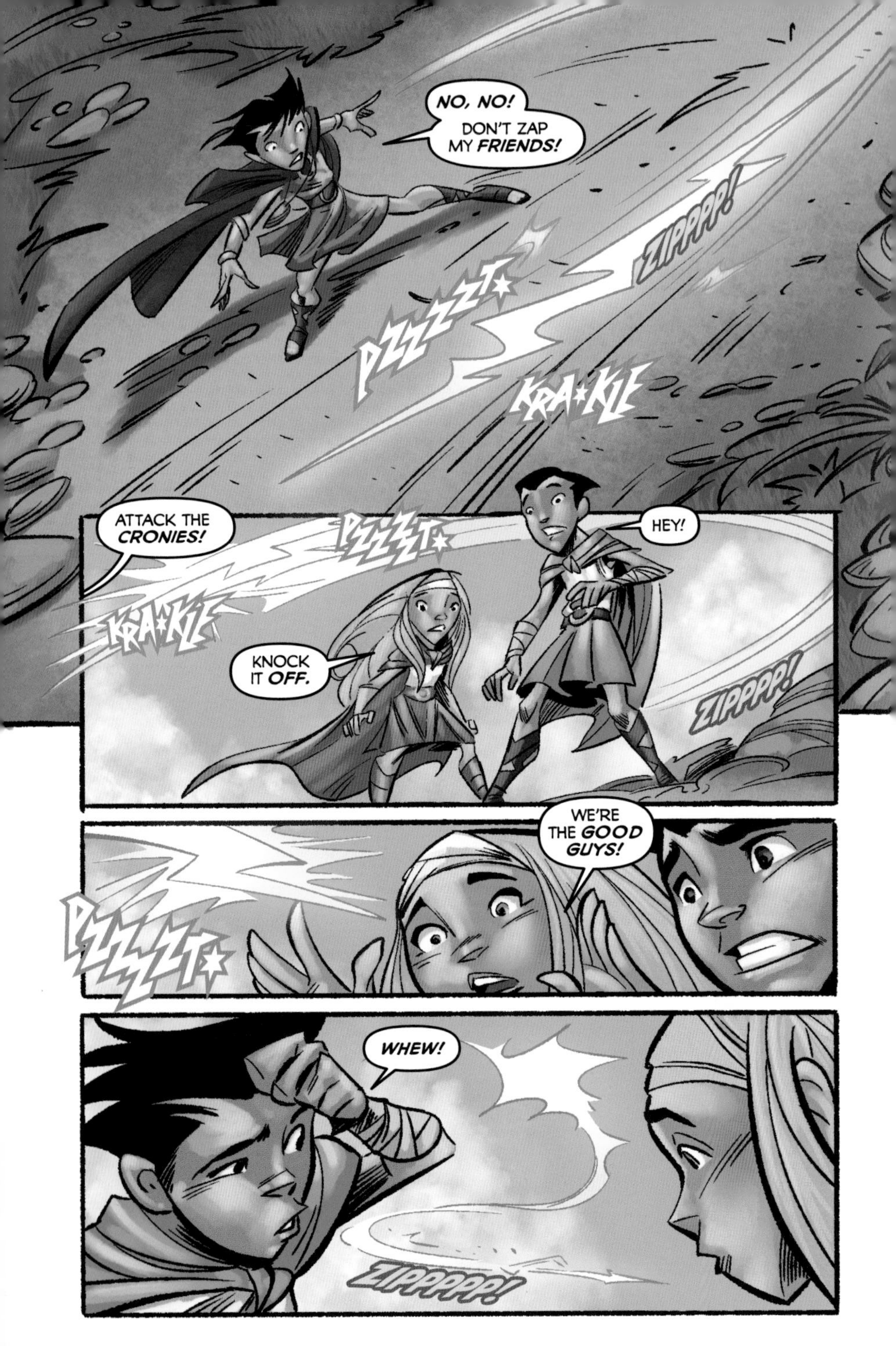

NO, NO! DON'T ZAP MY FRIENDS!
ZIPPPP!
PZZZZZT*
KRA*KLE
ATTACK THE CRONIES!
PZZZZT*
HEY!
KRA*KLE
KNOCK IT OFF.
ZIPPPP!
WE'RE THE GOOD GUYS!
PZZZZT*
WHEW!
ZIPPPPP!

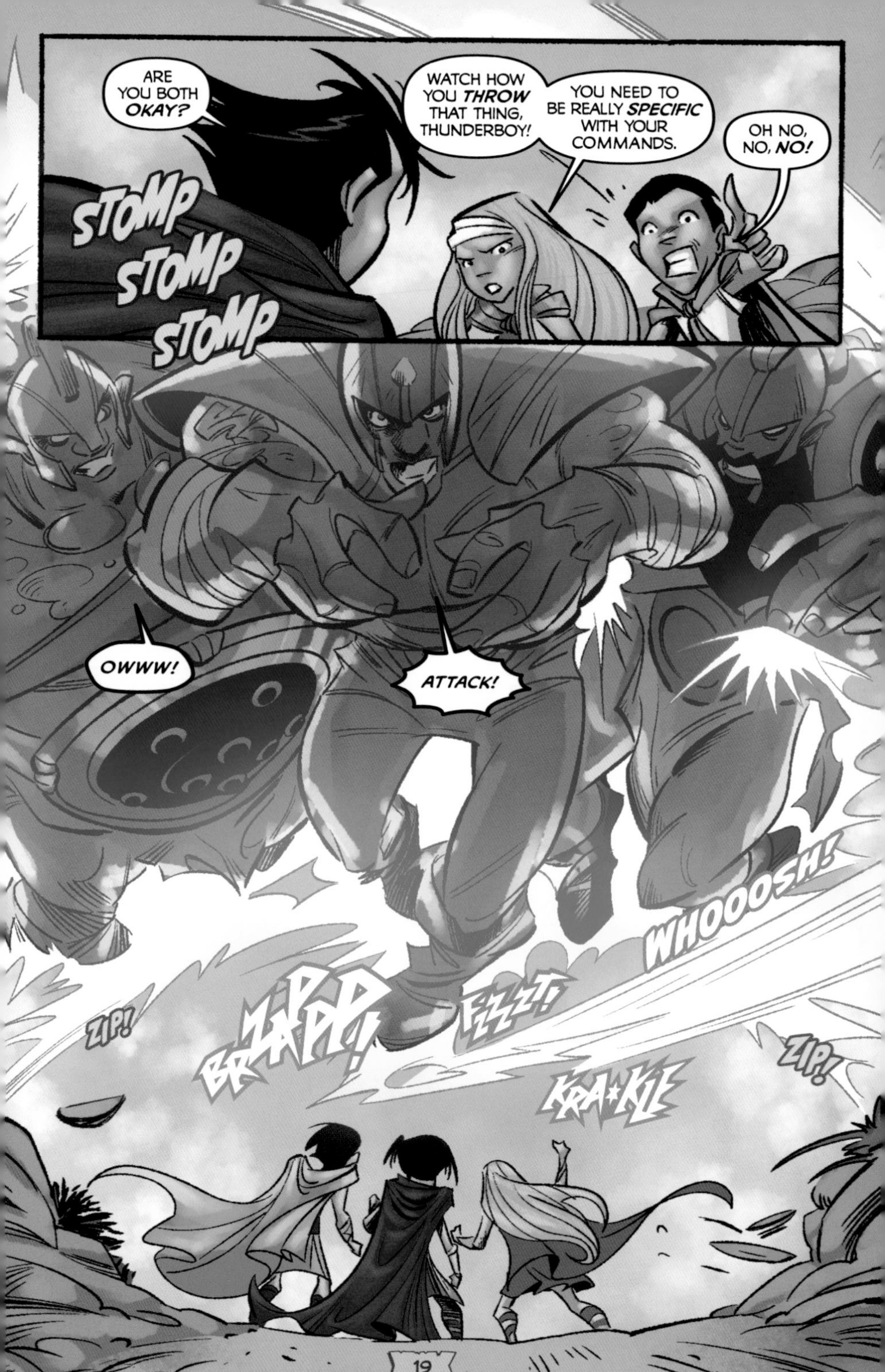
ARE YOU BOTH OKAY?
WATCH HOW YOU THROW THAT THING, THUNDERBOY!
YOU NEED TO BE REALLY SPECIFIC WITH YOUR COMMANDS.
OH NO, NO, NO!
STOMP
STOMP
STOMP
OWWW!
ATTACK!
WHOOOSH!
ZIP!
BRZAPPP!
FZZZT!
ZIP!
KRA*KLE

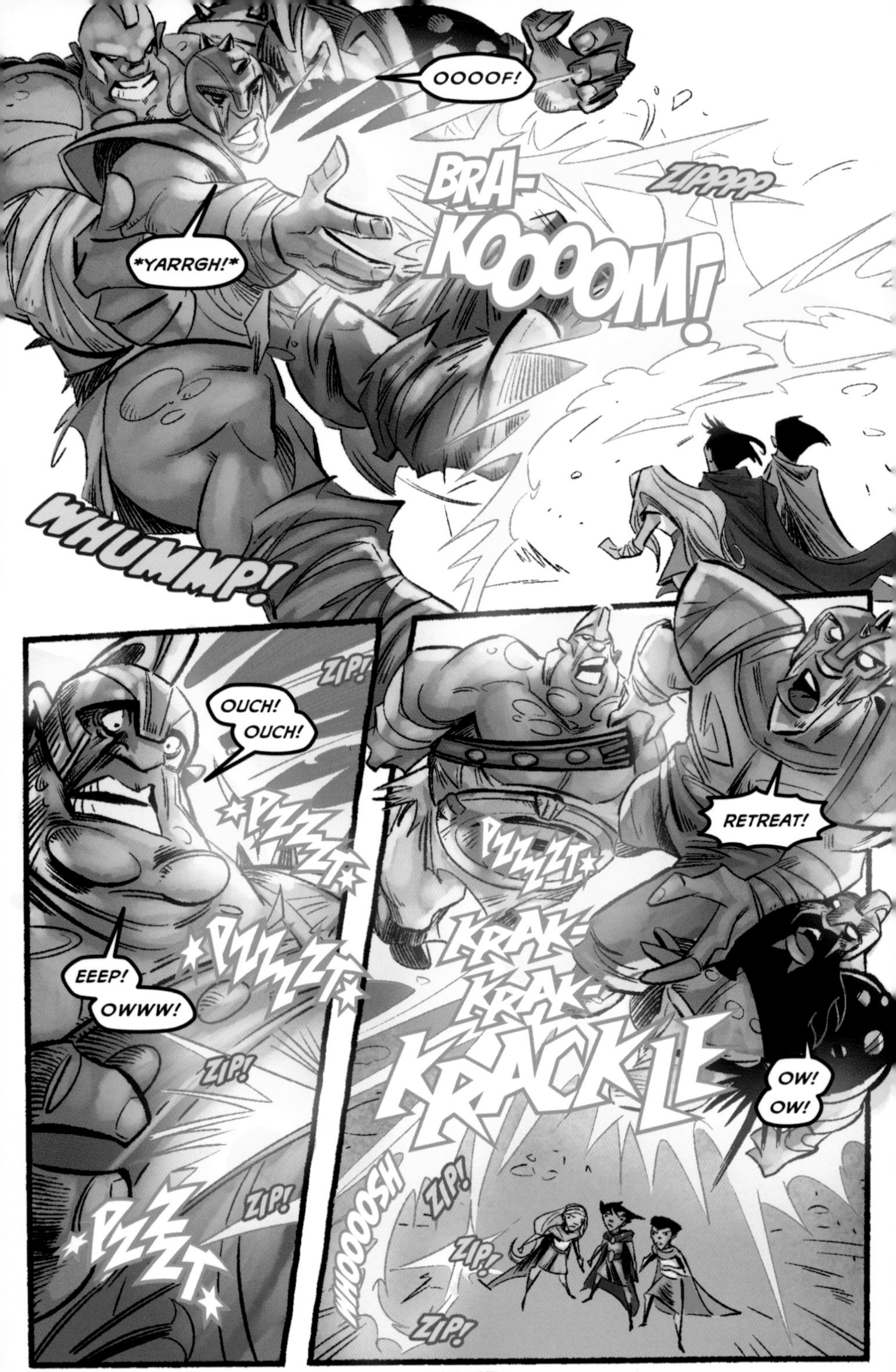
YARRGH!
OOOOF!
BRA-KOOOOM!
ZIPPPP
WHUMMP!
ZIP!
OUCH! OUCH!
PZZZT
PZZZZT
EEEP! OWWW!
ZIP!
ZIP!
PZZZT
RETREAT!
PZZZZT*
KRAK-KRAK-KRACKLE
OW! OW!
WHOOOOSH
ZIP!
ZIP!
ZIP!

CHAPTER TWO:
SEA JOURNEY

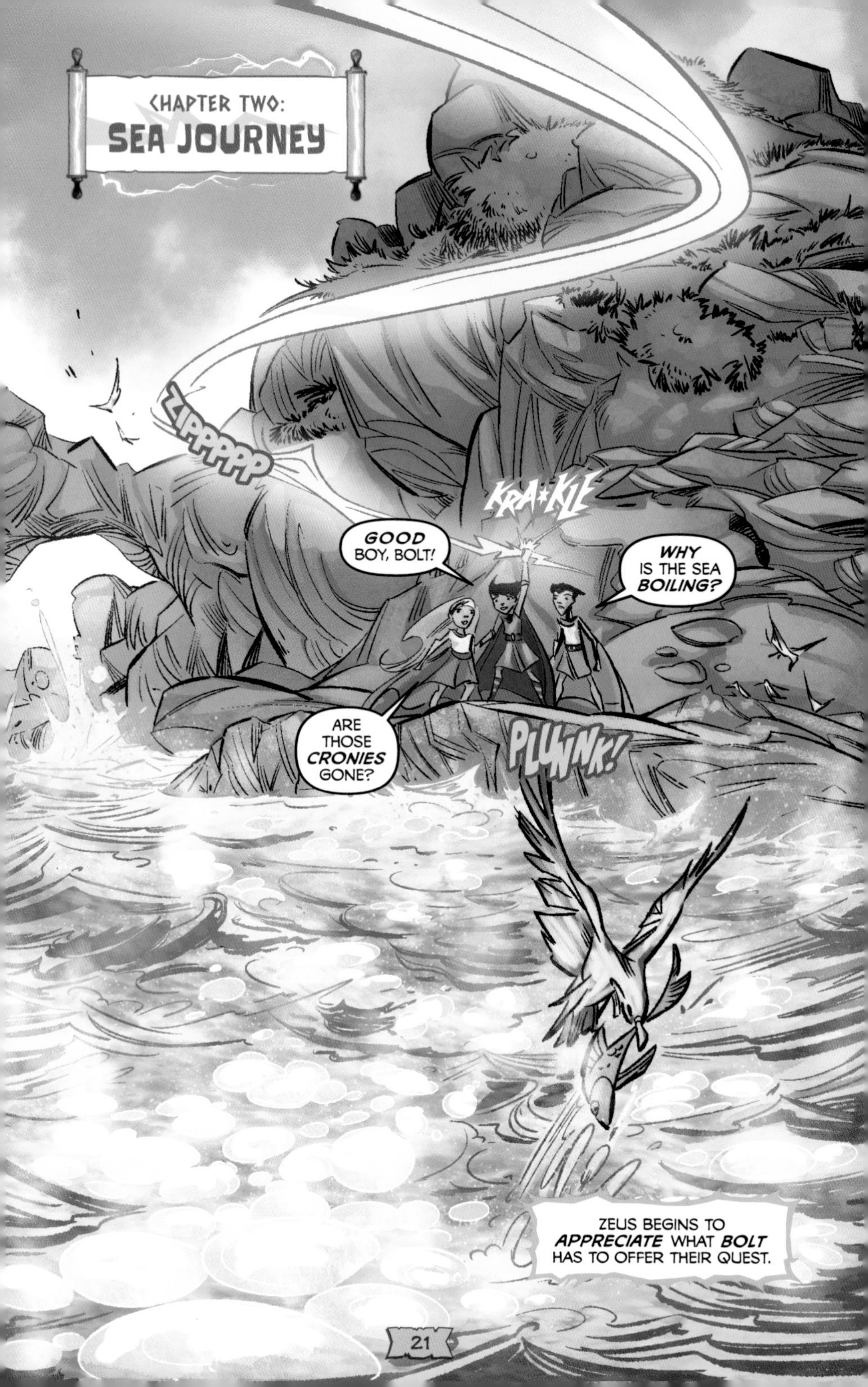
ZIPPPPPP
KRA★KLE
GOOD BOY, BOLT!
WHY IS THE SEA BOILING?
ARE THOSE CRONIES GONE?
PLUNNK!
ZEUS BEGINS TO APPRECIATE WHAT BOLT HAS TO OFFER THEIR QUEST.

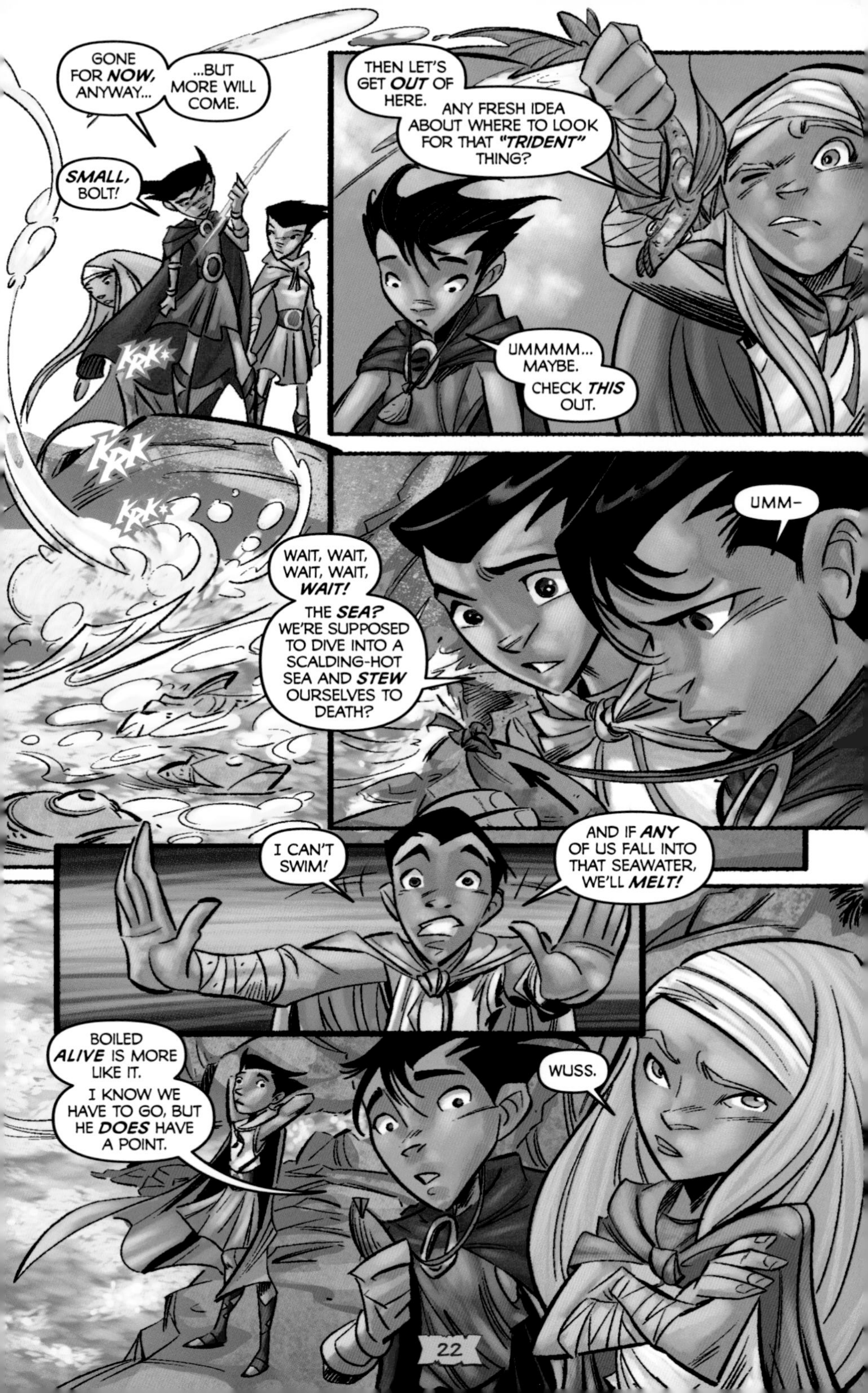

GONE FOR NOW, ANYWAY...
...BUT MORE WILL COME.
SMALL, BOLT!
KRK*
THEN LET'S GET OUT OF HERE.
ANY FRESH IDEA ABOUT WHERE TO LOOK FOR THAT "TRIDENT" THING?
UMMMM... MAYBE.
CHECK THIS OUT.
KRK
KRK*
UMM-
WAIT, WAIT, WAIT, WAIT, WAIT!
THE SEA? WE'RE SUPPOSED TO DIVE INTO A SCALDING-HOT SEA AND STEW OURSELVES TO DEATH?
I CAN'T SWIM!
AND IF ANY OF US FALL INTO THAT SEAWATER, WE'LL MELT!
BOILED ALIVE IS MORE LIKE IT.
I KNOW WE HAVE TO GO, BUT HE DOES HAVE A POINT.
WUSS.

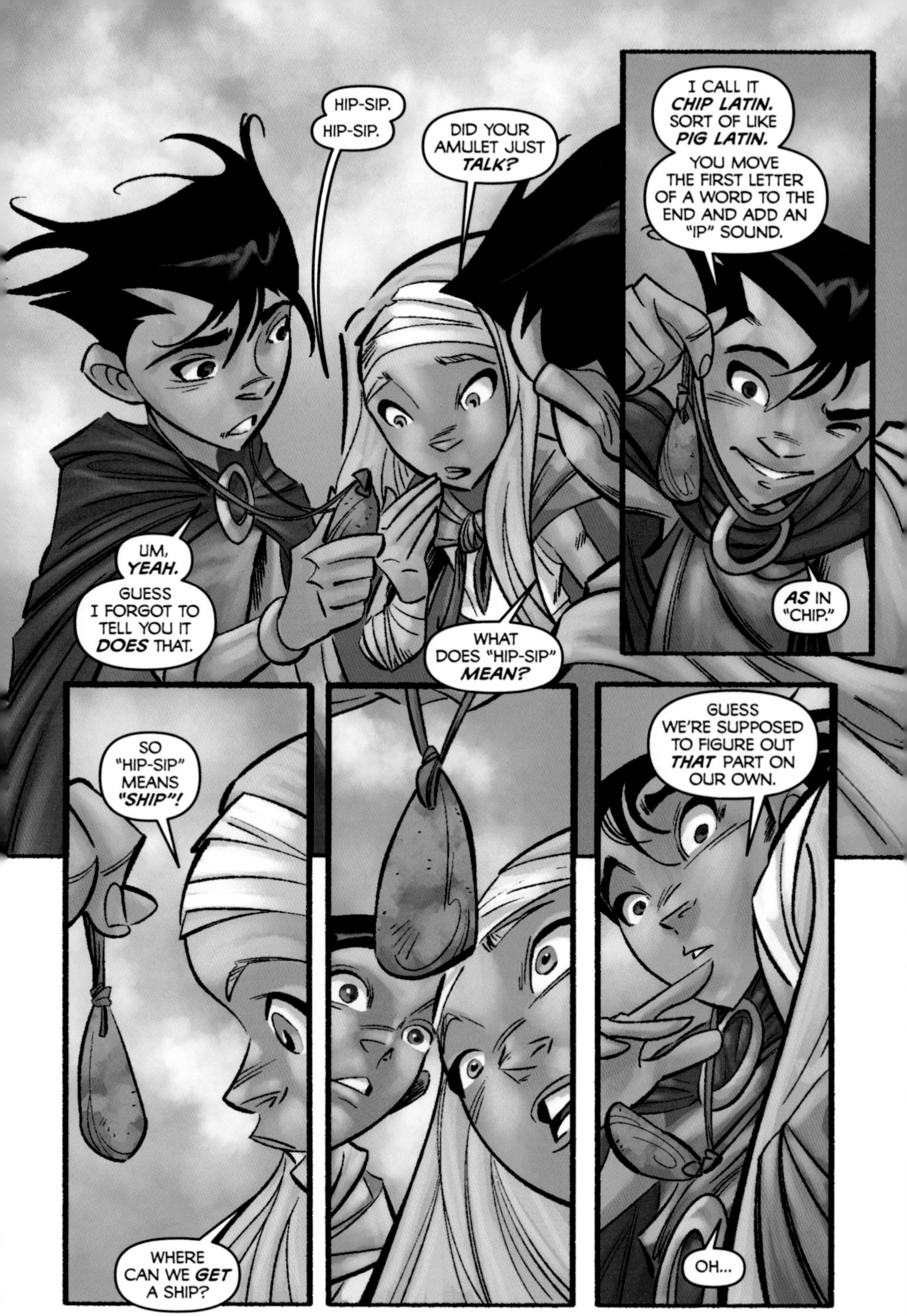
HIP-SIP.
HIP-SIP.
DID YOUR AMULET JUST TALK?
UM, YEAH.
GUESS I FORGOT TO TELL YOU IT DOES THAT.
I CALL IT CHIP LATIN. SORT OF LIKE PIG LATIN.
YOU MOVE THE FIRST LETTER OF A WORD TO THE END AND ADD AN "IP" SOUND.
AS IN "CHIP."
WHAT DOES "HIP-SIP" MEAN?
SO "HIP-SIP" MEANS "SHIP"!
WHERE CAN WE GET A SHIP?
GUESS WE'RE SUPPOSED TO FIGURE OUT THAT PART ON OUR OWN.
OH...

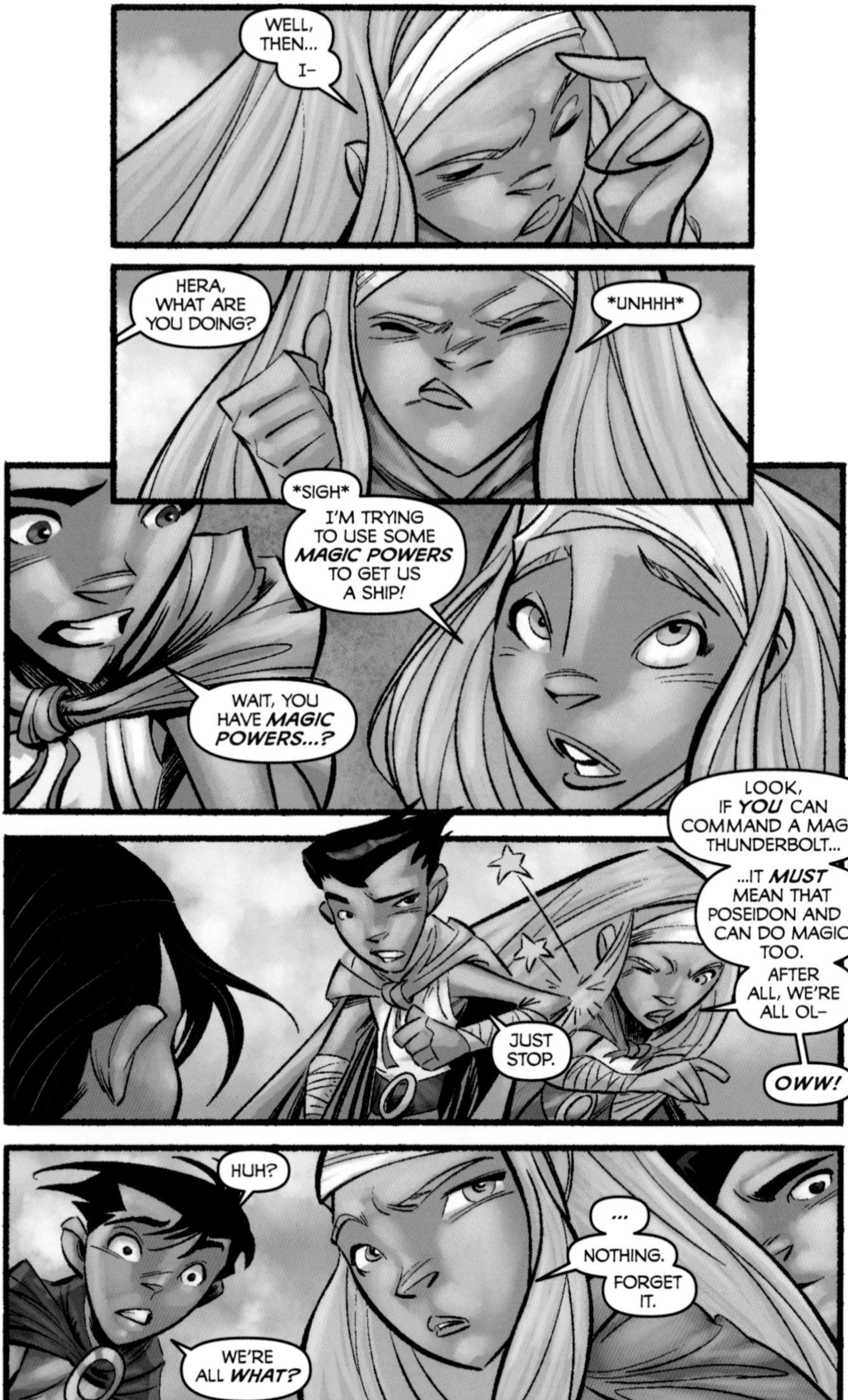
WELL, THEN...
I–
HERA, WHAT ARE YOU DOING?
UNHHH
SIGH
I'M TRYING TO USE SOME MAGIC POWERS TO GET US A SHIP!
WAIT, YOU HAVE MAGIC POWERS...?
LOOK, IF YOU CAN COMMAND A MAGIC THUNDERBOLT...
...IT MUST MEAN THAT POSEIDON AND I CAN DO MAGIC TOO.
AFTER ALL, WE'RE ALL OL–
JUST STOP.
OWW!
HUH?
...
NOTHING.
FORGET IT.
WE'RE ALL WHAT?

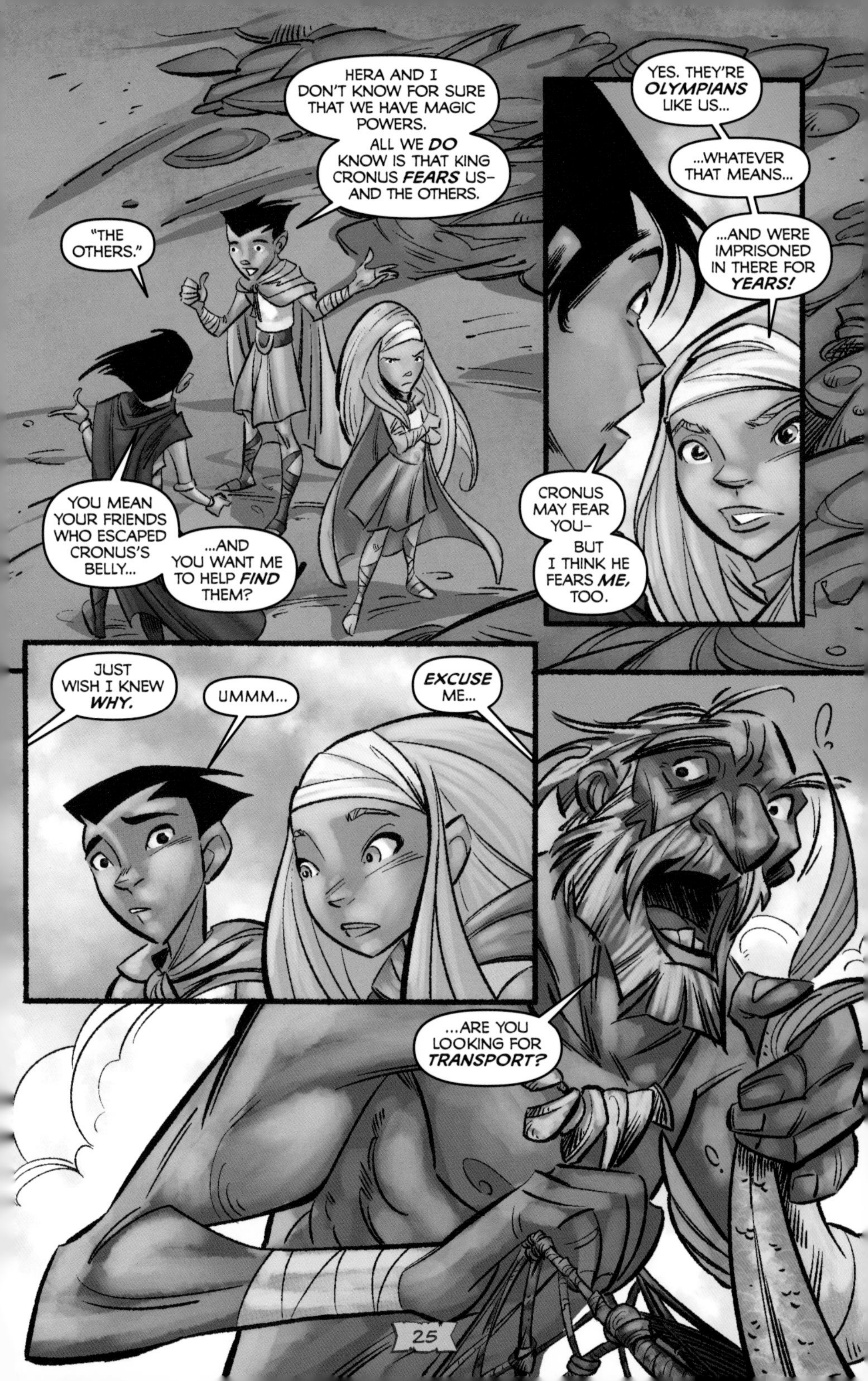
HERA AND I DON'T KNOW FOR SURE THAT WE HAVE MAGIC POWERS.
ALL WE *DO* KNOW IS THAT KING CRONUS *FEARS* US– AND THE OTHERS.
"THE OTHERS."
YOU MEAN YOUR FRIENDS WHO ESCAPED CRONUS'S BELLY...
...AND YOU WANT ME TO HELP *FIND* THEM?
YES. THEY'RE *OLYMPIANS* LIKE US...
...WHATEVER THAT MEANS...
...AND WERE IMPRISONED IN THERE FOR *YEARS!*
CRONUS MAY FEAR YOU–
BUT I THINK HE FEARS *ME,* TOO.
JUST WISH I KNEW *WHY.*
UMMM...
EXCUSE ME...
...ARE YOU LOOKING FOR *TRANSPORT?*

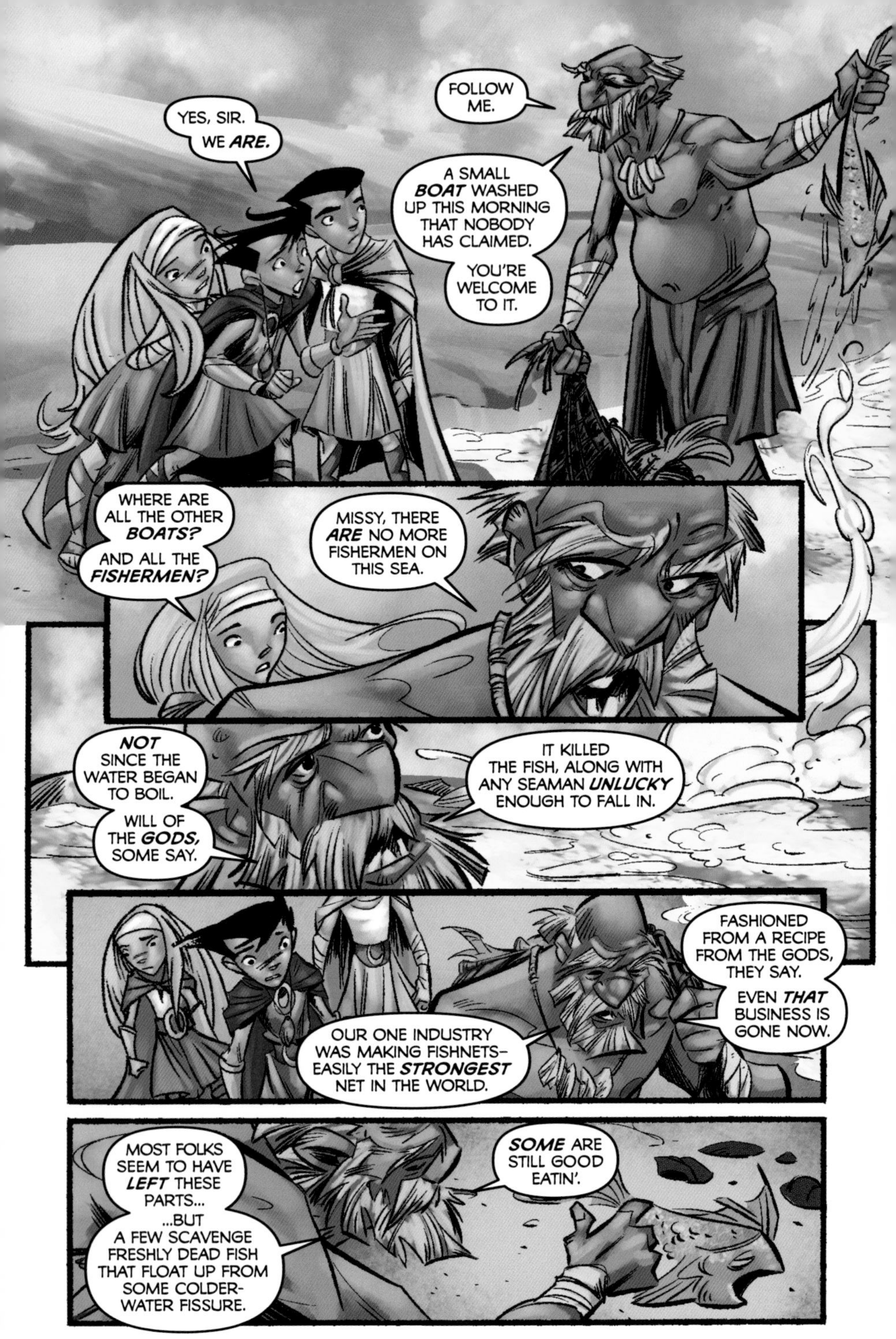
YES, SIR.
WE ARE.
FOLLOW ME.
A SMALL BOAT WASHED UP THIS MORNING THAT NOBODY HAS CLAIMED.
YOU'RE WELCOME TO IT.
WHERE ARE ALL THE OTHER BOATS?
AND ALL THE FISHERMEN?
MISSY, THERE ARE NO MORE FISHERMEN ON THIS SEA.
NOT SINCE THE WATER BEGAN TO BOIL.
WILL OF THE GODS, SOME SAY.
IT KILLED THE FISH, ALONG WITH ANY SEAMAN UNLUCKY ENOUGH TO FALL IN.
OUR ONE INDUSTRY WAS MAKING FISHNETS–EASILY THE STRONGEST NET IN THE WORLD.
FASHIONED FROM A RECIPE FROM THE GODS, THEY SAY.
EVEN THAT BUSINESS IS GONE NOW.
MOST FOLKS SEEM TO HAVE LEFT THESE PARTS...
...BUT A FEW SCAVENGE FRESHLY DEAD FISH THAT FLOAT UP FROM SOME COLDER-WATER FISSURE.
SOME ARE STILL GOOD EATIN'.

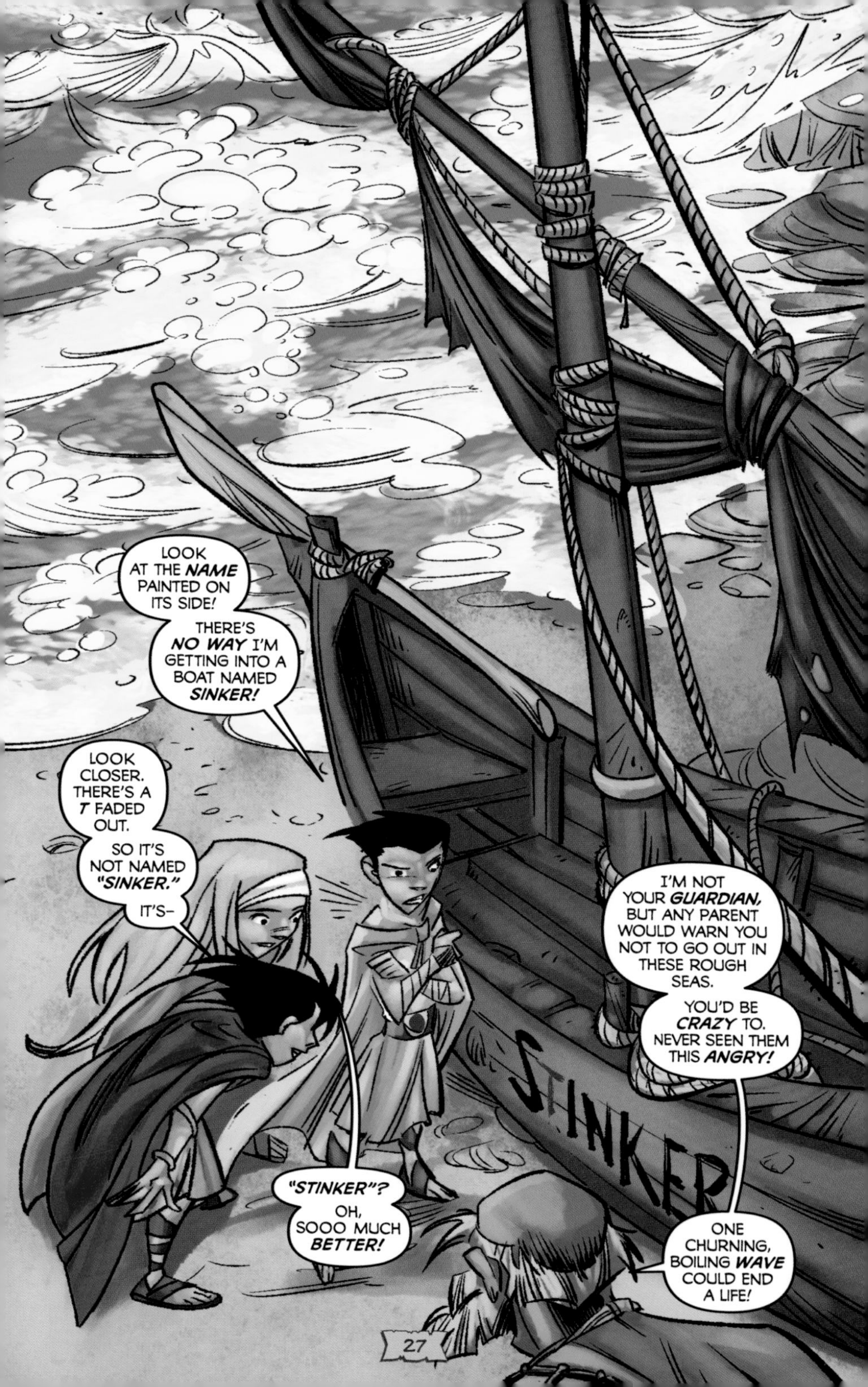
LOOK AT THE NAME PAINTED ON ITS SIDE!
THERE'S NO WAY I'M GETTING INTO A BOAT NAMED SINKER!
LOOK CLOSER. THERE'S A T FADED OUT.
SO IT'S NOT NAMED "SINKER."
IT'S-
"STINKER"? OH, SOOO MUCH BETTER!
STINKER
I'M NOT YOUR GUARDIAN, BUT ANY PARENT WOULD WARN YOU NOT TO GO OUT IN THESE ROUGH SEAS.
YOU'D BE CRAZY TO. NEVER SEEN THEM THIS ANGRY!
ONE CHURNING, BOILING WAVE COULD END A LIFE!

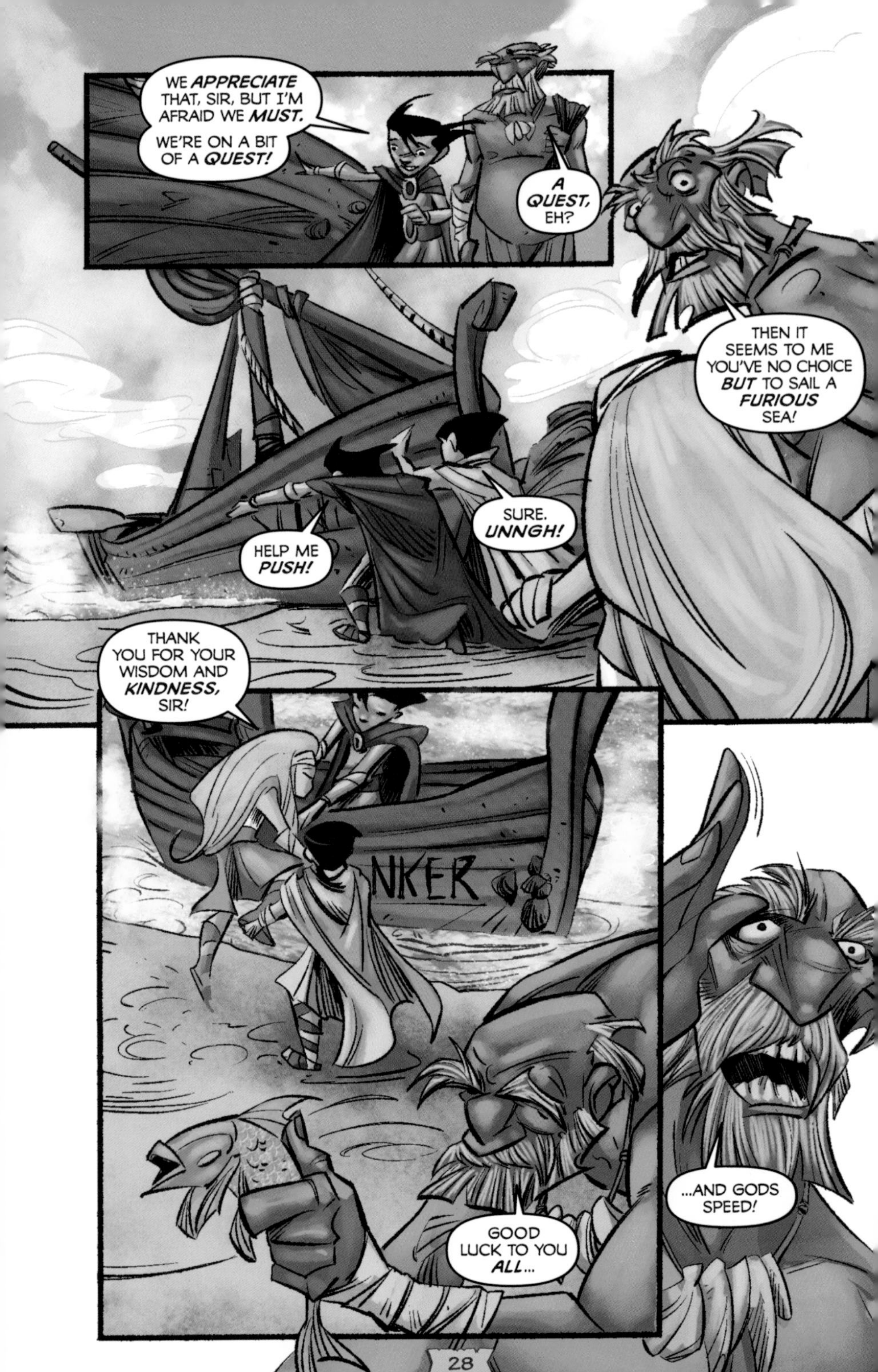
WE APPRECIATE THAT, SIR, BUT I'M AFRAID WE MUST.
WE'RE ON A BIT OF A QUEST!
A QUEST, EH?
THEN IT SEEMS TO ME YOU'VE NO CHOICE BUT TO SAIL A FURIOUS SEA!
HELP ME PUSH!
SURE. UNNGH!
THANK YOU FOR YOUR WISDOM AND KINDNESS, SIR!
NKER
GOOD LUCK TO YOU ALL...
...AND GODS SPEED!

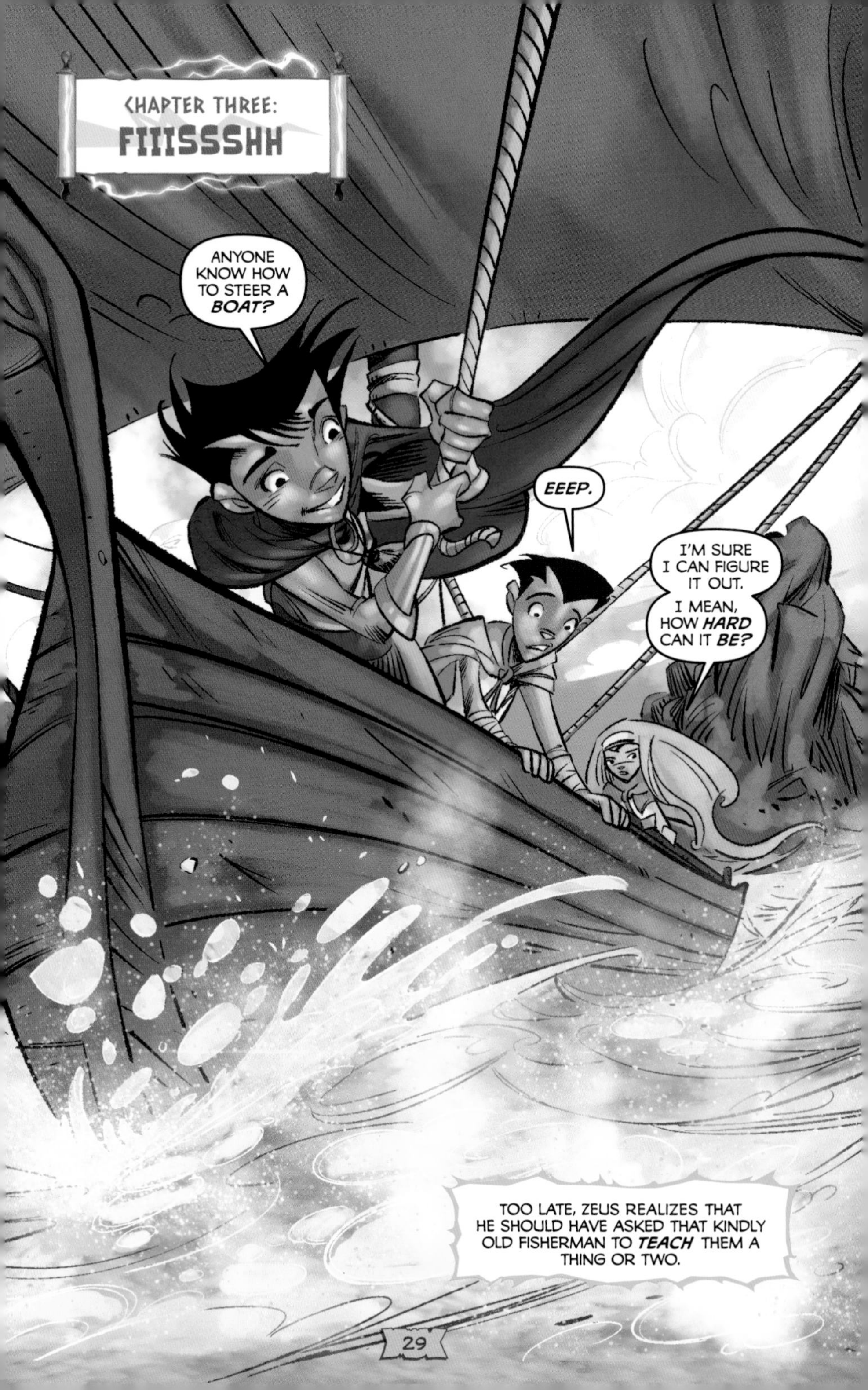
CHAPTER THREE:
FIIISSSHH
ANYONE KNOW HOW TO STEER A ***BOAT?***
EEEP.
I'M SURE I CAN FIGURE IT OUT.
I MEAN, HOW ***HARD*** CAN IT ***BE?***
TOO LATE, ZEUS REALIZES THAT HE SHOULD HAVE ASKED THAT KINDLY OLD FISHERMAN TO ***TEACH*** THEM A THING OR TWO.

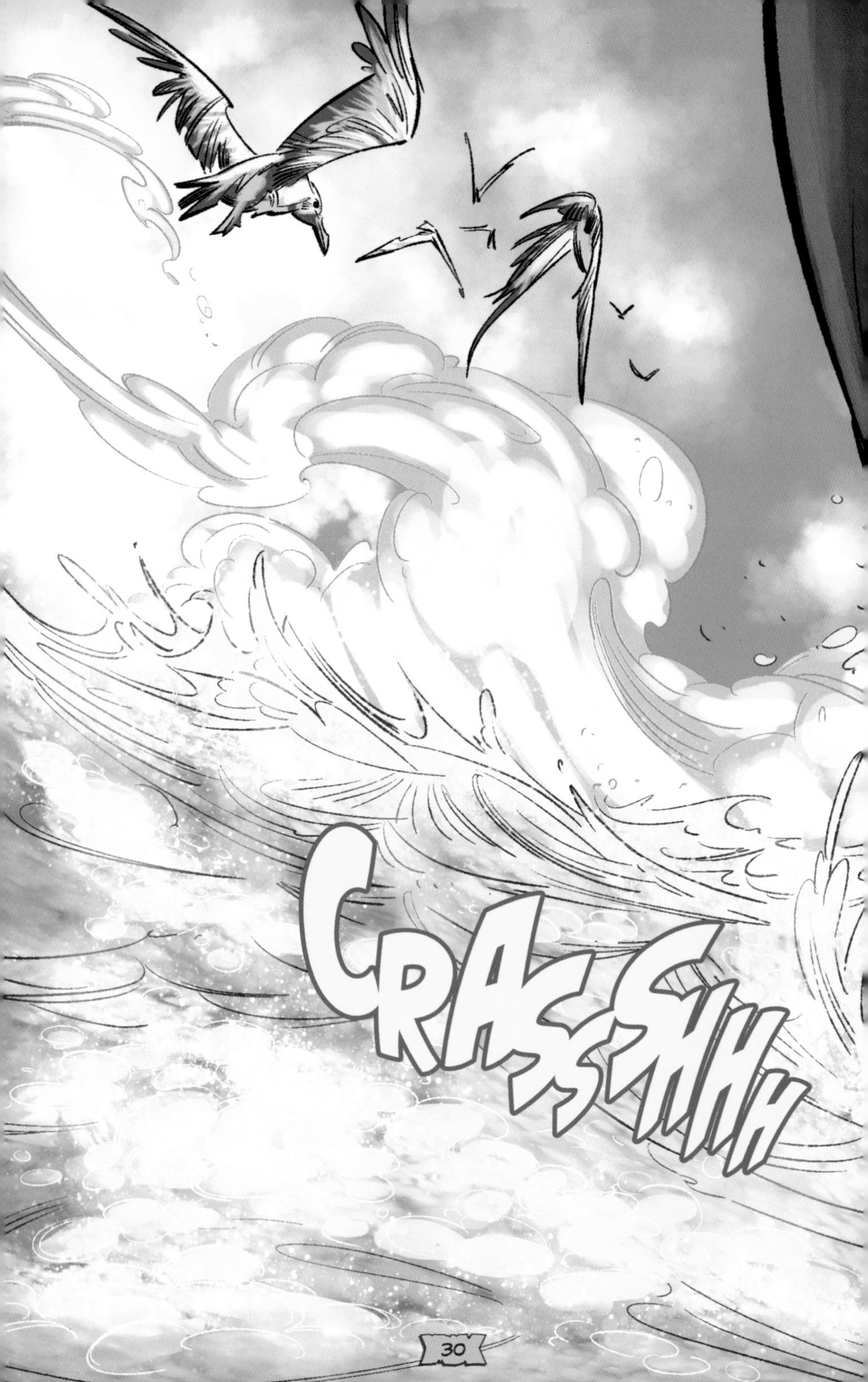
CRASSHHH

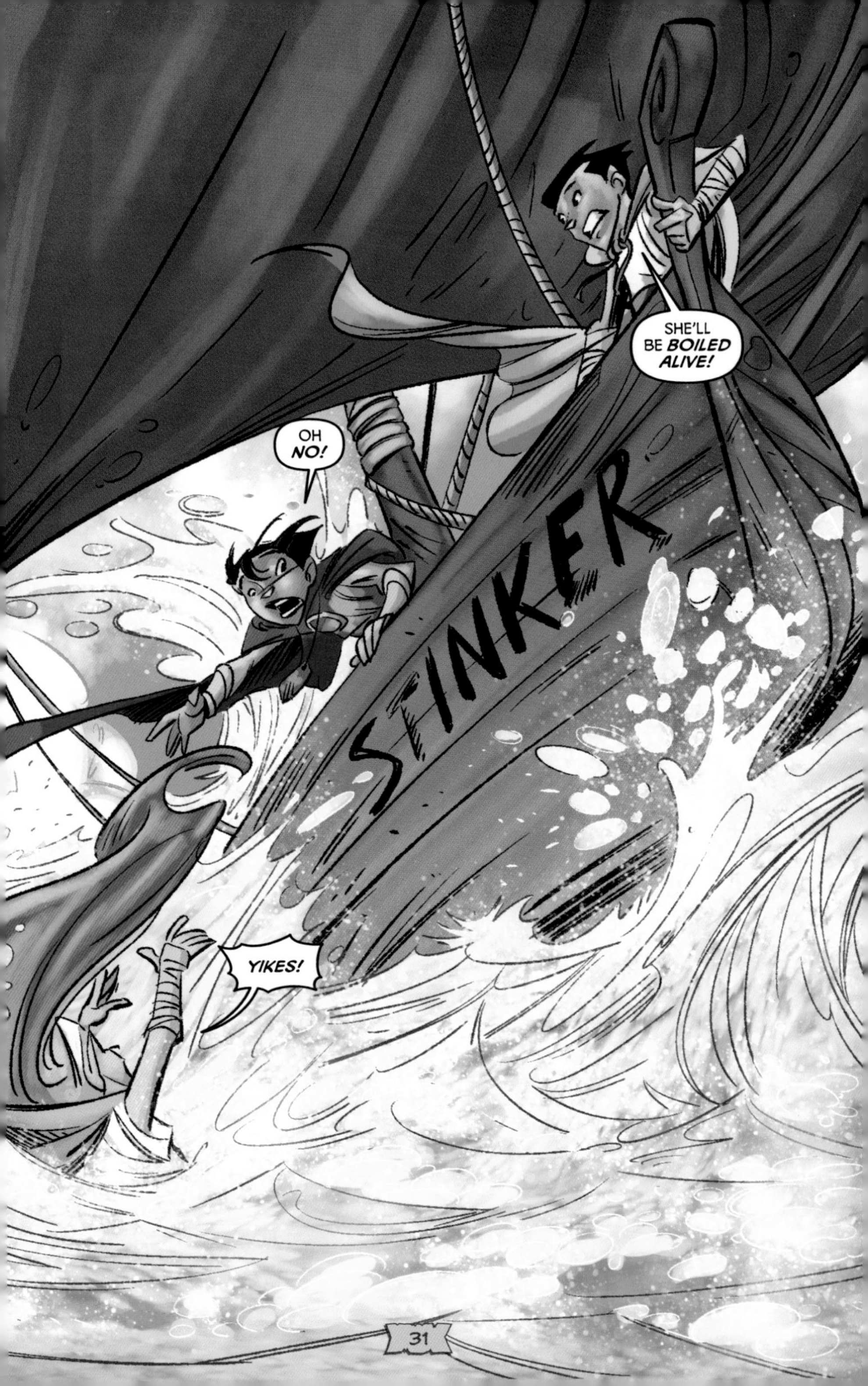
SHE'LL BE BOILED ALIVE!
OH NO!
STINKER
YIKES!

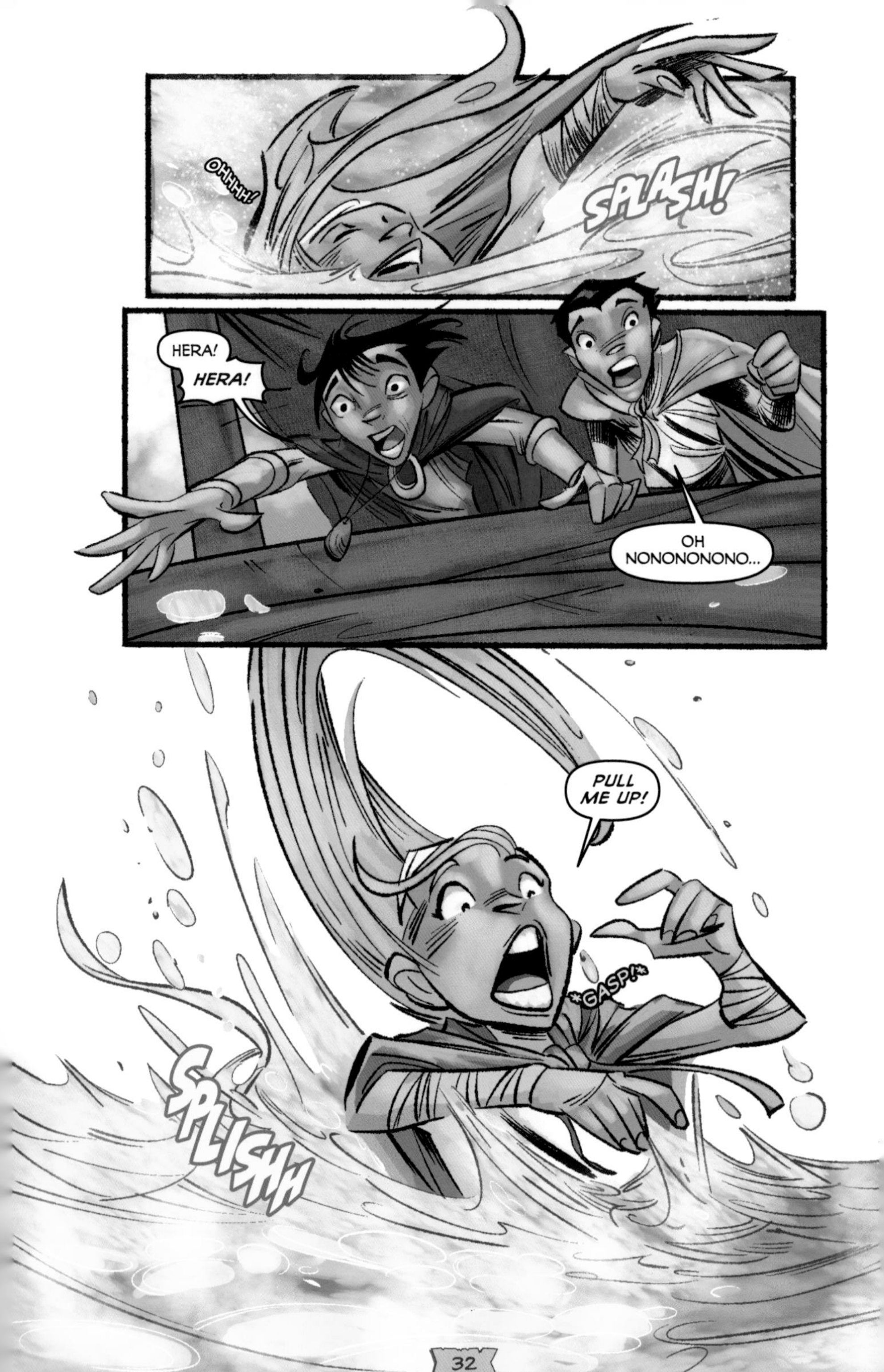
OHHHH!
SPLASH!
HERA!
HERA!
OH NONONONONO...
PULL ME UP!
GASP!
SPLISHH

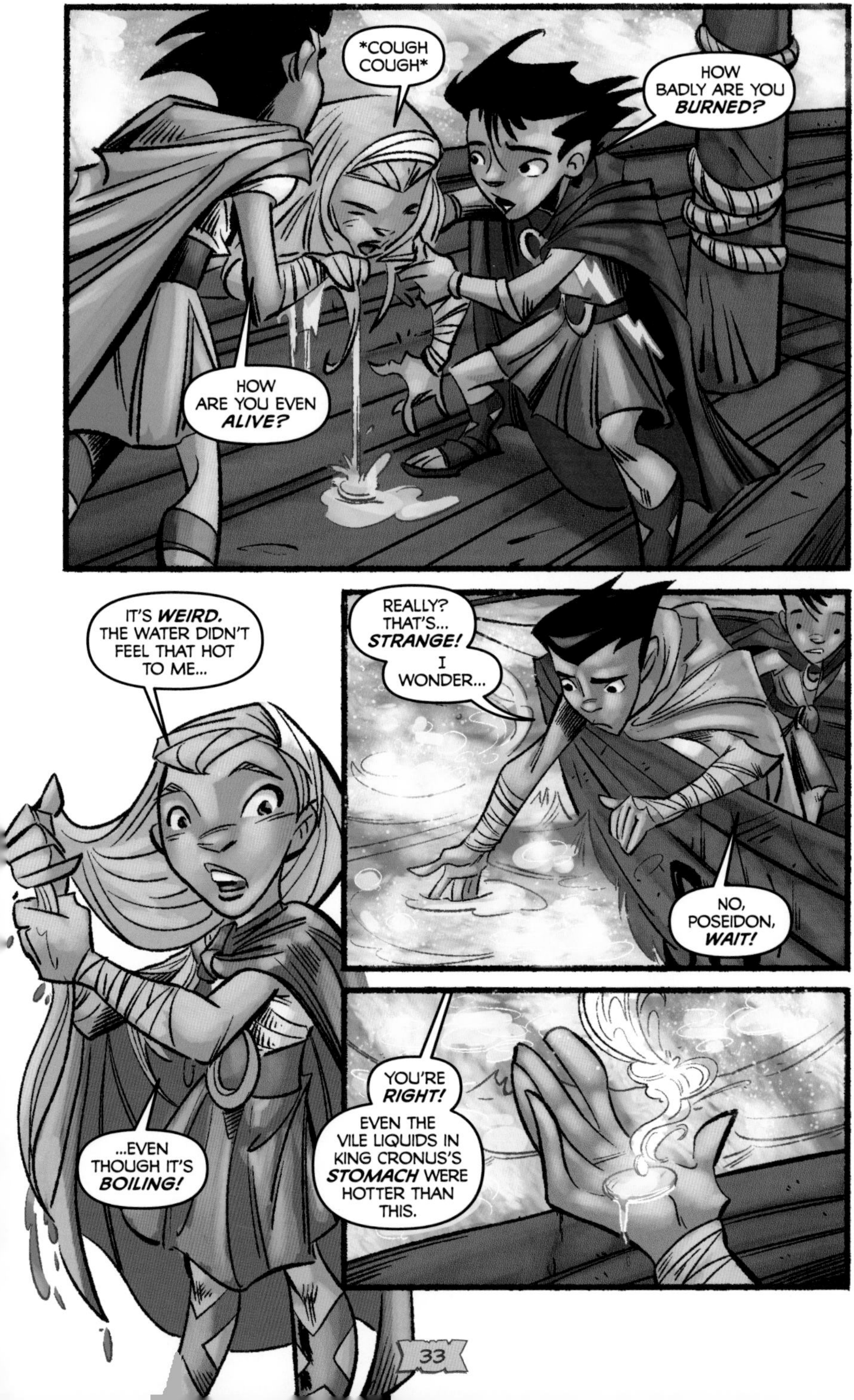
COUGH COUGH
HOW BADLY ARE YOU *BURNED?*
HOW ARE YOU EVEN *ALIVE?*
IT'S *WEIRD.* THE WATER DIDN'T FEEL THAT HOT TO ME...
...EVEN THOUGH IT'S *BOILING!*
REALLY? THAT'S... *STRANGE!*
I WONDER...
NO, POSEIDON, *WAIT!*
YOU'RE *RIGHT!*
EVEN THE VILE LIQUIDS IN KING CRONUS'S *STOMACH* WERE HOTTER THAN THIS.

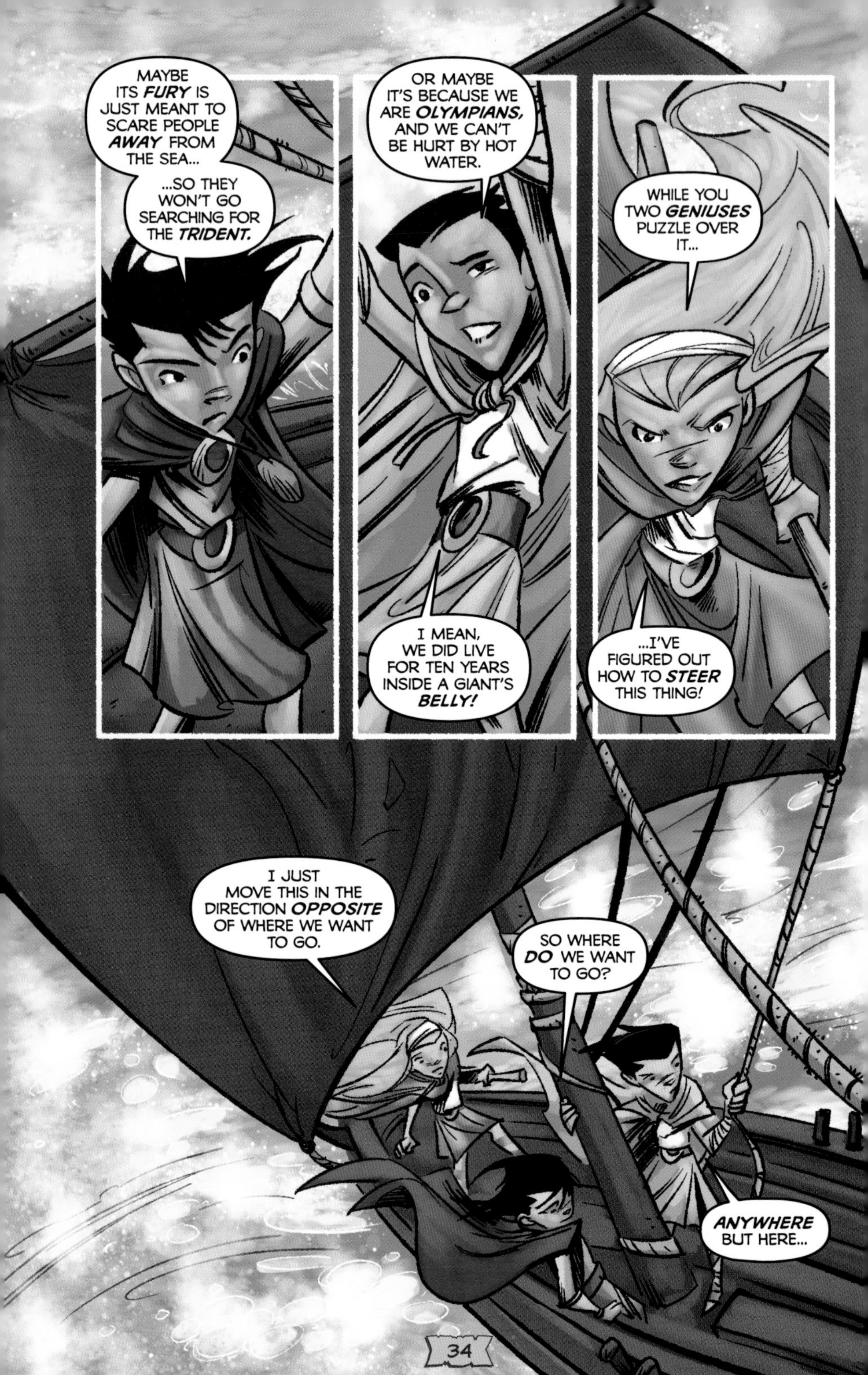
MAYBE ITS *FURY* IS JUST MEANT TO SCARE PEOPLE *AWAY* FROM THE SEA...
...SO THEY WON'T GO SEARCHING FOR THE *TRIDENT.*
OR MAYBE IT'S BECAUSE WE ARE *OLYMPIANS,* AND WE CAN'T BE HURT BY HOT WATER.
I MEAN, WE DID LIVE FOR TEN YEARS INSIDE A GIANT'S *BELLY!*
WHILE YOU TWO *GENIUSES* PUZZLE OVER IT...
...I'VE FIGURED OUT HOW TO *STEER* THIS THING!
I JUST MOVE THIS IN THE DIRECTION *OPPOSITE* OF WHERE WE WANT TO GO.
SO WHERE *DO* WE WANT TO GO?
ANYWHERE BUT HERE...

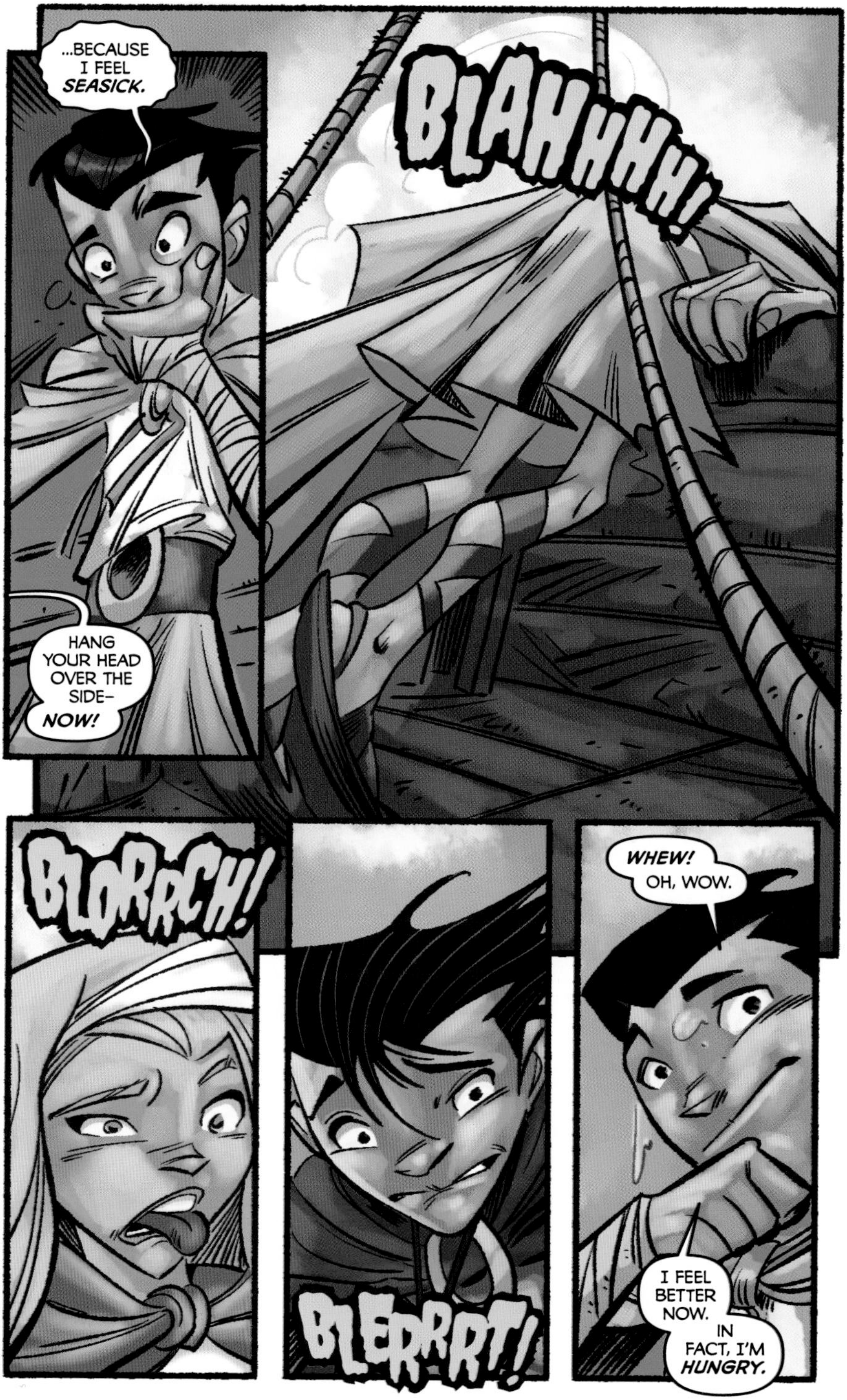
...BECAUSE I FEEL *SEASICK.*
HANG YOUR HEAD OVER THE SIDE– *NOW!*
BLAHHHHH!
BLORRCH!
BLERRRT!
WHEW! OH, WOW.
I FEEL BETTER NOW.
IN FACT, I'M *HUNGRY.*

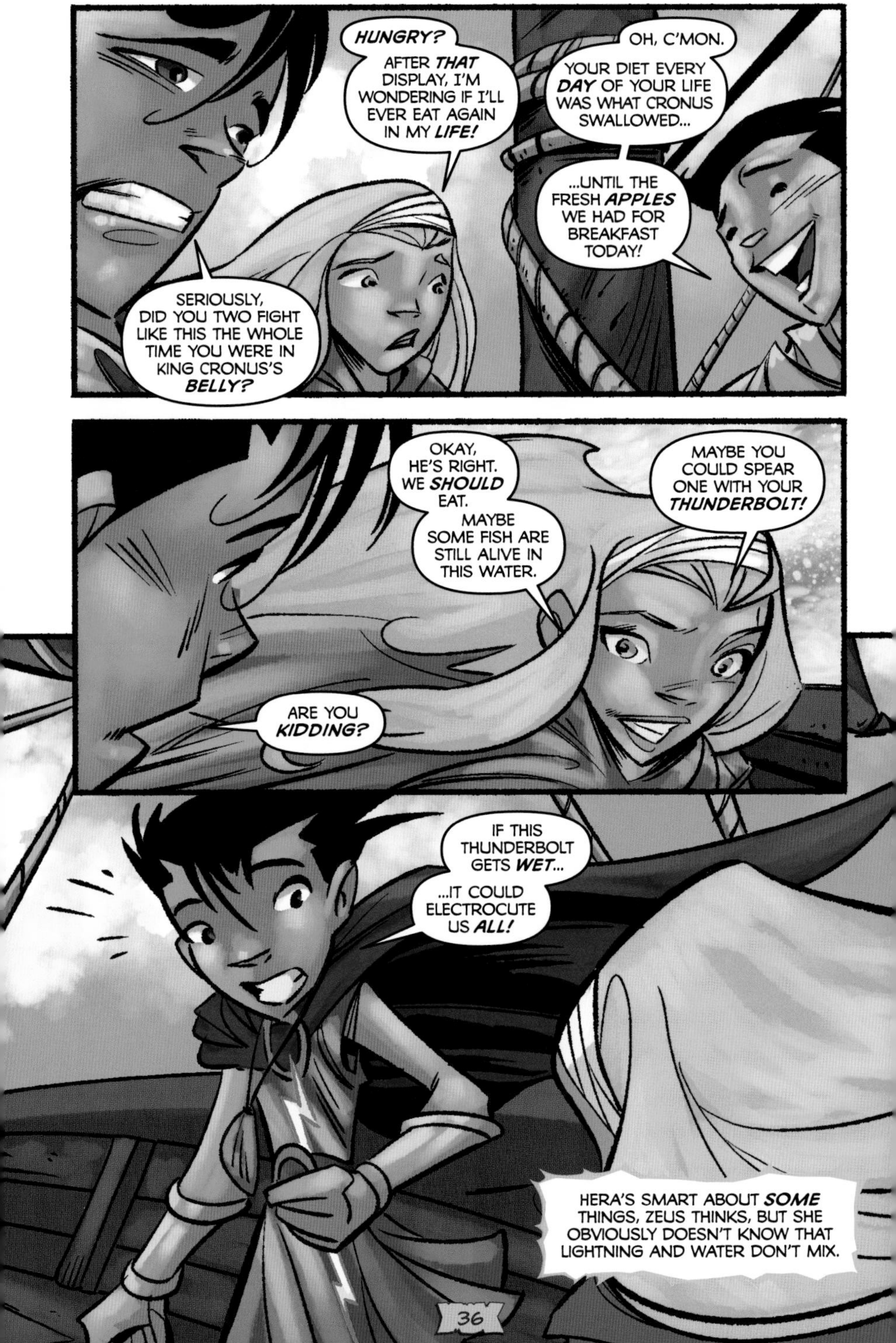
HUNGRY? AFTER THAT DISPLAY, I'M WONDERING IF I'LL EVER EAT AGAIN IN MY LIFE!
SERIOUSLY, DID YOU TWO FIGHT LIKE THIS THE WHOLE TIME YOU WERE IN KING CRONUS'S BELLY?
OH, C'MON.
YOUR DIET EVERY DAY OF YOUR LIFE WAS WHAT CRONUS SWALLOWED...
...UNTIL THE FRESH APPLES WE HAD FOR BREAKFAST TODAY!
OKAY, HE'S RIGHT. WE SHOULD EAT.
MAYBE SOME FISH ARE STILL ALIVE IN THIS WATER.
MAYBE YOU COULD SPEAR ONE WITH YOUR THUNDERBOLT!
ARE YOU KIDDING?
IF THIS THUNDERBOLT GETS WET...
...IT COULD ELECTROCUTE US ALL!
HERA'S SMART ABOUT SOME THINGS, ZEUS THINKS, BUT SHE OBVIOUSLY DOESN'T KNOW THAT LIGHTNING AND WATER DON'T MIX.

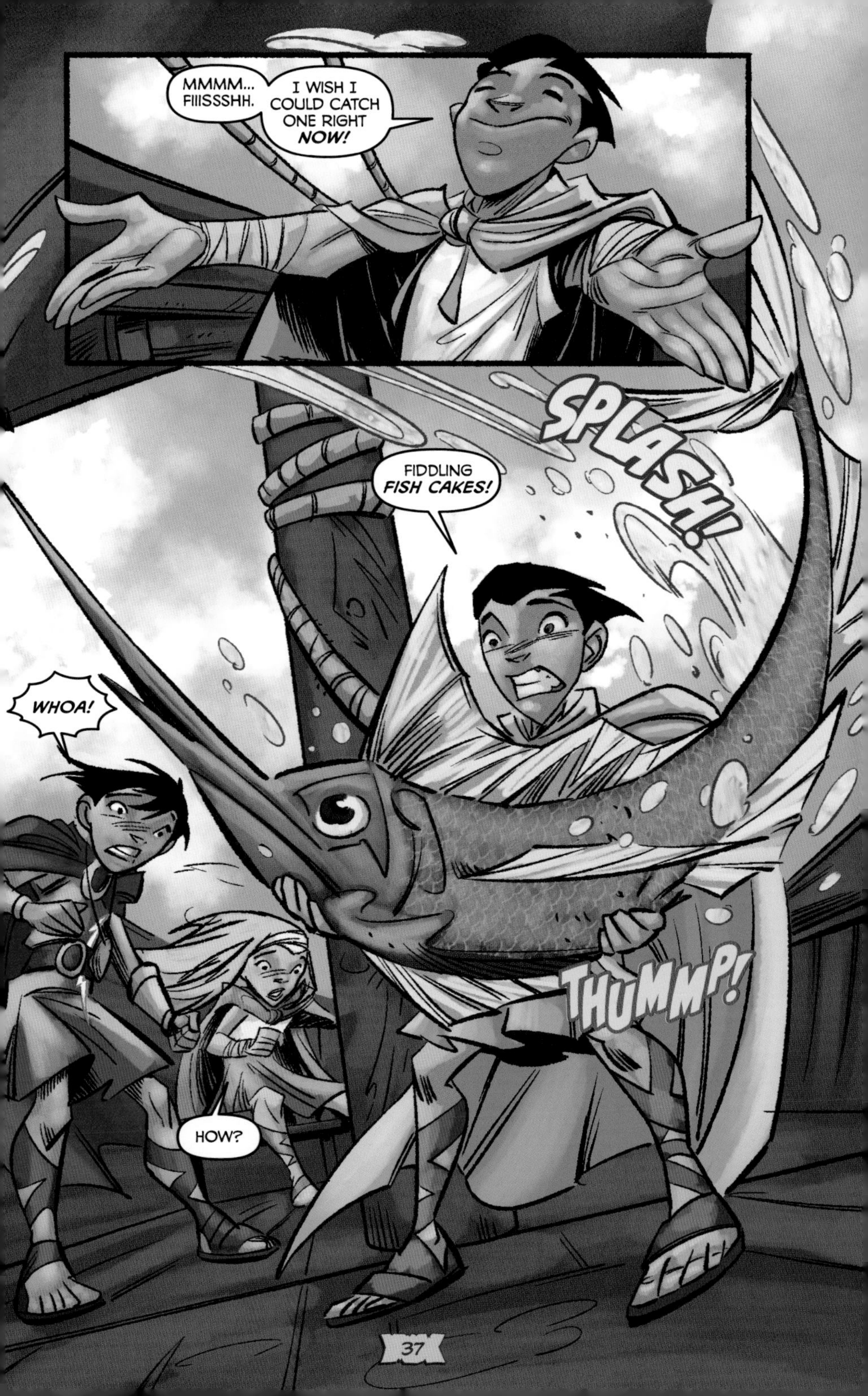
MMMM... FIIISSSHH.
I WISH I COULD CATCH ONE RIGHT NOW!
SPLASH!
FIDDLING FISH CAKES!
WHOA!
THUMMP!
HOW?

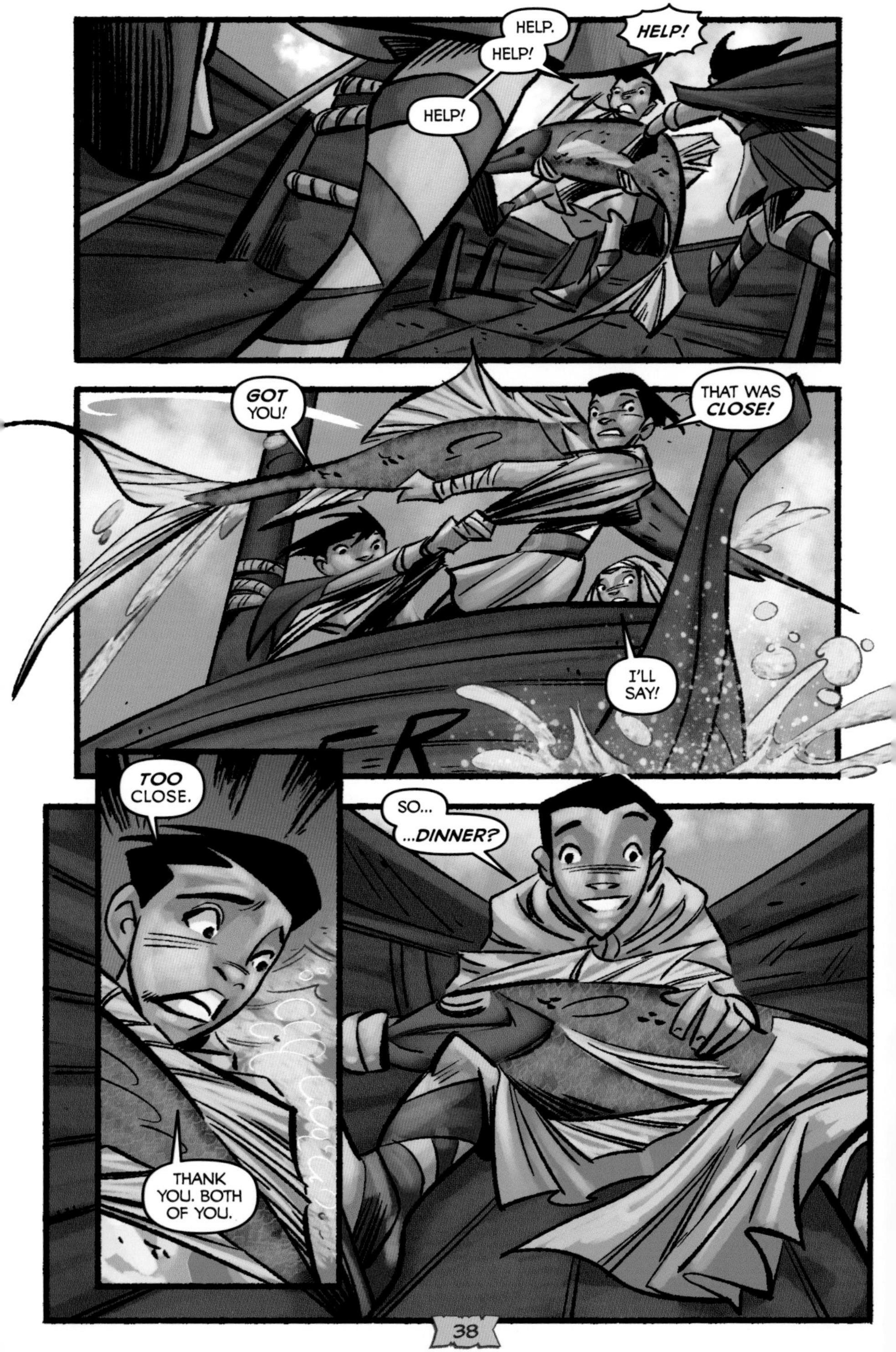
HELP.
HELP!
HELP!
HELP!
GOT YOU!
THAT WAS CLOSE!
I'LL SAY!
TOO CLOSE.
SO...
...DINNER?
THANK YOU. BOTH OF YOU.

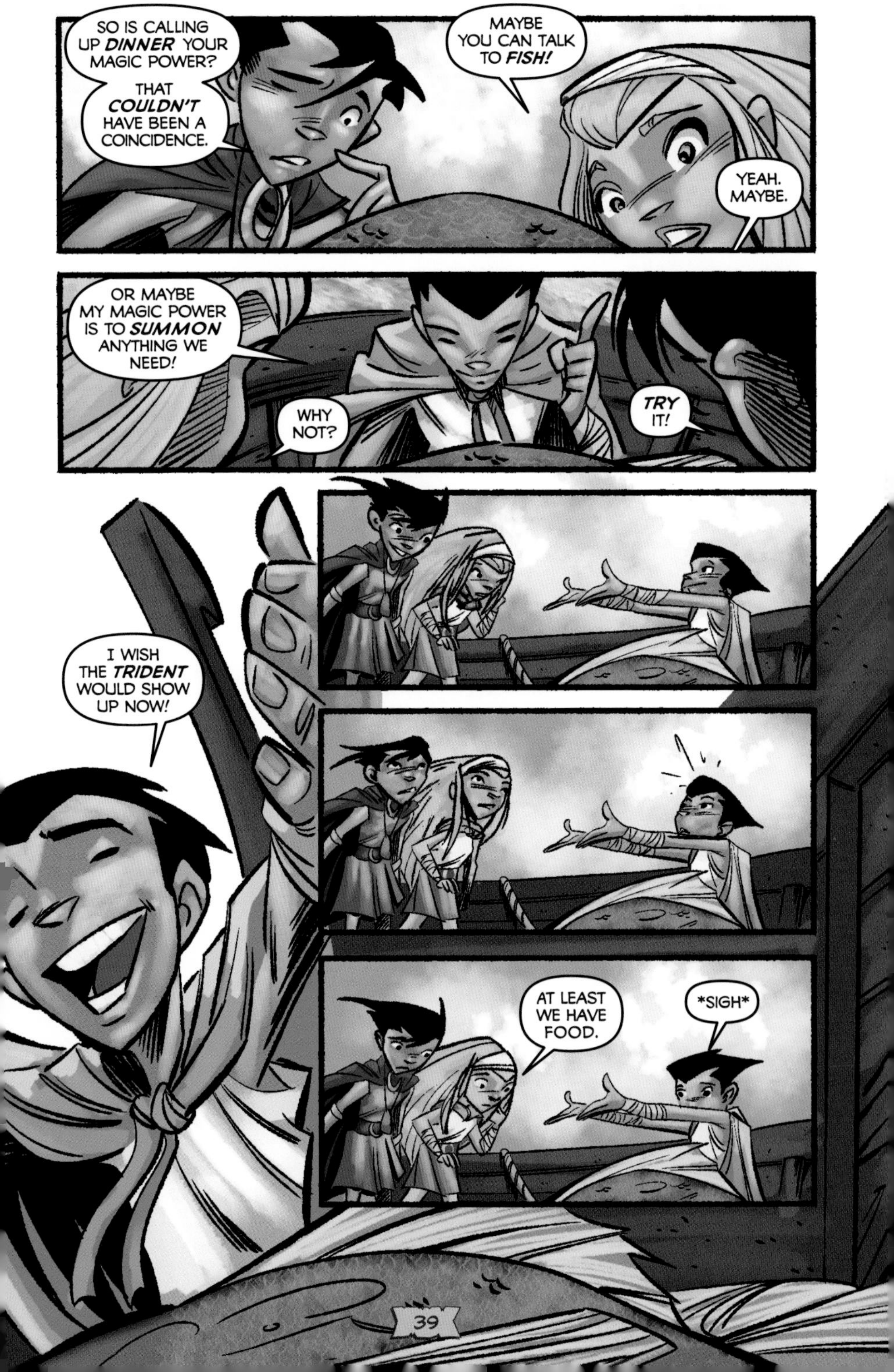
SO IS CALLING UP DINNER YOUR MAGIC POWER?
THAT COULDN'T HAVE BEEN A COINCIDENCE.
MAYBE YOU CAN TALK TO FISH!
YEAH. MAYBE.
OR MAYBE MY MAGIC POWER IS TO SUMMON ANYTHING WE NEED!
WHY NOT?
TRY IT!
I WISH THE TRIDENT WOULD SHOW UP NOW!
AT LEAST WE HAVE FOOD.
SIGH

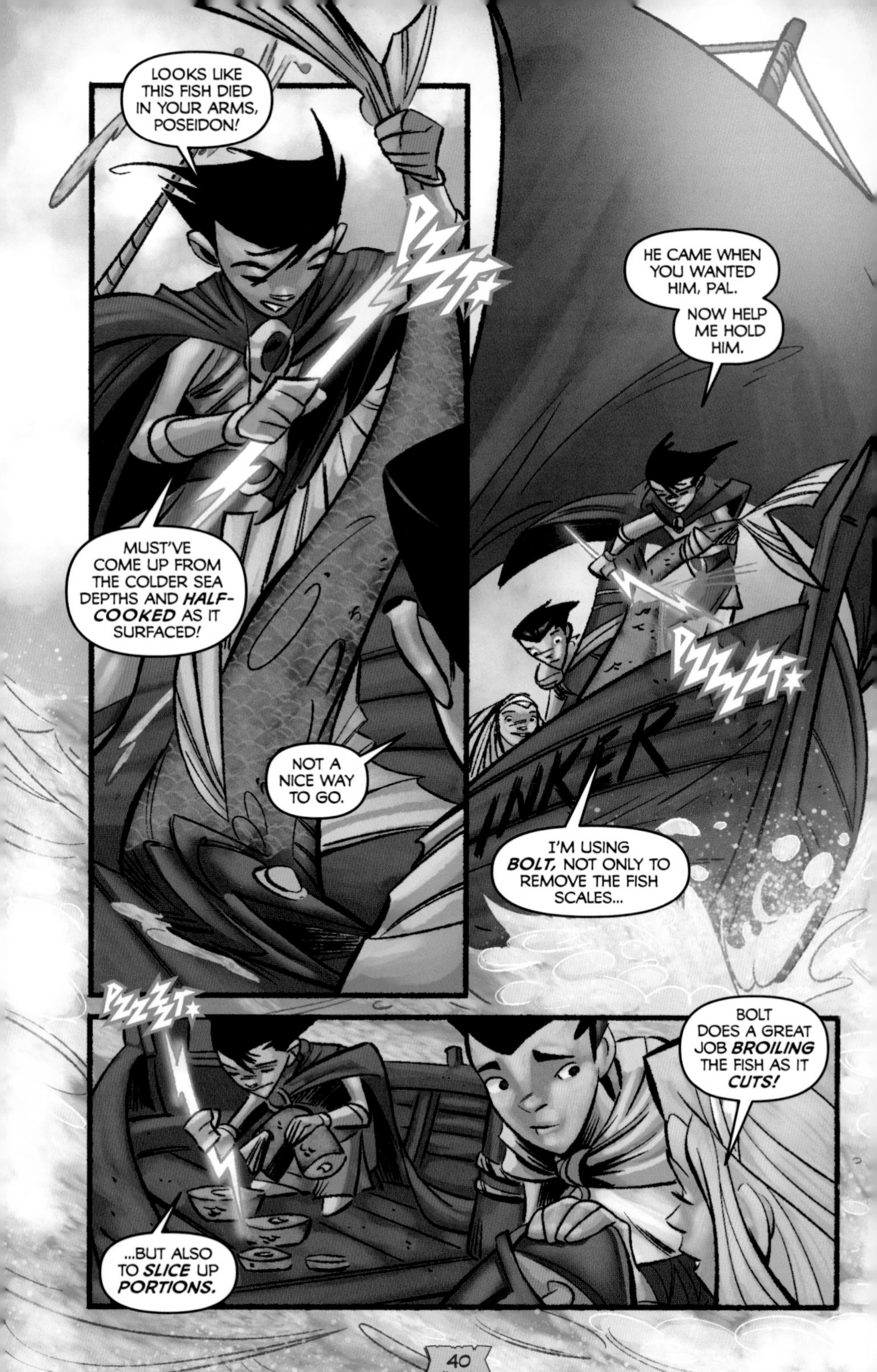
LOOKS LIKE THIS FISH DIED IN YOUR ARMS, POSEIDON!
PZZZT!
MUST'VE COME UP FROM THE COLDER SEA DEPTHS AND HALF-COOKED AS IT SURFACED!
NOT A NICE WAY TO GO.
HE CAME WHEN YOU WANTED HIM, PAL.
NOW HELP ME HOLD HIM.
PZZZZT!
INKER
I'M USING BOLT, NOT ONLY TO REMOVE THE FISH SCALES...
PZZZZT!
...BUT ALSO TO SLICE UP PORTIONS.
BOLT DOES A GREAT JOB BROILING THE FISH AS IT CUTS!

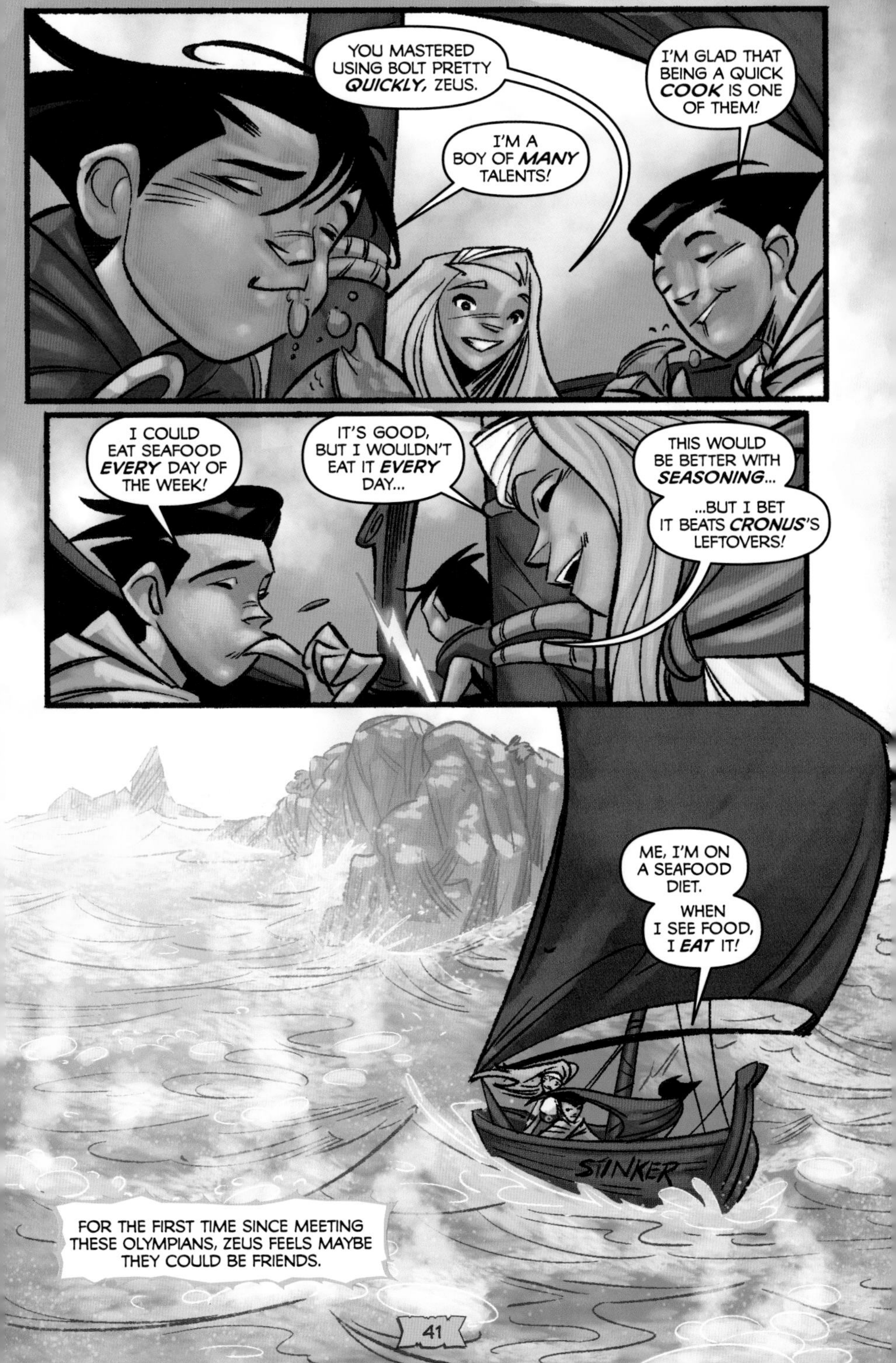
YOU MASTERED USING BOLT PRETTY QUICKLY, ZEUS.
I'M A BOY OF MANY TALENTS!
I'M GLAD THAT BEING A QUICK COOK IS ONE OF THEM!
I COULD EAT SEAFOOD EVERY DAY OF THE WEEK!
IT'S GOOD, BUT I WOULDN'T EAT IT EVERY DAY...
THIS WOULD BE BETTER WITH SEASONING...
...BUT I BET IT BEATS CRONUS'S LEFTOVERS!
ME, I'M ON A SEAFOOD DIET.
WHEN I SEE FOOD, I EAT IT!
STINKER
FOR THE FIRST TIME SINCE MEETING THESE OLYMPIANS, ZEUS FEELS MAYBE THEY COULD BE FRIENDS.

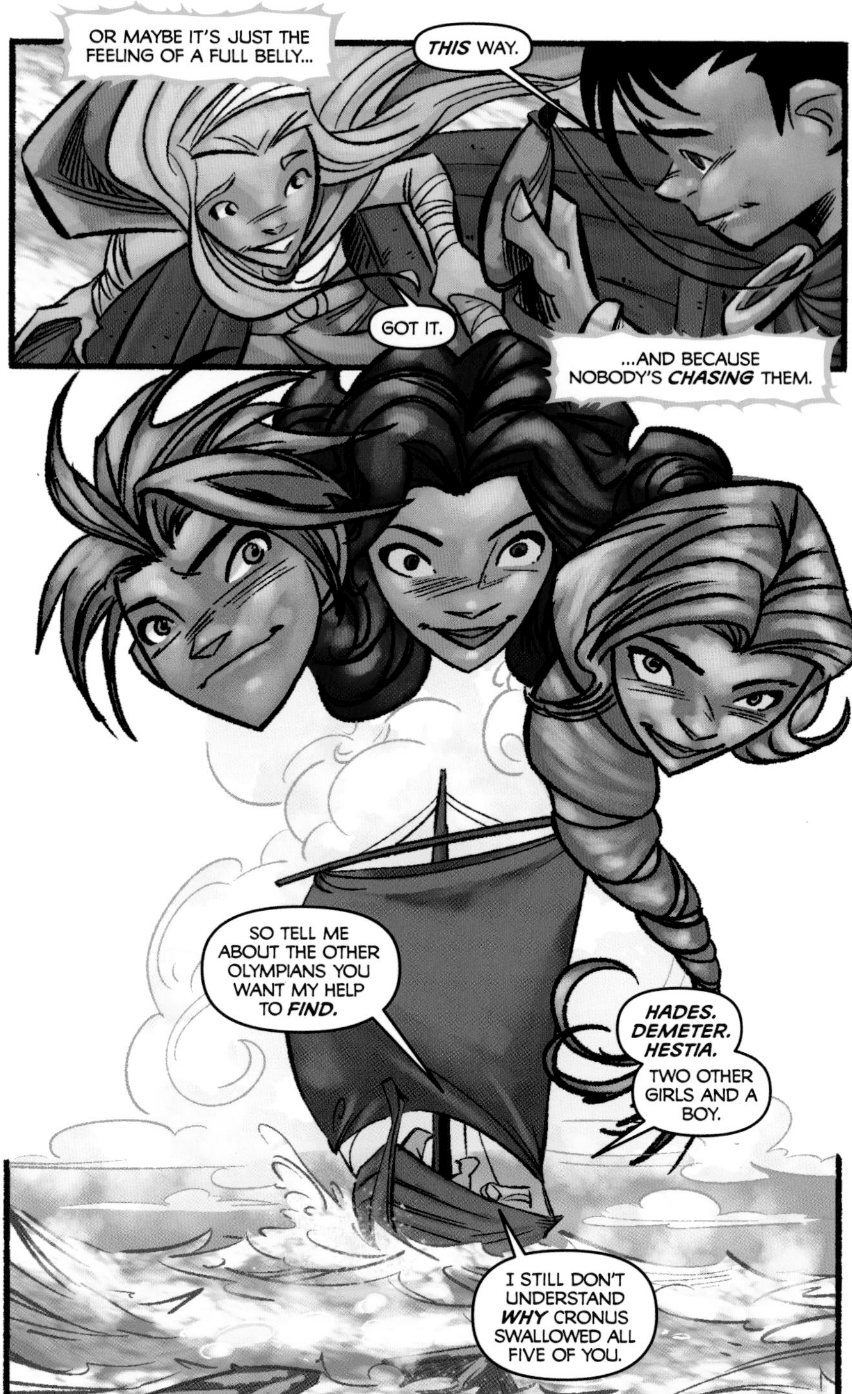
OR MAYBE IT'S JUST THE FEELING OF A FULL BELLY...
THIS WAY.
GOT IT.
...AND BECAUSE NOBODY'S CHASING THEM.
SO TELL ME ABOUT THE OTHER OLYMPIANS YOU WANT MY HELP TO FIND.
HADES. DEMETER. HESTIA.
TWO OTHER GIRLS AND A BOY.
I STILL DON'T UNDERSTAND WHY CRONUS SWALLOWED ALL FIVE OF YOU.

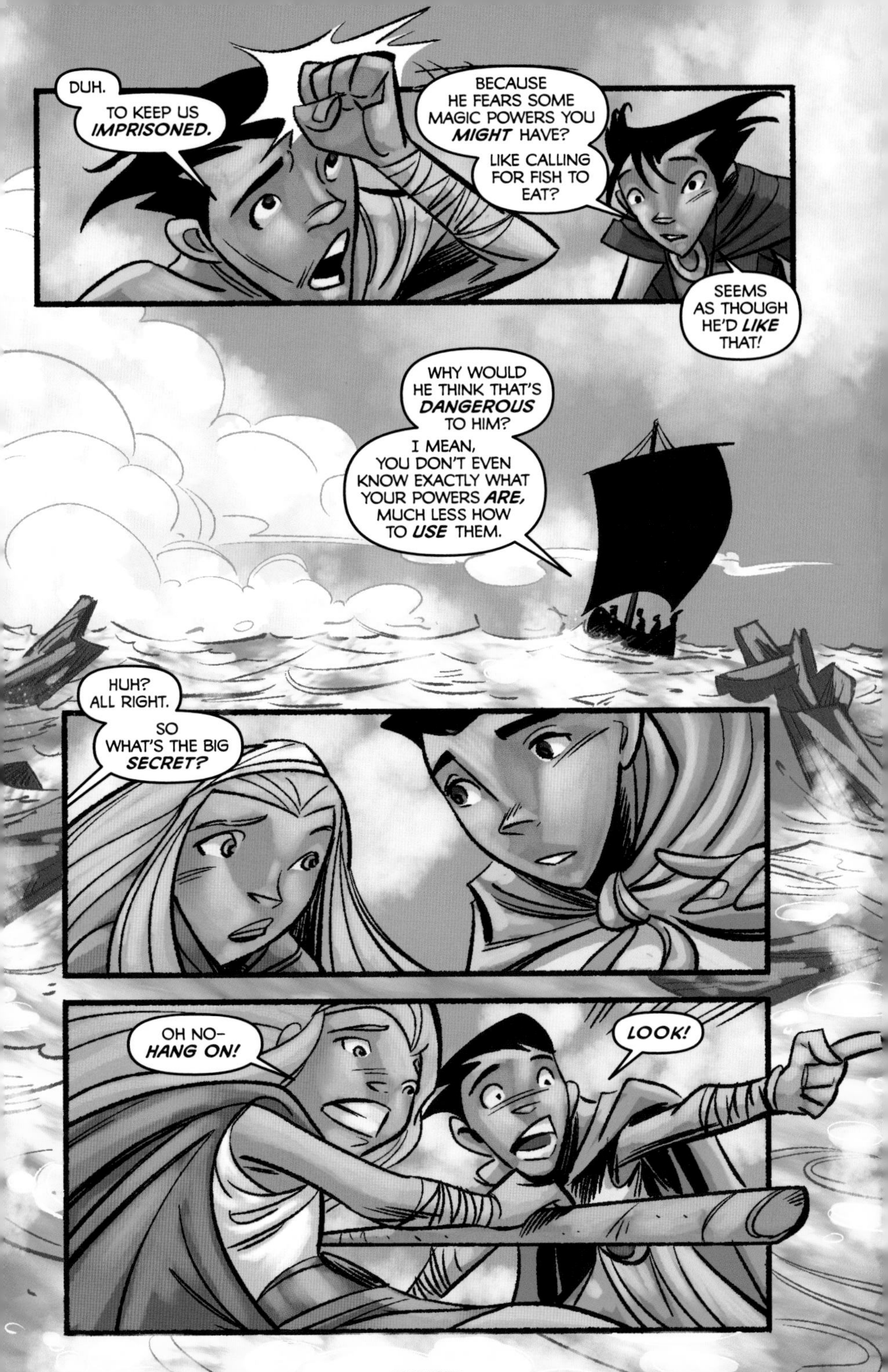
DUH.
TO KEEP US IMPRISONED.
BECAUSE HE FEARS SOME MAGIC POWERS YOU MIGHT HAVE?
LIKE CALLING FOR FISH TO EAT?
SEEMS AS THOUGH HE'D LIKE THAT!
WHY WOULD HE THINK THAT'S DANGEROUS TO HIM?
I MEAN, YOU DON'T EVEN KNOW EXACTLY WHAT YOUR POWERS ARE, MUCH LESS HOW TO USE THEM.
HUH? ALL RIGHT.
SO WHAT'S THE BIG SECRET?
OH NO– HANG ON!
LOOK!

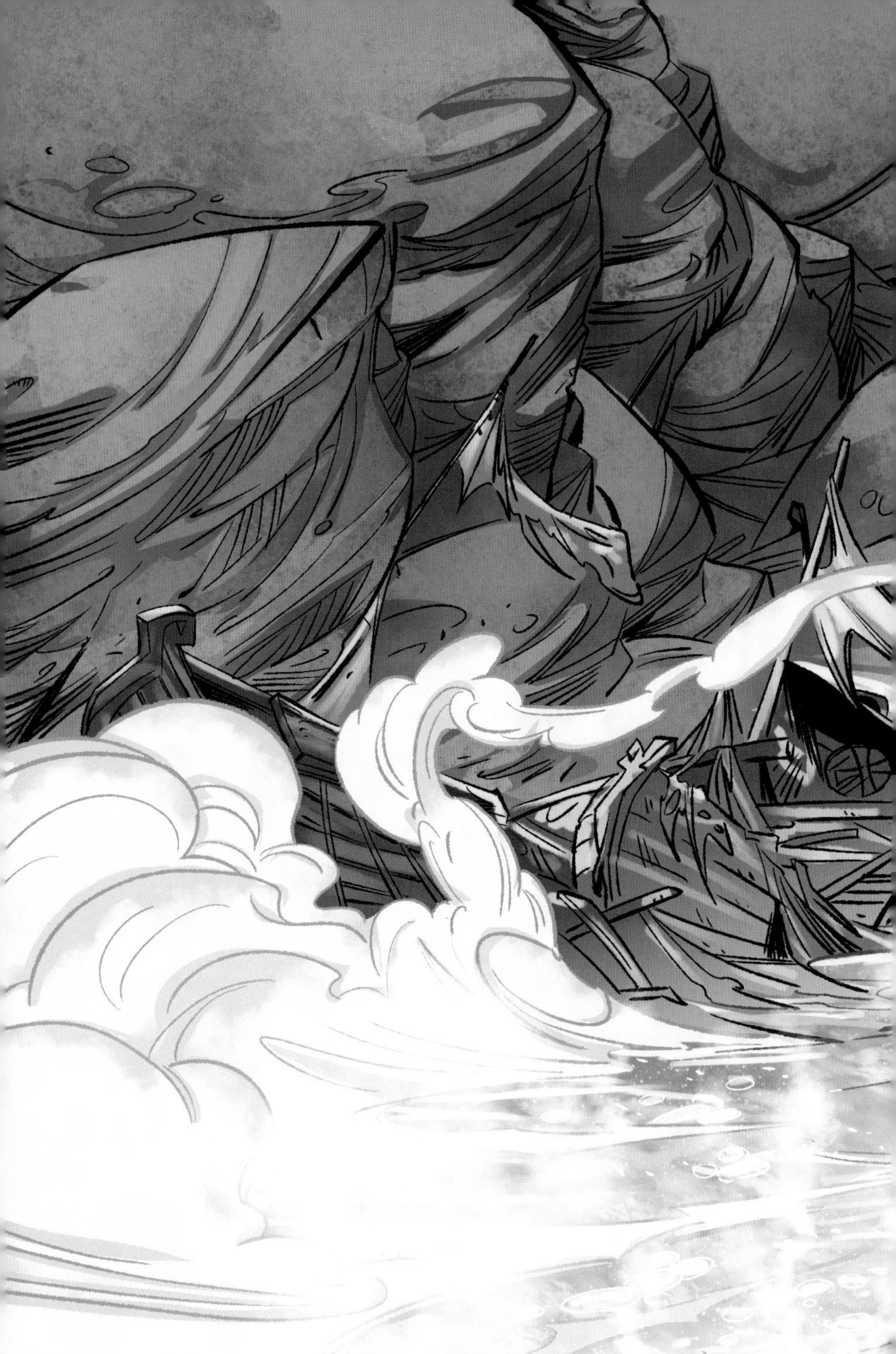

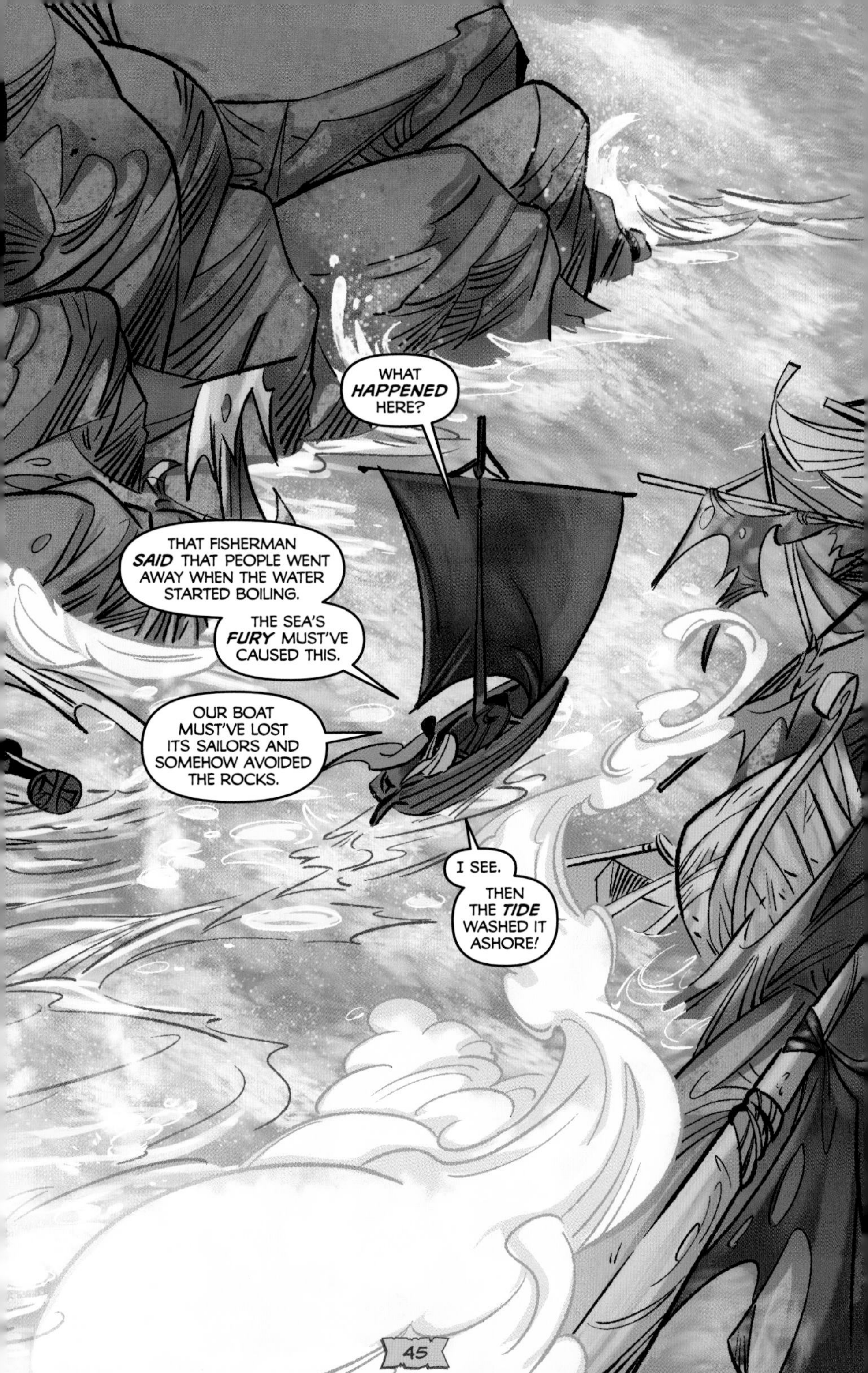
WHAT *HAPPENED* HERE?
THAT FISHERMAN *SAID* THAT PEOPLE WENT AWAY WHEN THE WATER STARTED BOILING.
THE SEA'S *FURY* MUST'VE CAUSED THIS.
OUR BOAT MUST'VE LOST ITS SAILORS AND SOMEHOW AVOIDED THE ROCKS.
I SEE.
THEN THE *TIDE* WASHED IT ASHORE!

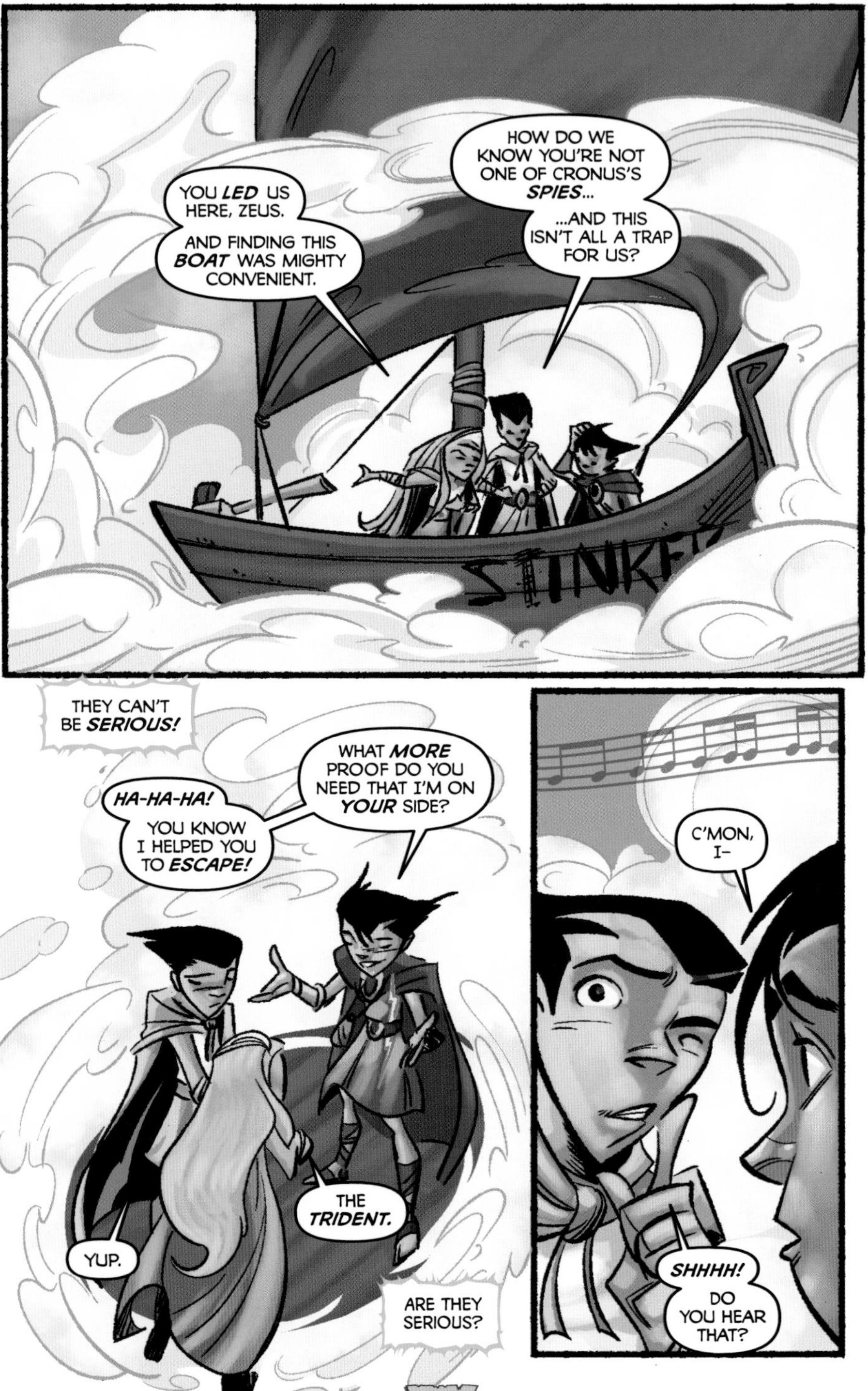
YOU LED US HERE, ZEUS.
AND FINDING THIS BOAT WAS MIGHTY CONVENIENT.
HOW DO WE KNOW YOU'RE NOT ONE OF CRONUS'S SPIES...
...AND THIS ISN'T ALL A TRAP FOR US?
STINKED
THEY CAN'T BE SERIOUS!
HA-HA-HA! YOU KNOW I HELPED YOU TO ESCAPE!
WHAT MORE PROOF DO YOU NEED THAT I'M ON YOUR SIDE?
THE TRIDENT.
YUP.
ARE THEY SERIOUS?
C'MON, I–
SHHHH! DO YOU HEAR THAT?

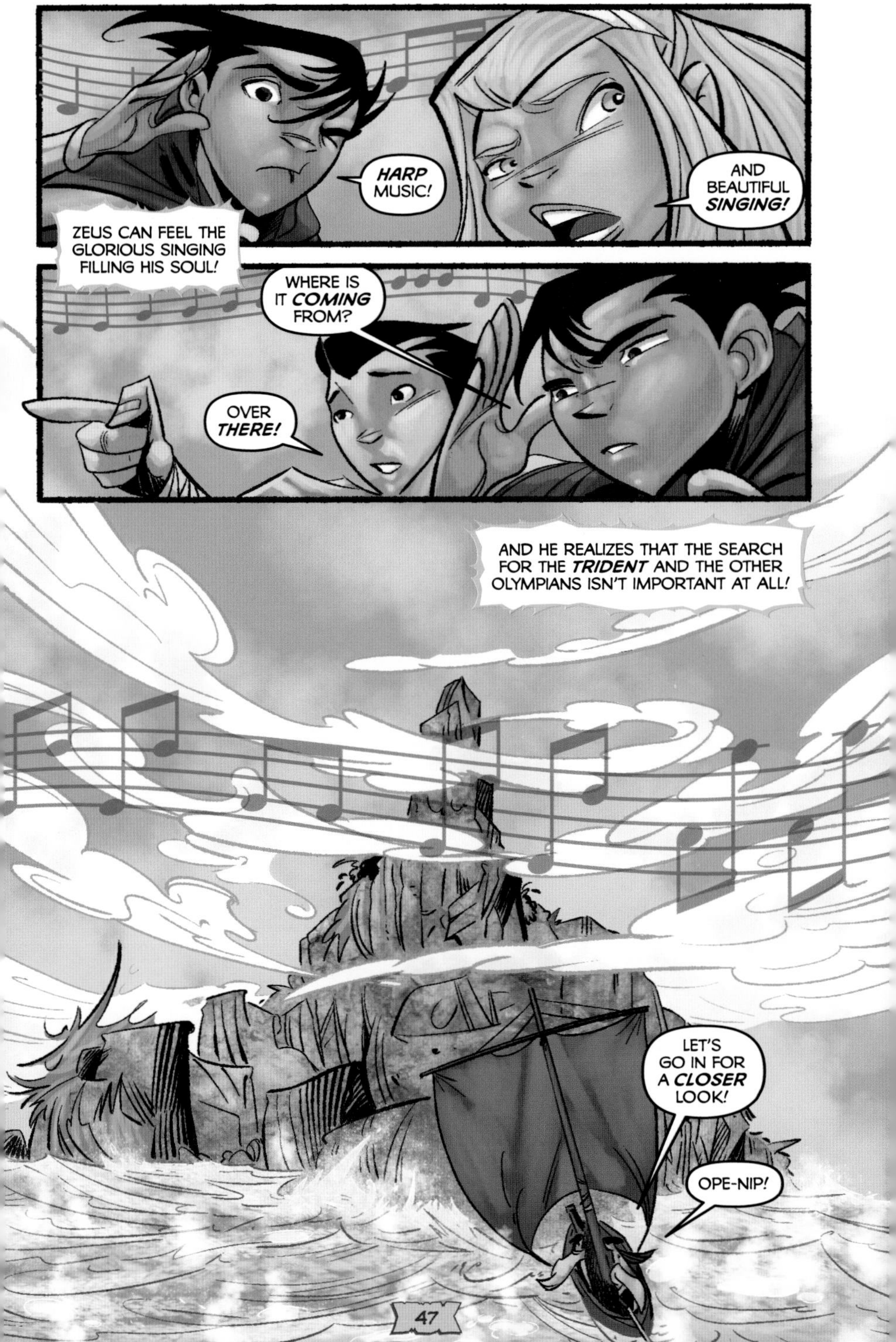
HARP MUSIC!
AND BEAUTIFUL SINGING!
ZEUS CAN FEEL THE GLORIOUS SINGING FILLING HIS SOUL!
WHERE IS IT COMING FROM?
OVER THERE!
AND HE REALIZES THAT THE SEARCH FOR THE TRIDENT AND THE OTHER OLYMPIANS ISN'T IMPORTANT AT ALL!
LET'S GO IN FOR A CLOSER LOOK!
OPE-NIP!

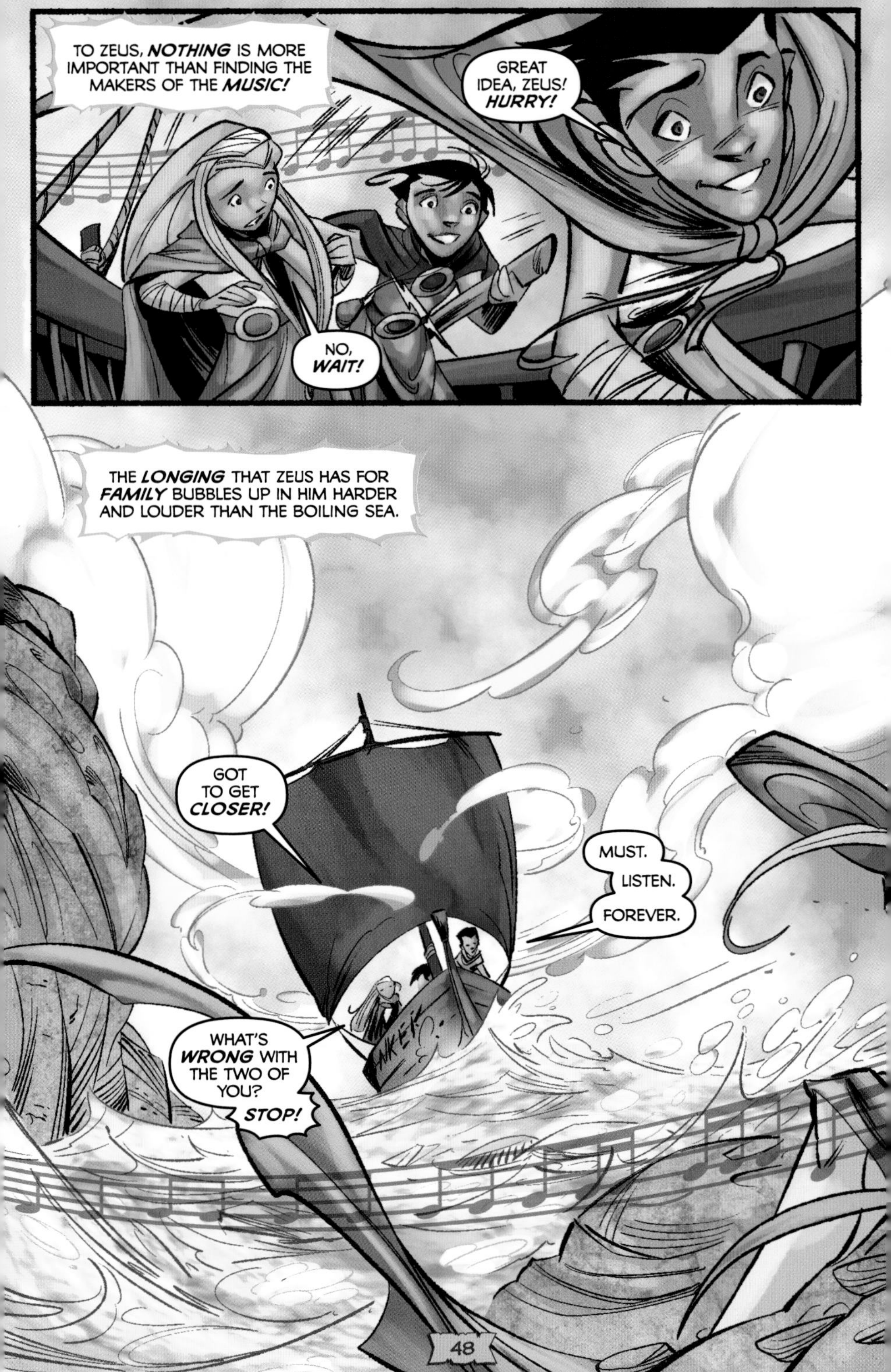
TO ZEUS, NOTHING IS MORE IMPORTANT THAN FINDING THE MAKERS OF THE MUSIC!
GREAT IDEA, ZEUS! HURRY!
NO, WAIT!
THE LONGING THAT ZEUS HAS FOR FAMILY BUBBLES UP IN HIM HARDER AND LOUDER THAN THE BOILING SEA.
GOT TO GET CLOSER!
MUST. LISTEN. FOREVER.
WHAT'S WRONG WITH THE TWO OF YOU? STOP!

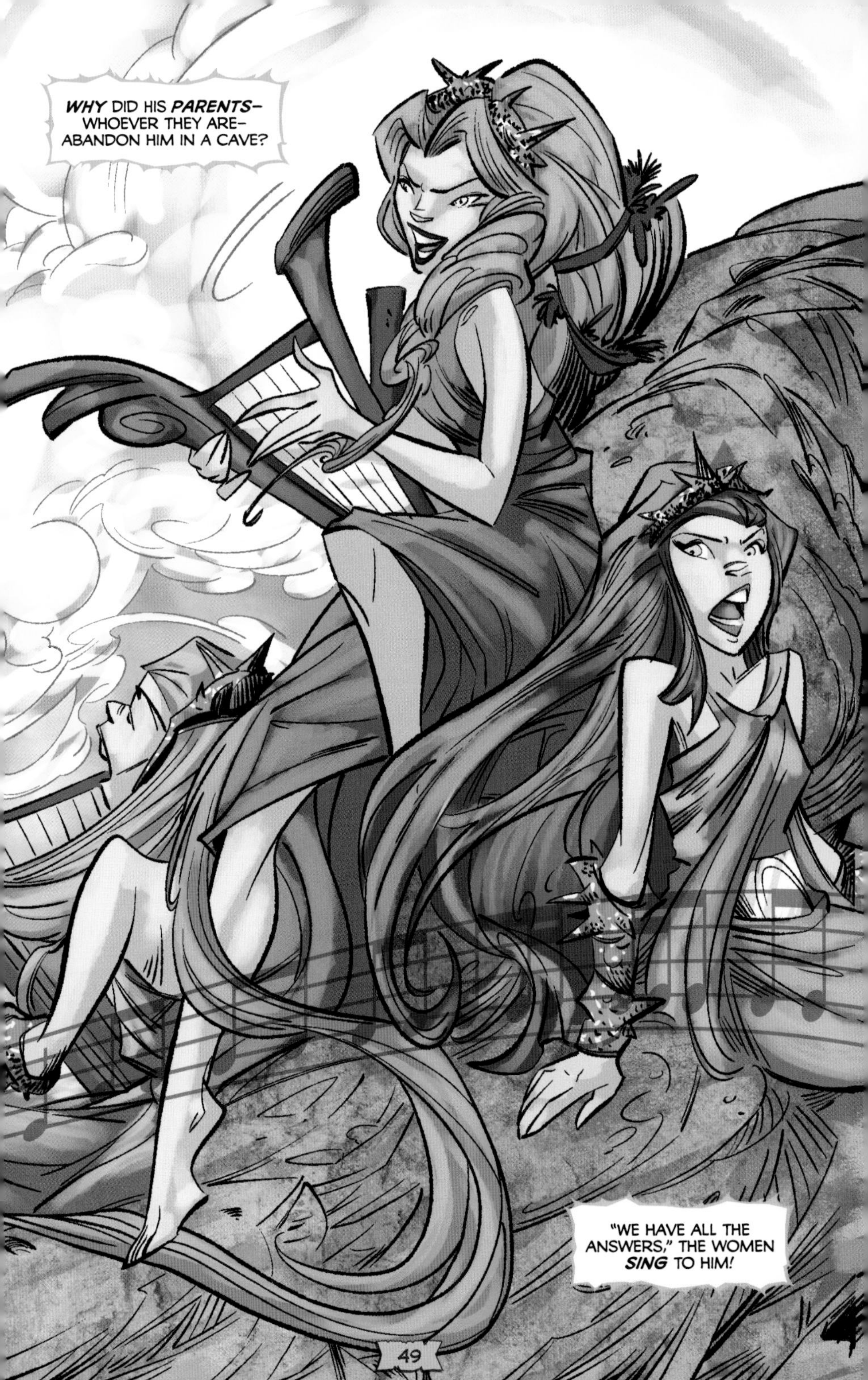

WHY DID HIS **PARENTS**– WHOEVER THEY ARE– ABANDON HIM IN A CAVE?
"WE HAVE ALL THE ANSWERS," THE WOMEN **SING** TO HIM!

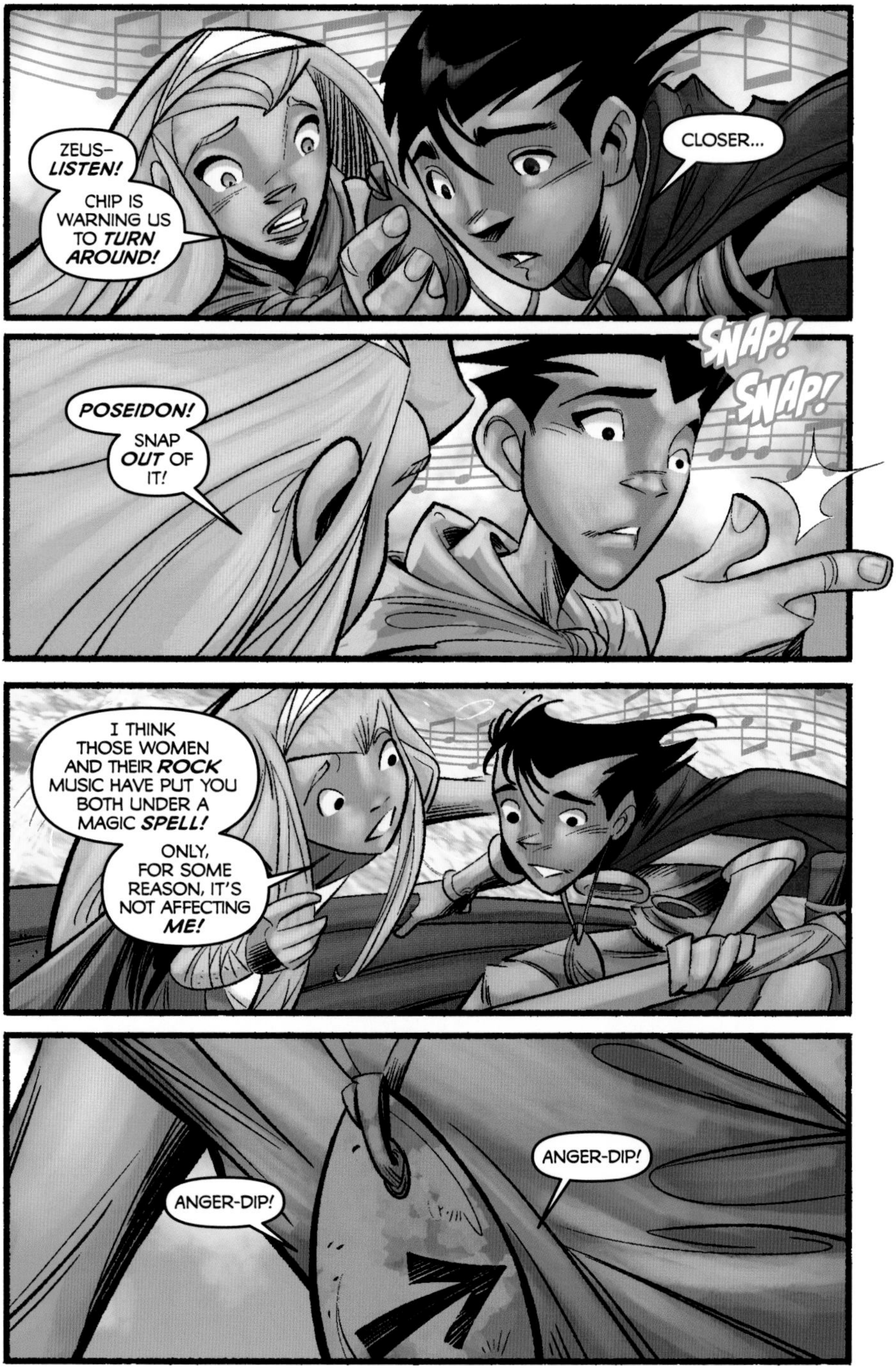
ZEUS–
LISTEN!
CHIP IS WARNING US TO ***TURN AROUND!***
CLOSER...
POSEIDON!
SNAP ***OUT*** OF IT!
SNAP! SNAP!
I THINK THOSE WOMEN AND THEIR ***ROCK*** MUSIC HAVE PUT YOU BOTH UNDER A MAGIC ***SPELL!***
ONLY, FOR SOME REASON, IT'S NOT AFFECTING ***ME!***
ANGER-DIP!
ANGER-DIP!

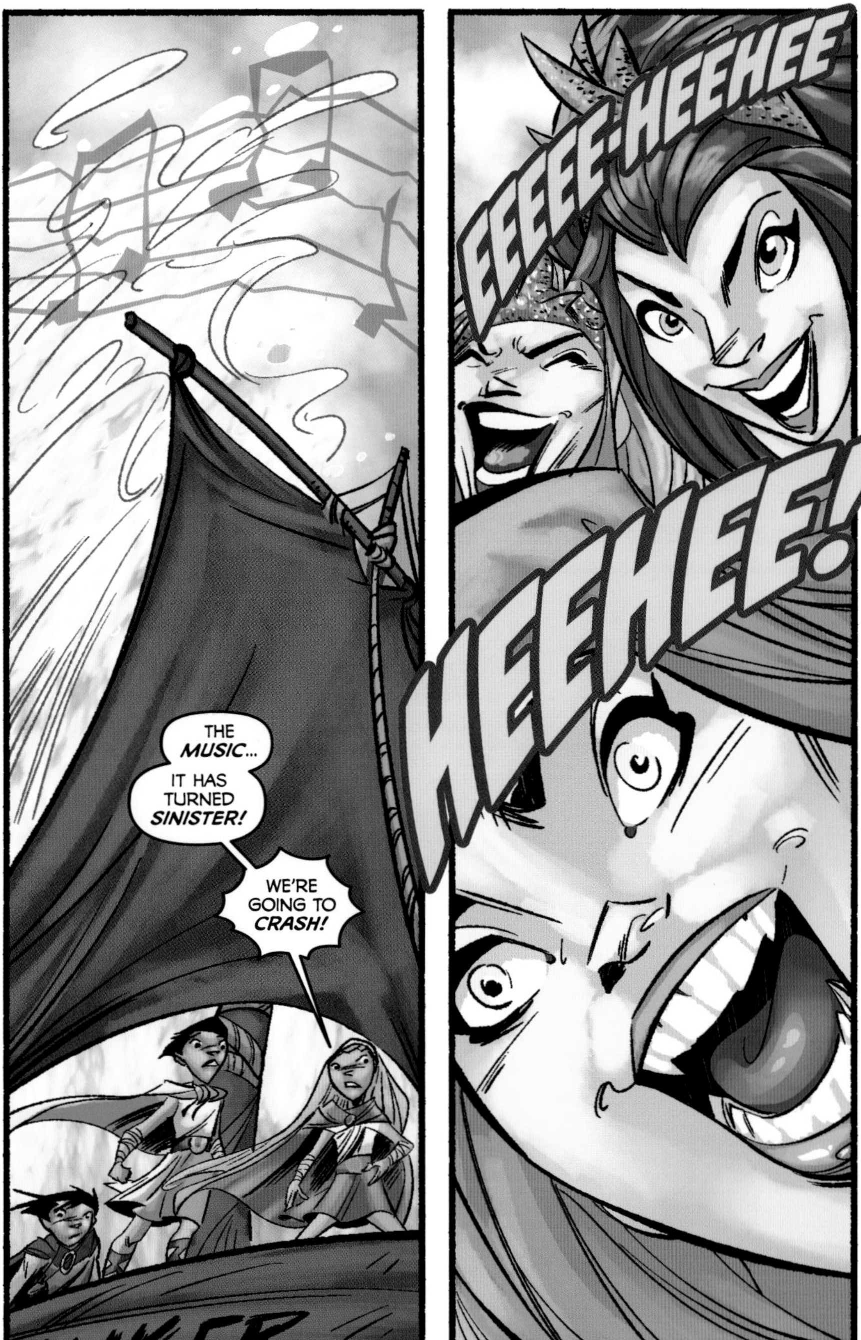
THE MUSIC...
IT HAS TURNED SINISTER!
WE'RE GOING TO CRASH!
EEEEE-HEEHEE
HEEHEE!

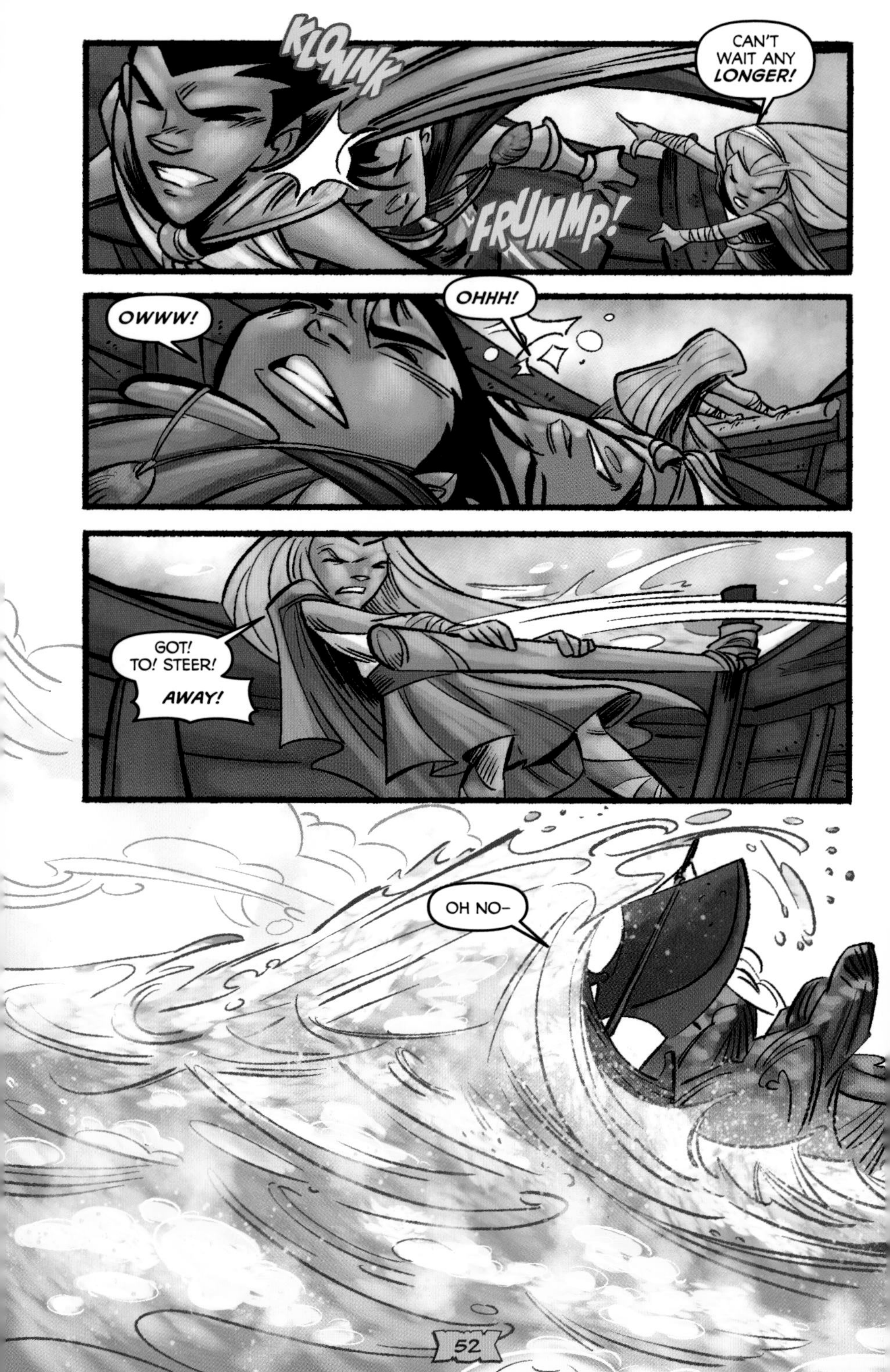
KLONK
CAN'T WAIT ANY LONGER!
FRUMMP!
OWWW!
OHHH!
GOT! TO! STEER! AWAY!
OH NO–

CHAPTER FOUR:
SEA SERPENTS AND MERPEOPLE

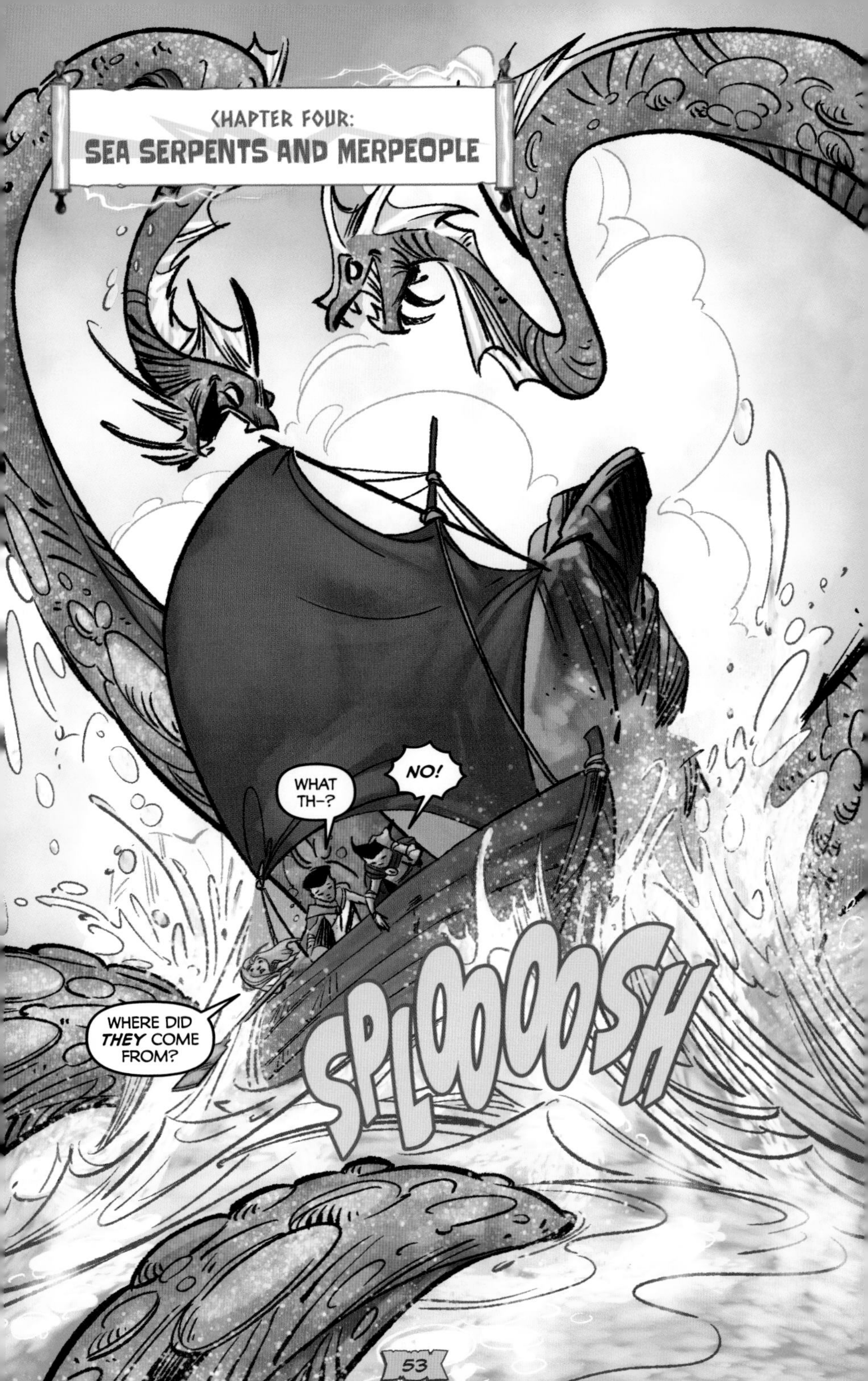
WHAT TH–?
NO!
WHERE DID *THEY* COME FROM?
SPLOOOOSH

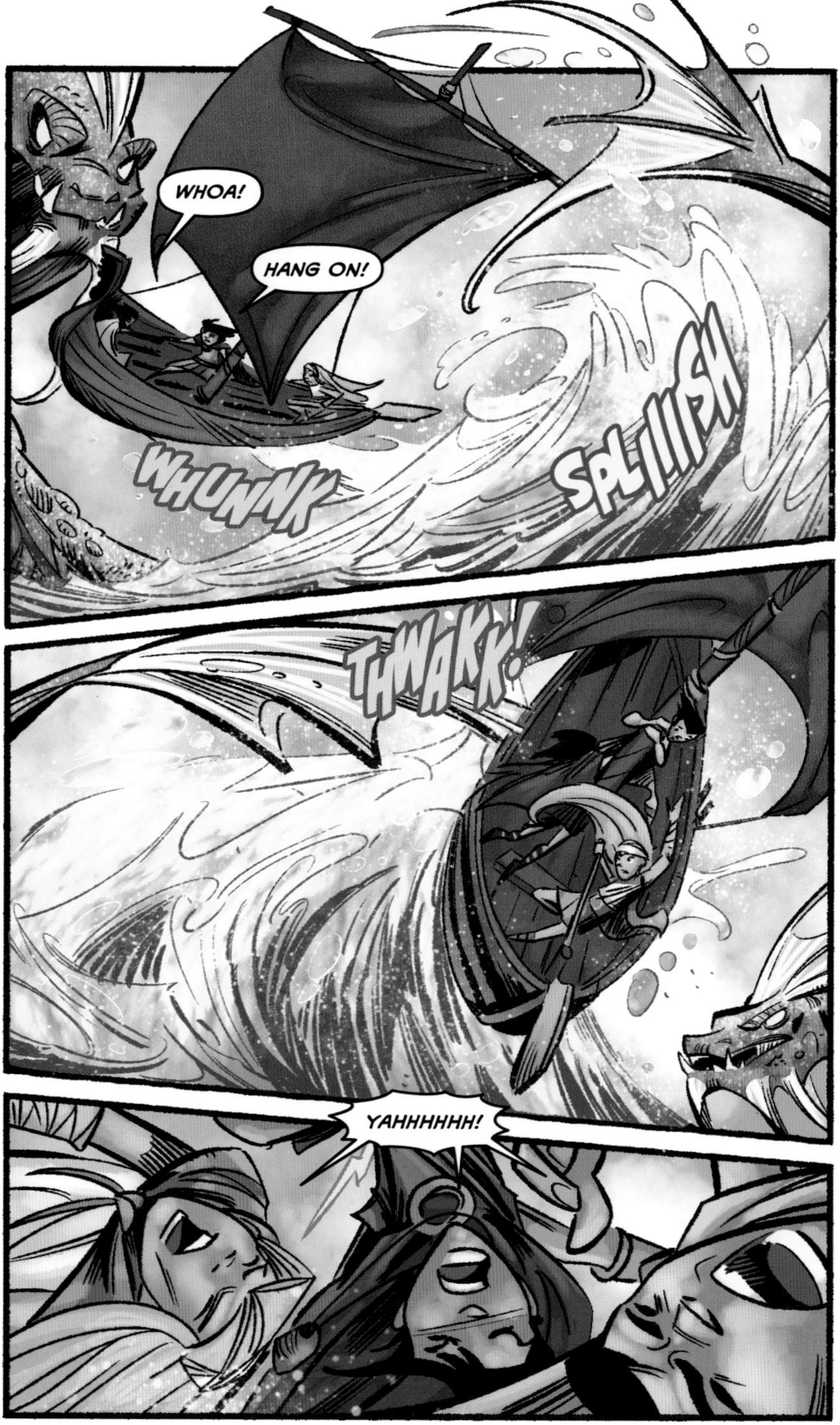
WHOA!
HANG ON!
WHUNNK
SPLIIISH
THWAKK!
YAHHHHHH!

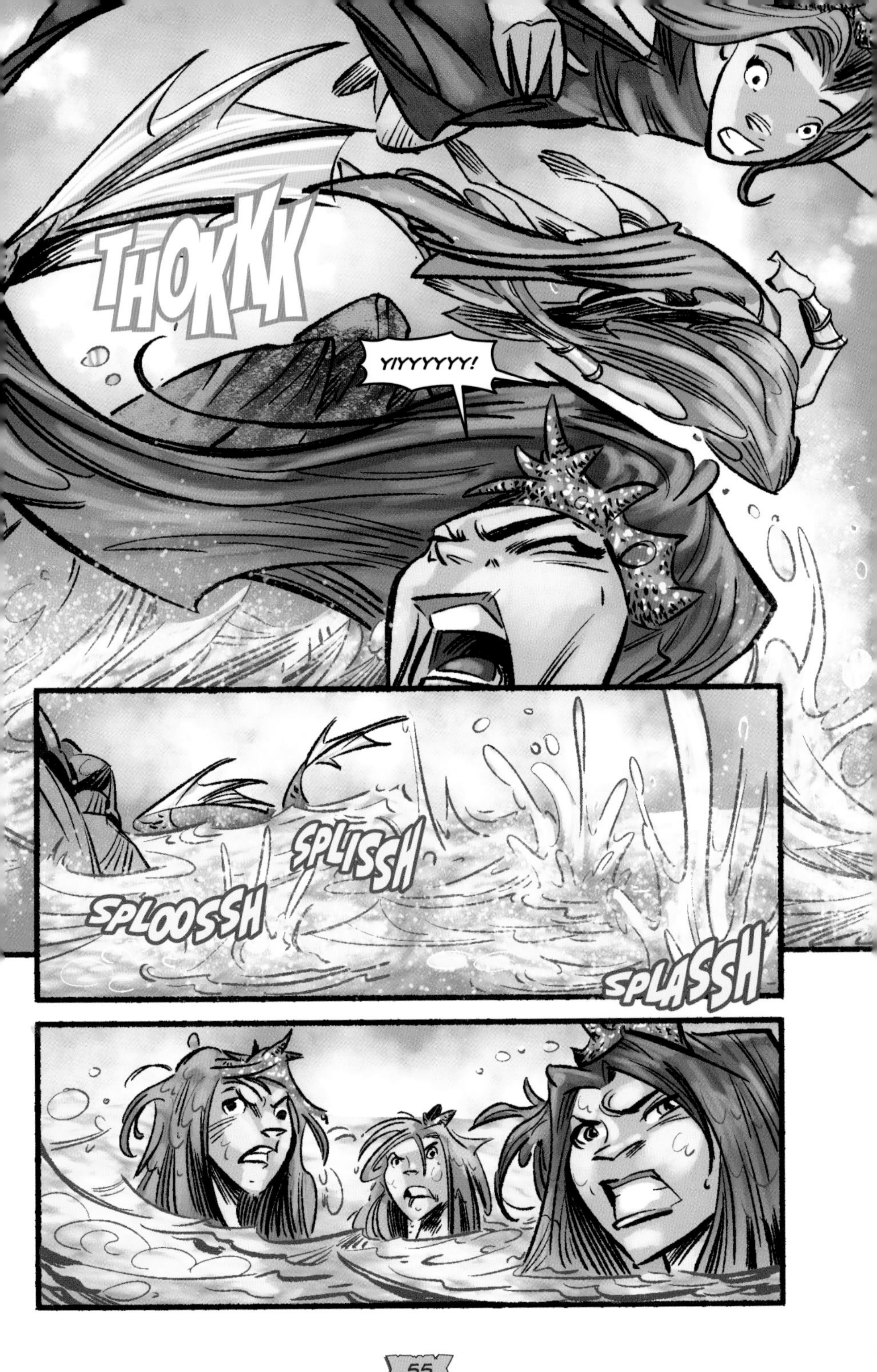
THOKKK
YIYYYYYY!
SPLISSH
SPLOOSSH
SPLASSH

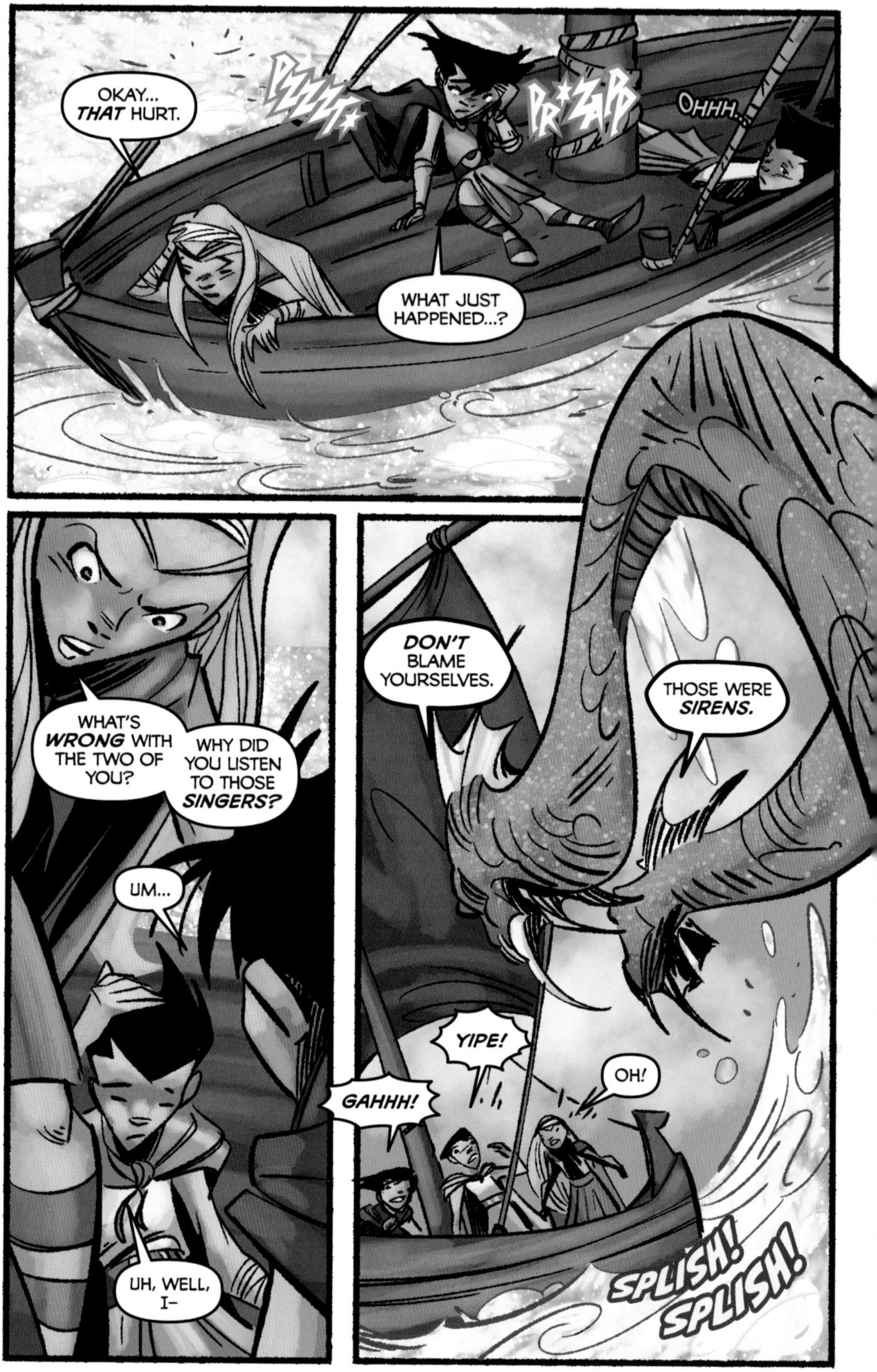

OKAY... *THAT* HURT.
PZZZT
PR*ZAP
OHHH...
WHAT JUST HAPPENED...?
WHAT'S *WRONG* WITH THE TWO OF YOU?
WHY DID YOU LISTEN TO THOSE *SINGERS?*
UM...
UH, WELL, I–
DON'T BLAME YOURSELVES.
THOSE WERE *SIRENS.*
YIPE!
OH!
GAHHH!
SPLISH! SPLISH!

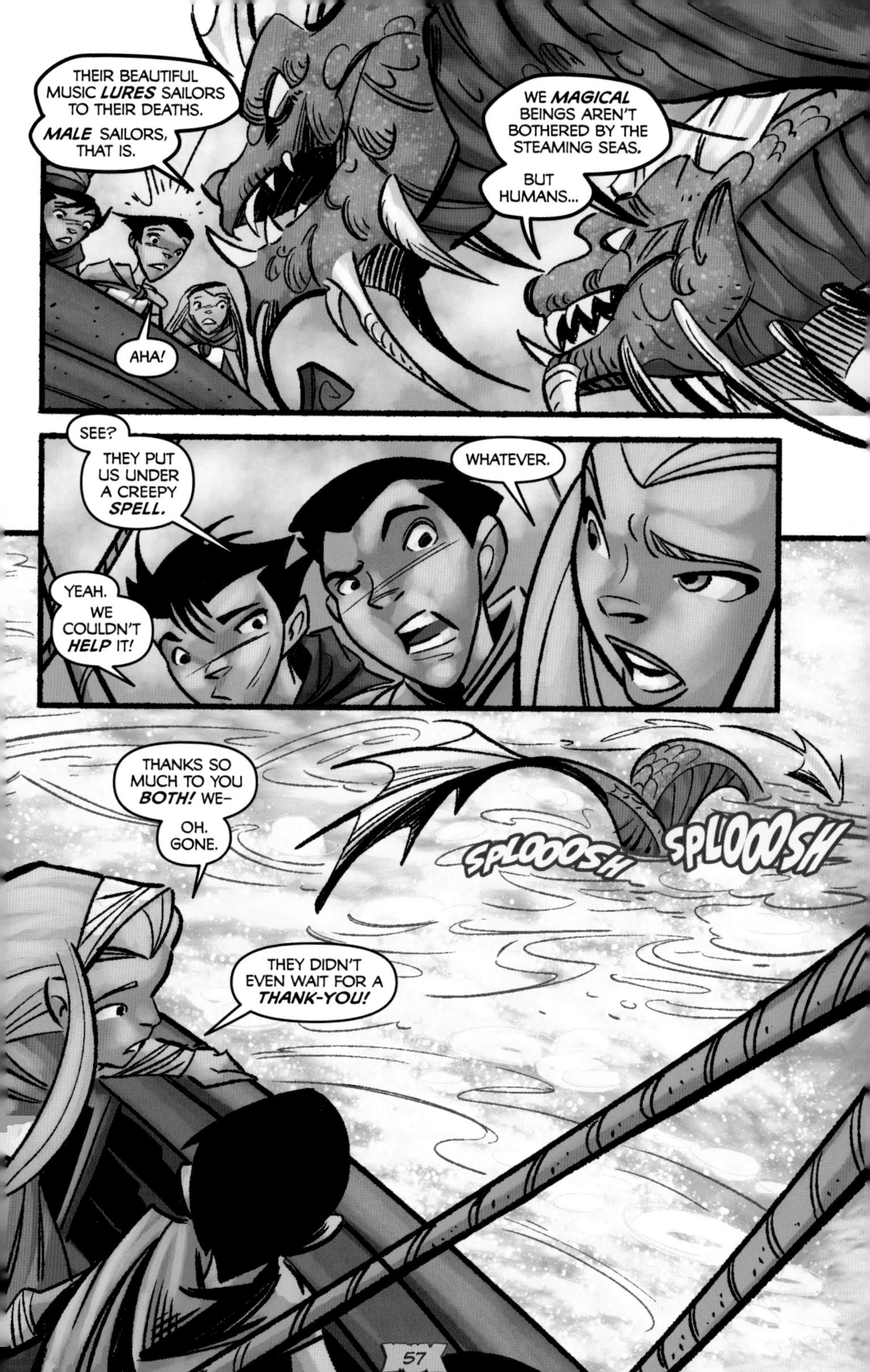
THEIR BEAUTIFUL MUSIC LURES SAILORS TO THEIR DEATHS.
MALE SAILORS, THAT IS.
AHA!
WE MAGICAL BEINGS AREN'T BOTHERED BY THE STEAMING SEAS.
BUT HUMANS...
SEE?
THEY PUT US UNDER A CREEPY SPELL.
YEAH.
WE COULDN'T HELP IT!
WHATEVER.
THANKS SO MUCH TO YOU BOTH! WE–
OH. GONE.
SPLOOOSH
SPLOOOSH
THEY DIDN'T EVEN WAIT FOR A THANK-YOU!

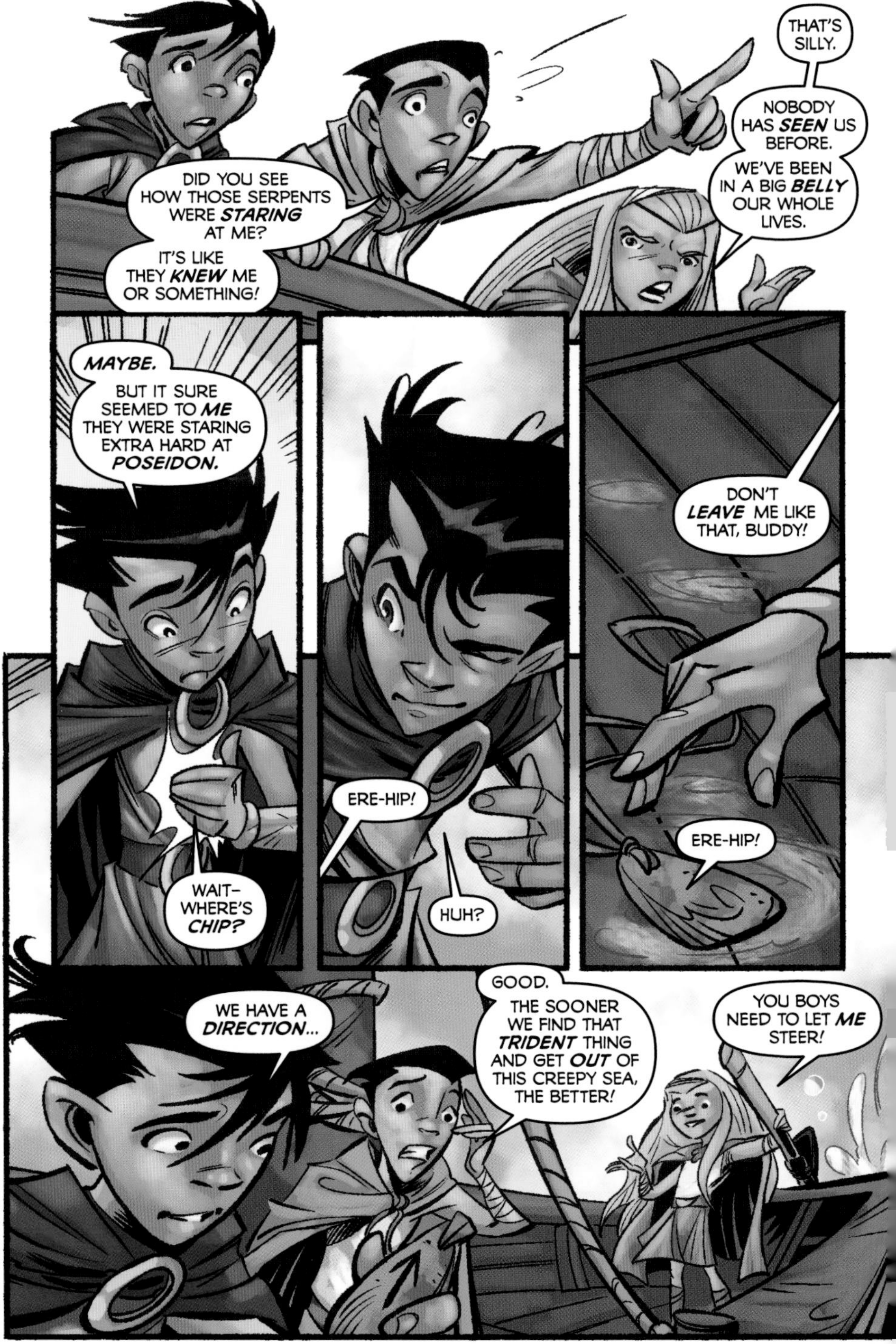
DID YOU SEE HOW THOSE SERPENTS WERE STARING AT ME?
IT'S LIKE THEY KNEW ME OR SOMETHING!
THAT'S SILLY.
NOBODY HAS SEEN US BEFORE.
WE'VE BEEN IN A BIG BELLY OUR WHOLE LIVES.
MAYBE.
BUT IT SURE SEEMED TO ME THEY WERE STARING EXTRA HARD AT POSEIDON.
WAIT— WHERE'S CHIP?
ERE-HIP!
HUH?
DON'T LEAVE ME LIKE THAT, BUDDY!
ERE-HIP!
WE HAVE A DIRECTION...
GOOD.
THE SOONER WE FIND THAT TRIDENT THING AND GET OUT OF THIS CREEPY SEA, THE BETTER!
YOU BOYS NEED TO LET ME STEER!

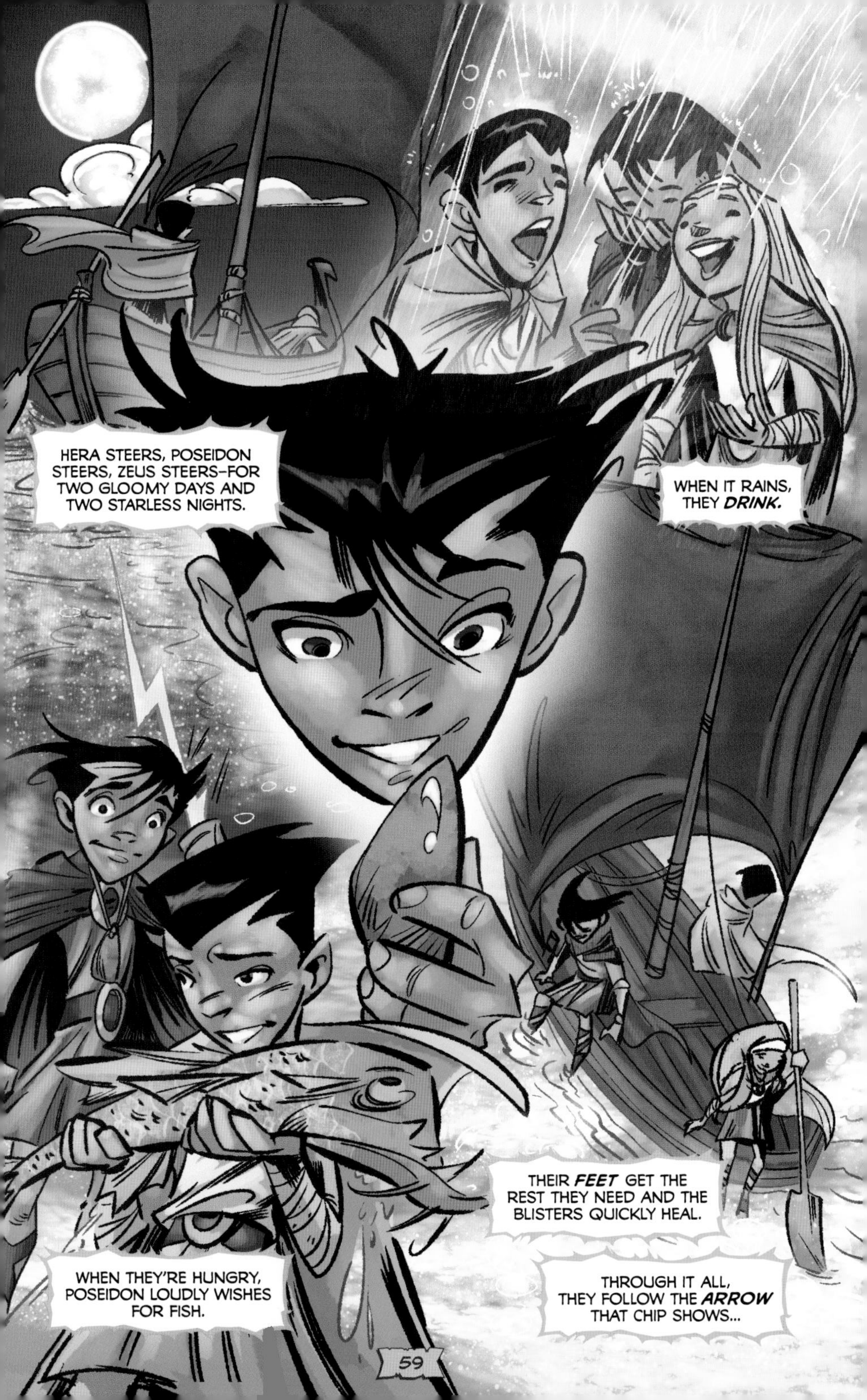
HERA STEERS, POSEIDON STEERS, ZEUS STEERS–FOR TWO GLOOMY DAYS AND TWO STARLESS NIGHTS.
WHEN IT RAINS, THEY ***DRINK.***
WHEN THEY'RE HUNGRY, POSEIDON LOUDLY WISHES FOR FISH.
THEIR ***FEET*** GET THE REST THEY NEED AND THE BLISTERS QUICKLY HEAL.
THROUGH IT ALL, THEY FOLLOW THE ***ARROW*** THAT CHIP SHOWS...

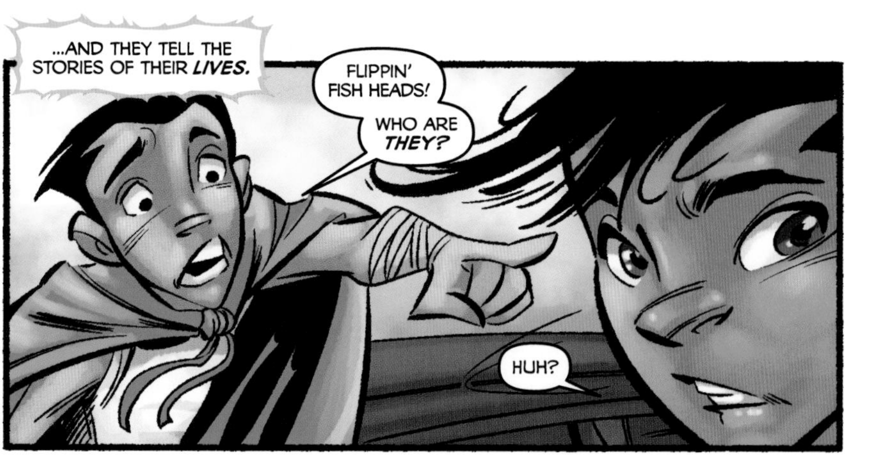
...AND THEY TELL THE STORIES OF THEIR *LIVES.*
FLIPPIN' FISH HEADS!
WHO ARE *THEY?*
HUH?

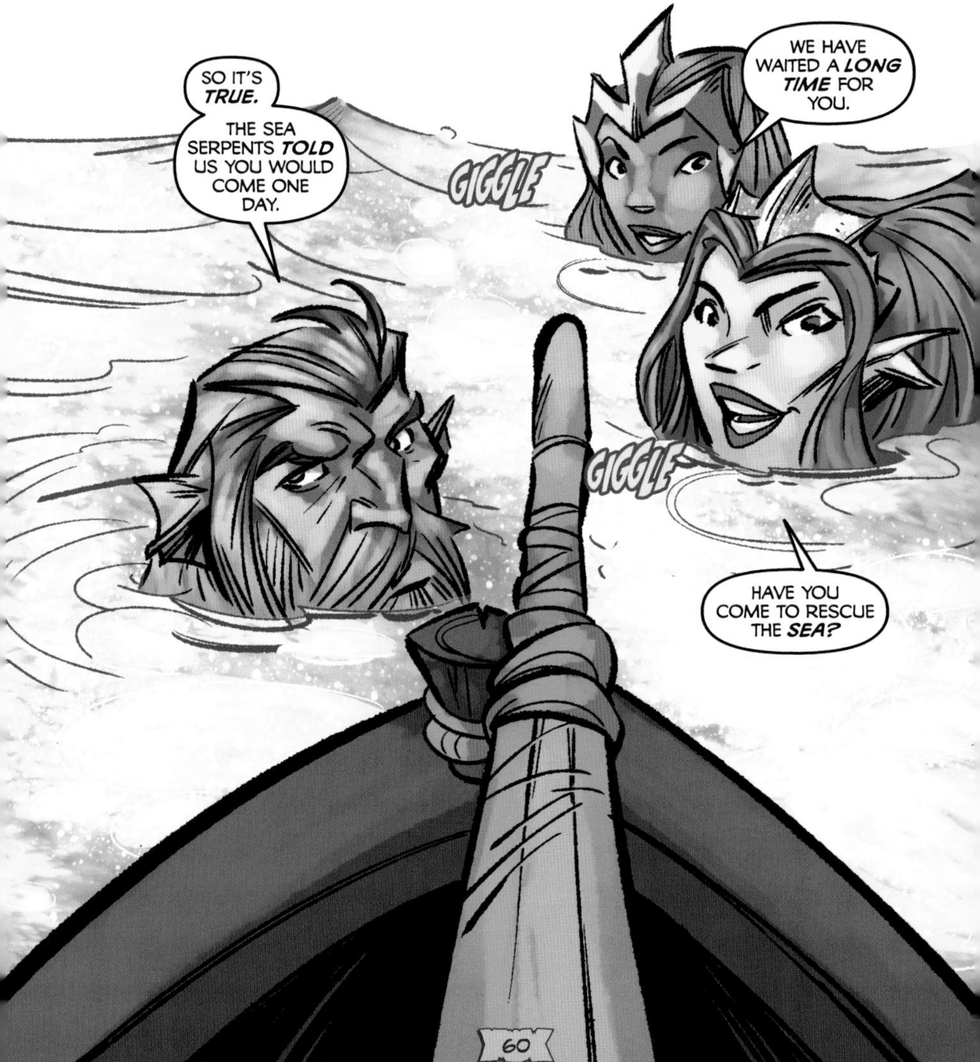
SO IT'S *TRUE.*
THE SEA SERPENTS *TOLD* US YOU WOULD COME ONE DAY.
WE HAVE WAITED A *LONG TIME* FOR YOU.
GIGGLE
GIGGLE
HAVE YOU COME TO RESCUE THE *SEA?*

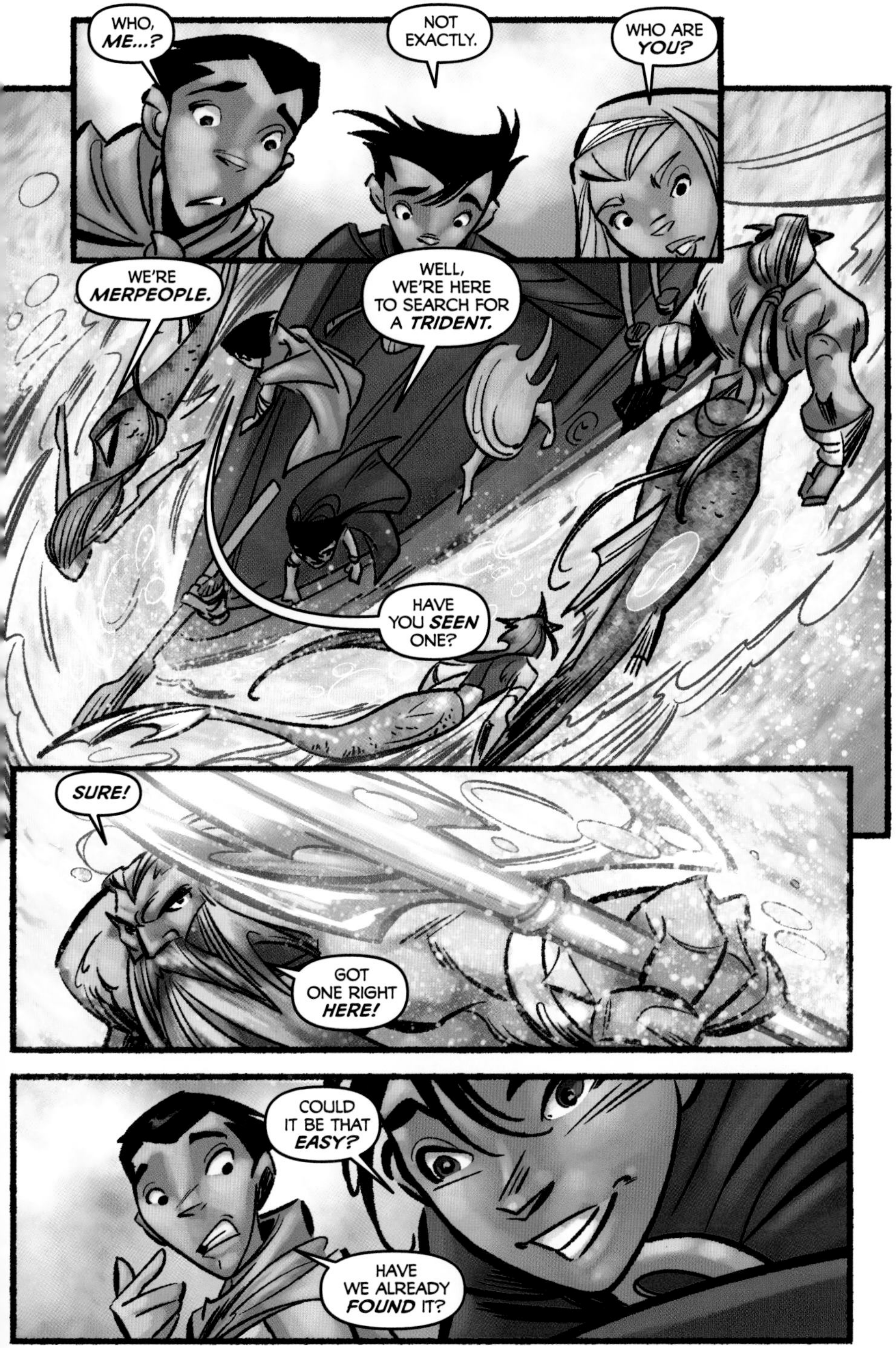
WHO, ME...?
NOT EXACTLY.
WHO ARE YOU?
WE'RE MERPEOPLE.
WELL, WE'RE HERE TO SEARCH FOR A TRIDENT.
HAVE YOU SEEN ONE?
SURE!
GOT ONE RIGHT HERE!
COULD IT BE THAT EASY?
HAVE WE ALREADY FOUND IT?

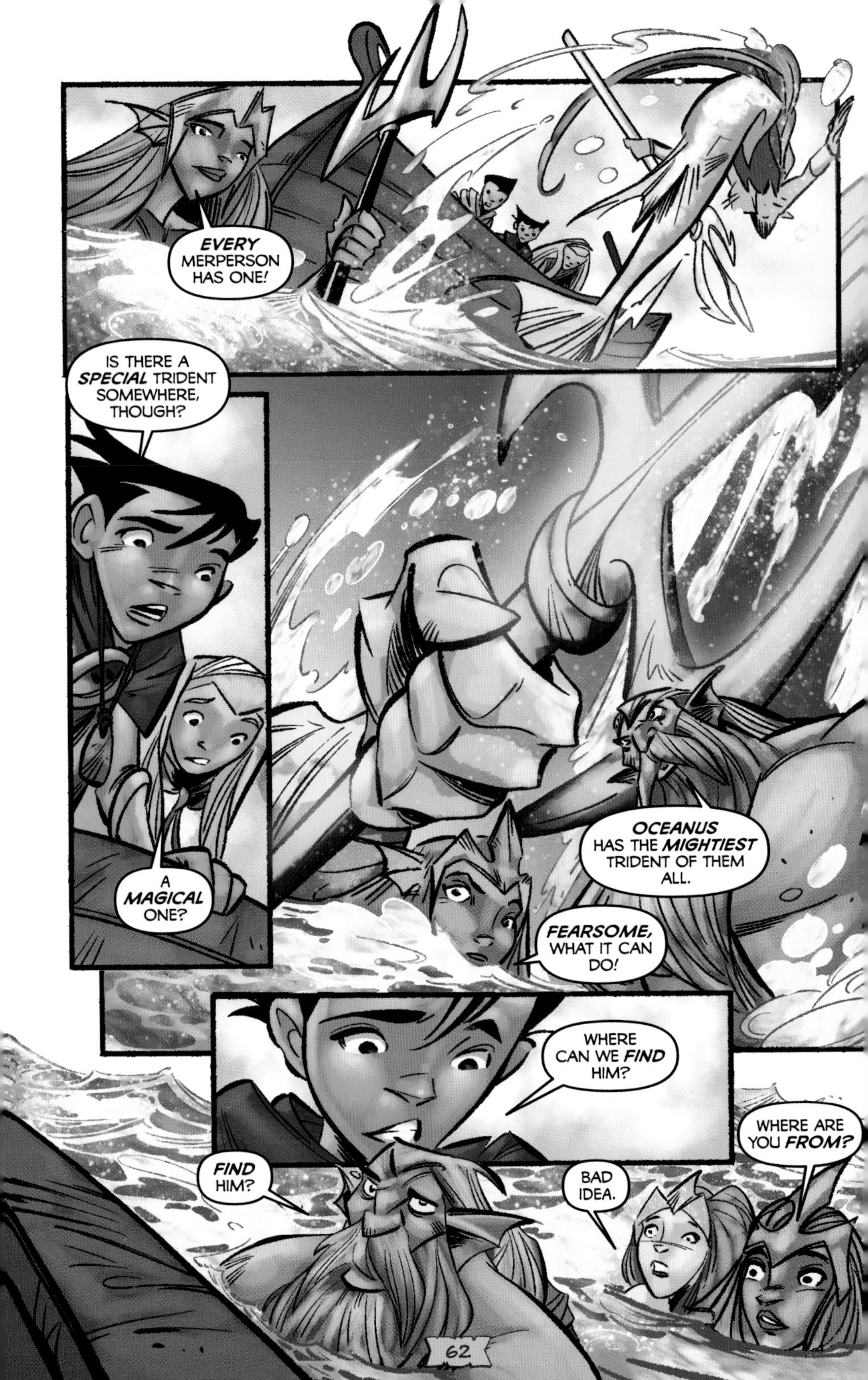

EVERY MERPERSON HAS ONE!
IS THERE A SPECIAL TRIDENT SOMEWHERE, THOUGH?
A MAGICAL ONE?
OCEANUS HAS THE MIGHTIEST TRIDENT OF THEM ALL.
FEARSOME, WHAT IT CAN DO!
WHERE CAN WE FIND HIM?
FIND HIM?
BAD IDEA.
WHERE ARE YOU FROM?

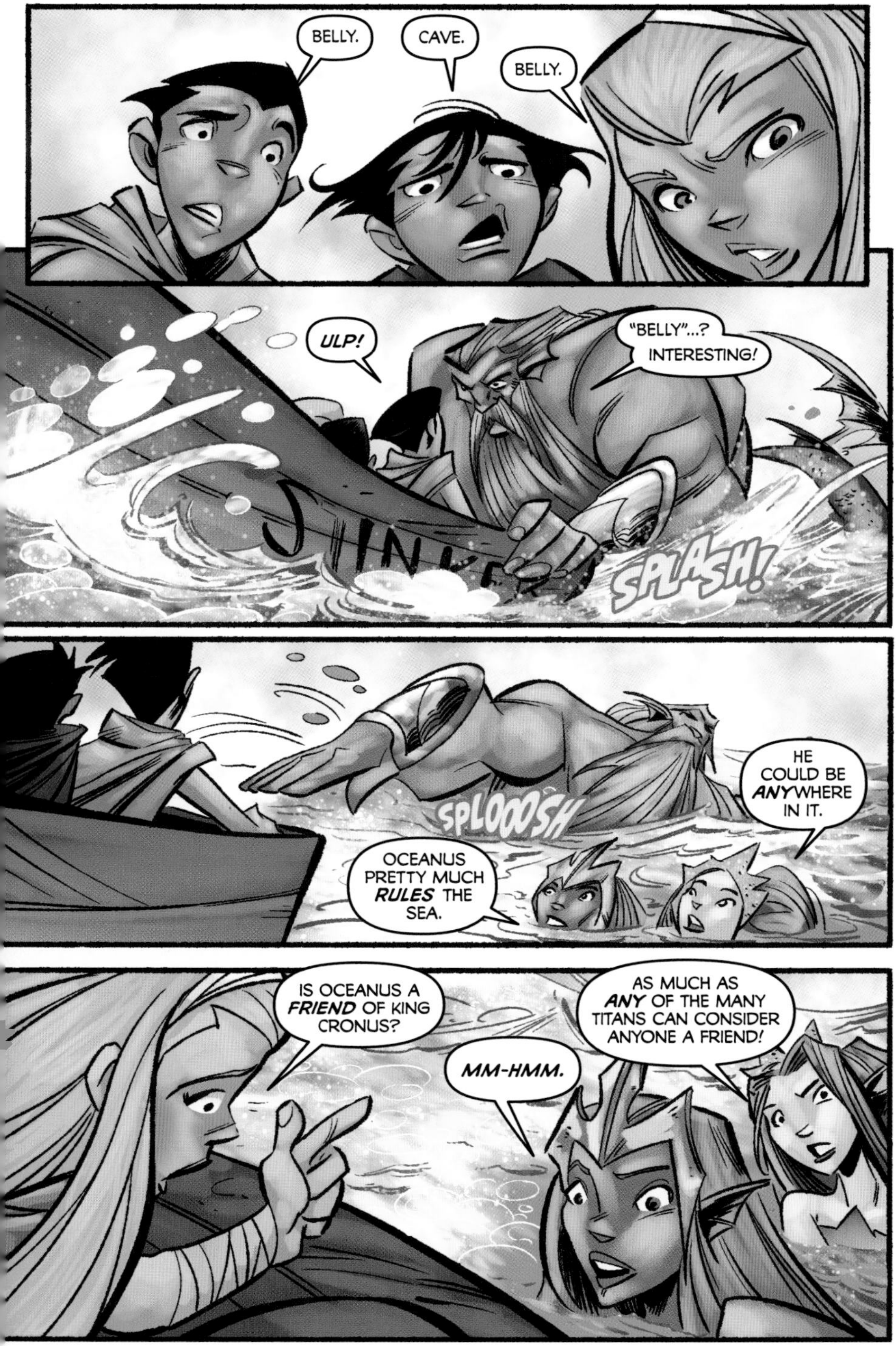
BELLY.
CAVE.
BELLY.
ULP!
"BELLY"...? INTERESTING!
SPLASH!
SPLOOOSH
HE COULD BE ANYWHERE IN IT.
OCEANUS PRETTY MUCH RULES THE SEA.
IS OCEANUS A FRIEND OF KING CRONUS?
AS MUCH AS ANY OF THE MANY TITANS CAN CONSIDER ANYONE A FRIEND!
MM-HMM.

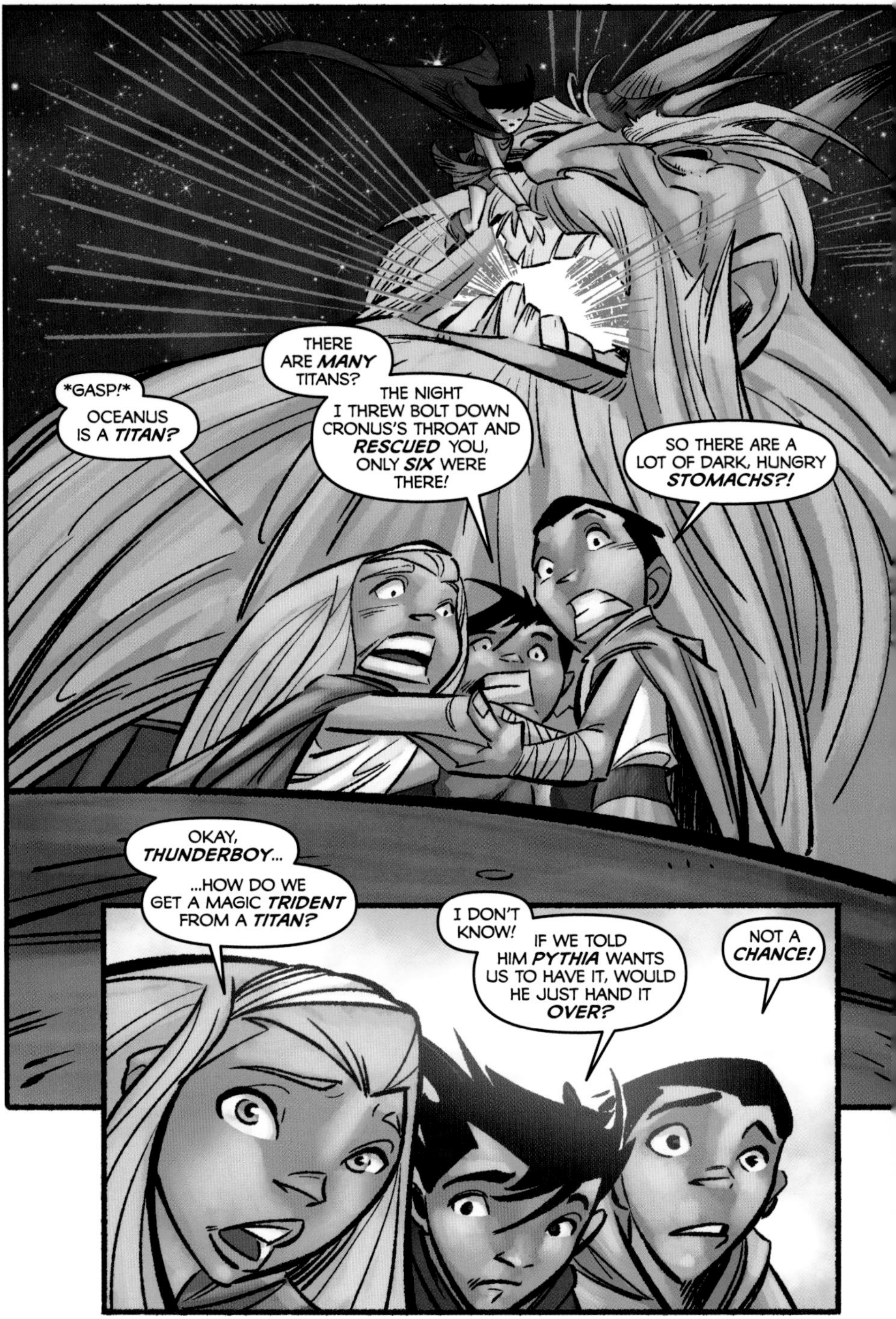
GASP! OCEANUS IS A TITAN?
THERE ARE MANY TITANS?
THE NIGHT I THREW BOLT DOWN CRONUS'S THROAT AND RESCUED YOU, ONLY SIX WERE THERE!
SO THERE ARE A LOT OF DARK, HUNGRY STOMACHS?!
OKAY, THUNDERBOY...
...HOW DO WE GET A MAGIC TRIDENT FROM A TITAN?
I DON'T KNOW!
IF WE TOLD HIM PYTHIA WANTS US TO HAVE IT, WOULD HE JUST HAND IT OVER?
NOT A CHANCE!

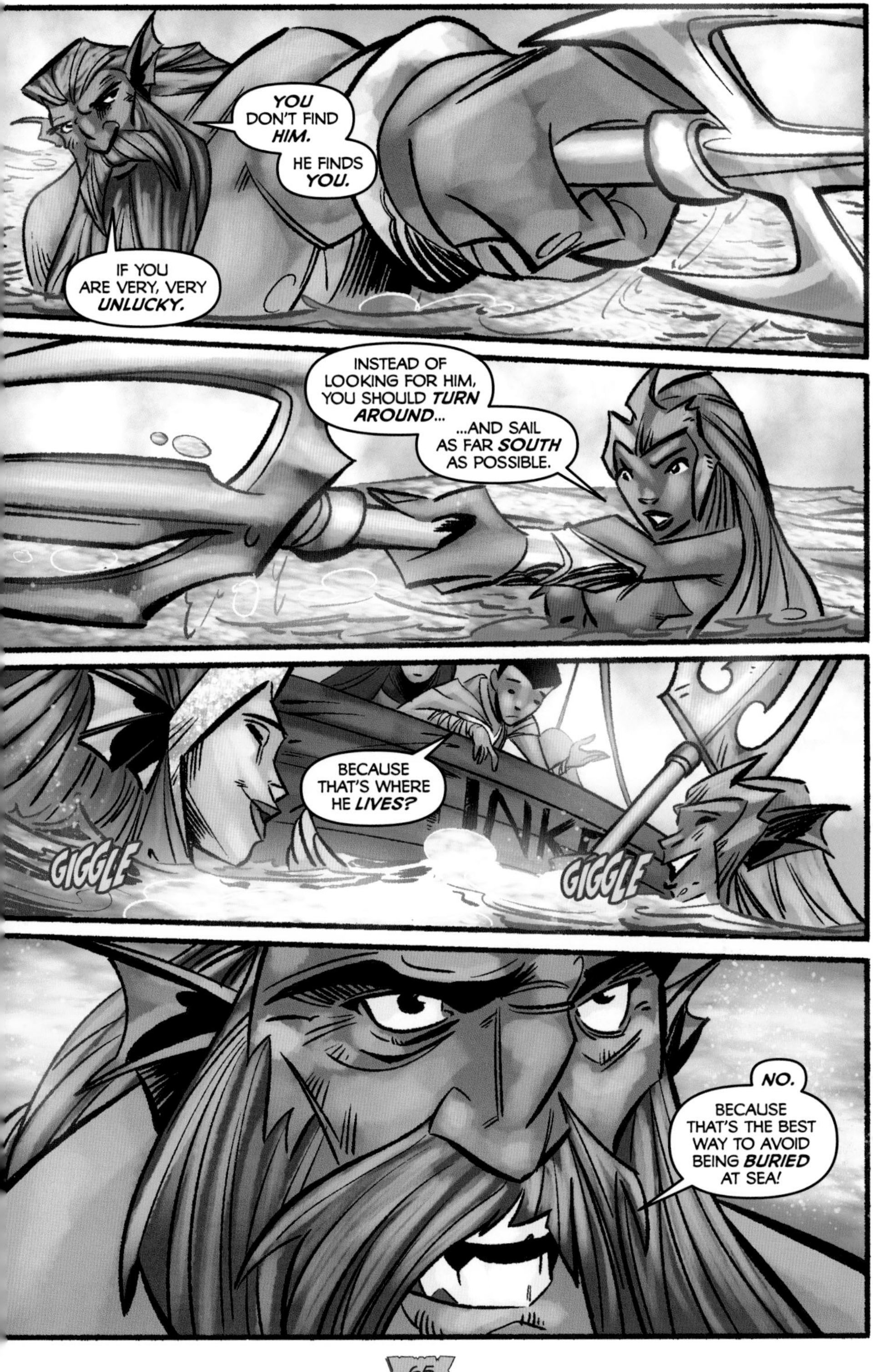
YOU DON'T FIND HIM.
HE FINDS YOU.
IF YOU ARE VERY, VERY UNLUCKY.
INSTEAD OF LOOKING FOR HIM, YOU SHOULD TURN AROUND...
...AND SAIL AS FAR SOUTH AS POSSIBLE.
BECAUSE THAT'S WHERE HE LIVES?
GIGGLE
GIGGLE
NO.
BECAUSE THAT'S THE BEST WAY TO AVOID BEING BURIED AT SEA!

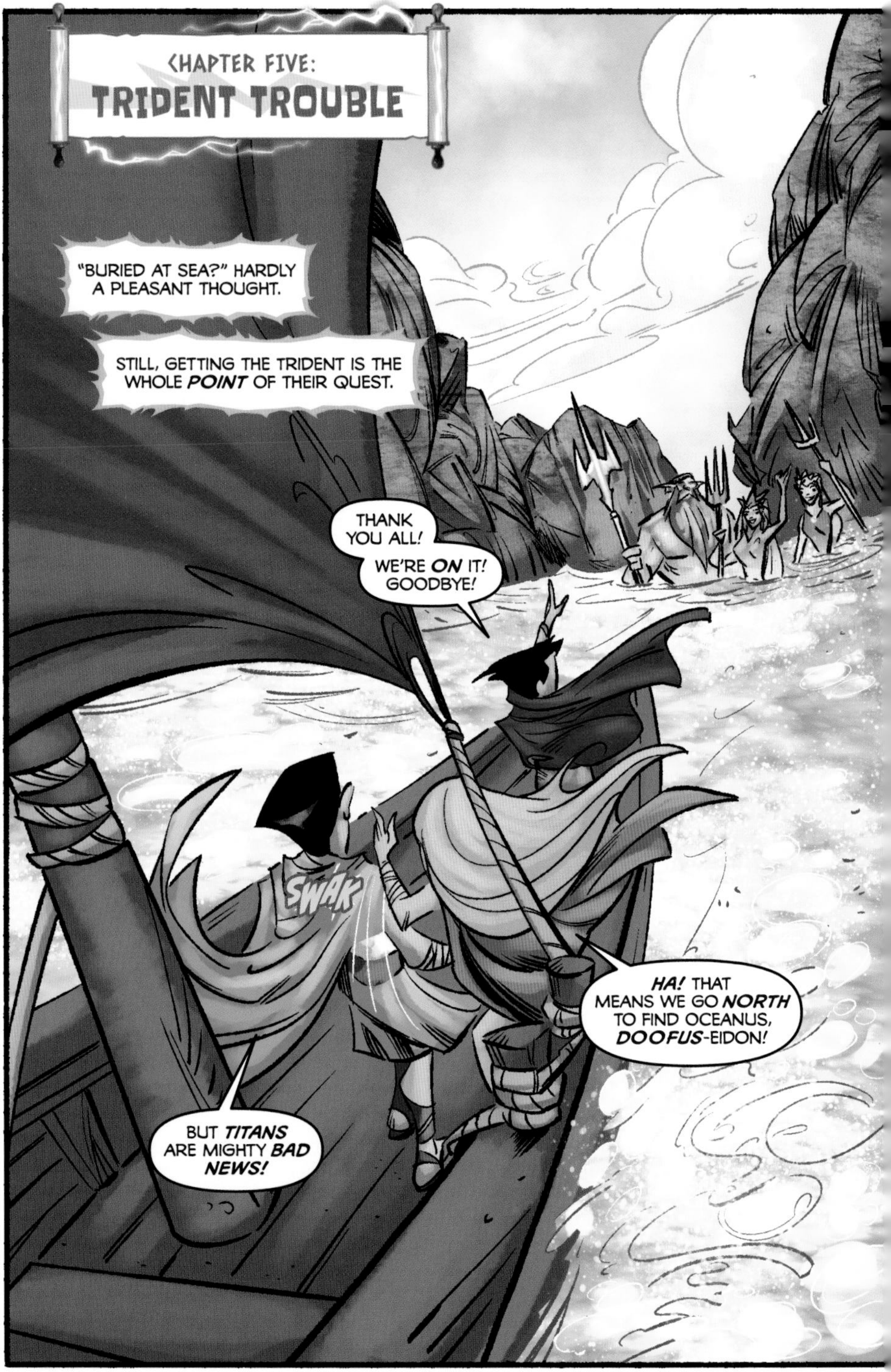
CHAPTER FIVE:
TRIDENT TROUBLE
"BURIED AT SEA?" HARDLY A PLEASANT THOUGHT.
STILL, GETTING THE TRIDENT IS THE WHOLE POINT OF THEIR QUEST.
THANK YOU ALL!
WE'RE ON IT! GOODBYE!
SWAK
HA! THAT MEANS WE GO NORTH TO FIND OCEANUS, DOOFUS-EIDON!
BUT TITANS ARE MIGHTY BAD NEWS!

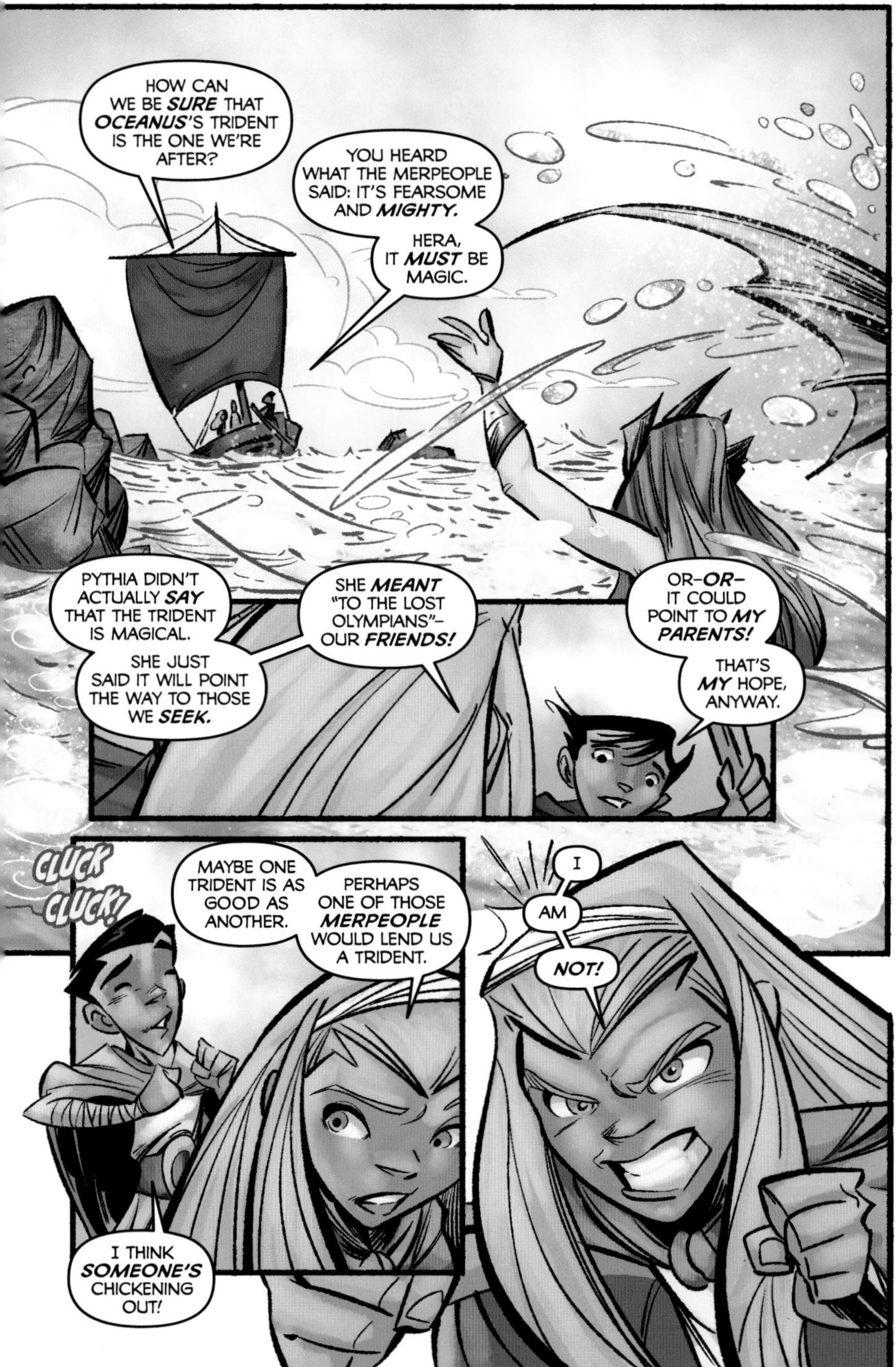
HOW CAN WE BE *SURE* THAT *OCEANUS*'S TRIDENT IS THE ONE WE'RE AFTER?
YOU HEARD WHAT THE MERPEOPLE SAID: IT'S FEARSOME AND *MIGHTY.*
HERA, IT *MUST* BE MAGIC.
PYTHIA DIDN'T ACTUALLY *SAY* THAT THE TRIDENT IS MAGICAL.
SHE JUST SAID IT WILL POINT THE WAY TO THOSE WE *SEEK.*
SHE *MEANT* "TO THE LOST OLYMPIANS"– OUR *FRIENDS!*
OR–*OR*– IT COULD POINT TO *MY PARENTS!*
THAT'S *MY* HOPE, ANYWAY.
CLUCK CLUCK!
MAYBE ONE TRIDENT IS AS GOOD AS ANOTHER.
PERHAPS ONE OF THOSE *MERPEOPLE* WOULD LEND US A TRIDENT.
I THINK *SOMEONE'S* CHICKENING OUT!
I
AM
NOT!

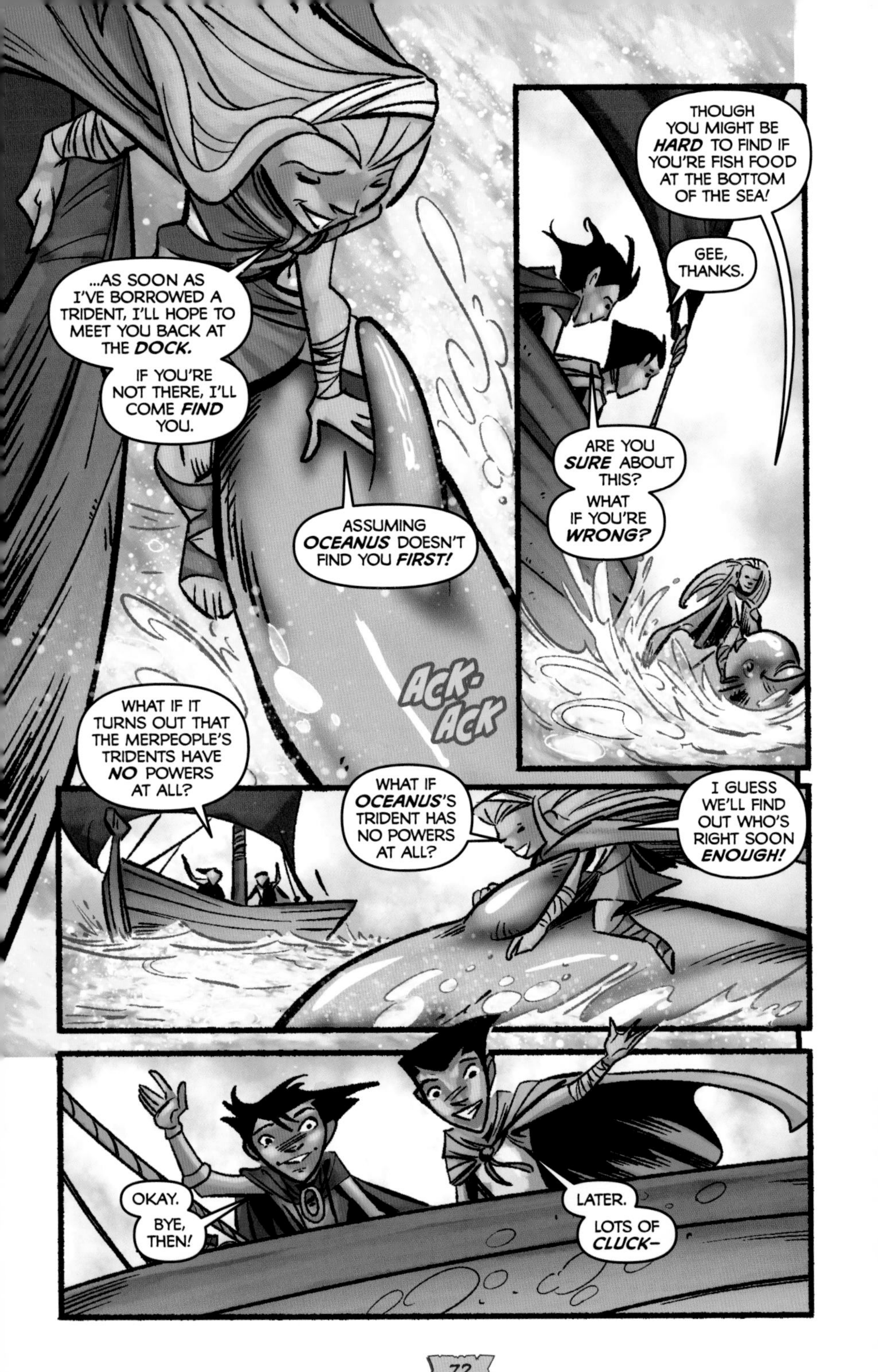
...AS SOON AS I'VE BORROWED A TRIDENT, I'LL HOPE TO MEET YOU BACK AT THE DOCK.
IF YOU'RE NOT THERE, I'LL COME FIND YOU.
ASSUMING OCEANUS DOESN'T FIND YOU FIRST!
THOUGH YOU MIGHT BE HARD TO FIND IF YOU'RE FISH FOOD AT THE BOTTOM OF THE SEA!
GEE, THANKS.
ARE YOU SURE ABOUT THIS?
WHAT IF YOU'RE WRONG?
ACK-ACK
WHAT IF IT TURNS OUT THAT THE MERPEOPLE'S TRIDENTS HAVE NO POWERS AT ALL?
WHAT IF OCEANUS'S TRIDENT HAS NO POWERS AT ALL?
I GUESS WE'LL FIND OUT WHO'S RIGHT SOON ENOUGH!
OKAY.
BYE, THEN!
LATER.
LOTS OF CLUCK–

POSEIDON, FOR SOMEONE SO SCARED OF THE *SEA...*

...YOU HAVE AN ODD EFFECT ON ITS *CREATURES!*

WELL, *I'M* THINKING ABOUT HOW ALL THESE CREATURES ARE SURVIVING THE BOILING SEA— JUST LIKE *WE* ARE!

AND IT *COULD* BE THAT SOME OF THEM ARE PROTECTED BY MAGIC, LIKE MAYBE *WE* ARE.

COULD BE COLD POCKETS FROM DEEP DOWN, LIKE THE *FISHERMAN* SAID.

SAY, WHAT DID YOU *SEE* WHEN THOSE SIRENS CALLED TO US?

YOU *FIRST!*

WHAT DID *YOU* SEE?

NOTHING.

IT'S *DUMB.*

LET'S JUST *GO.*

HE LOOKS *SORRY* THAT HE BROUGHT UP THE SUBJECT!

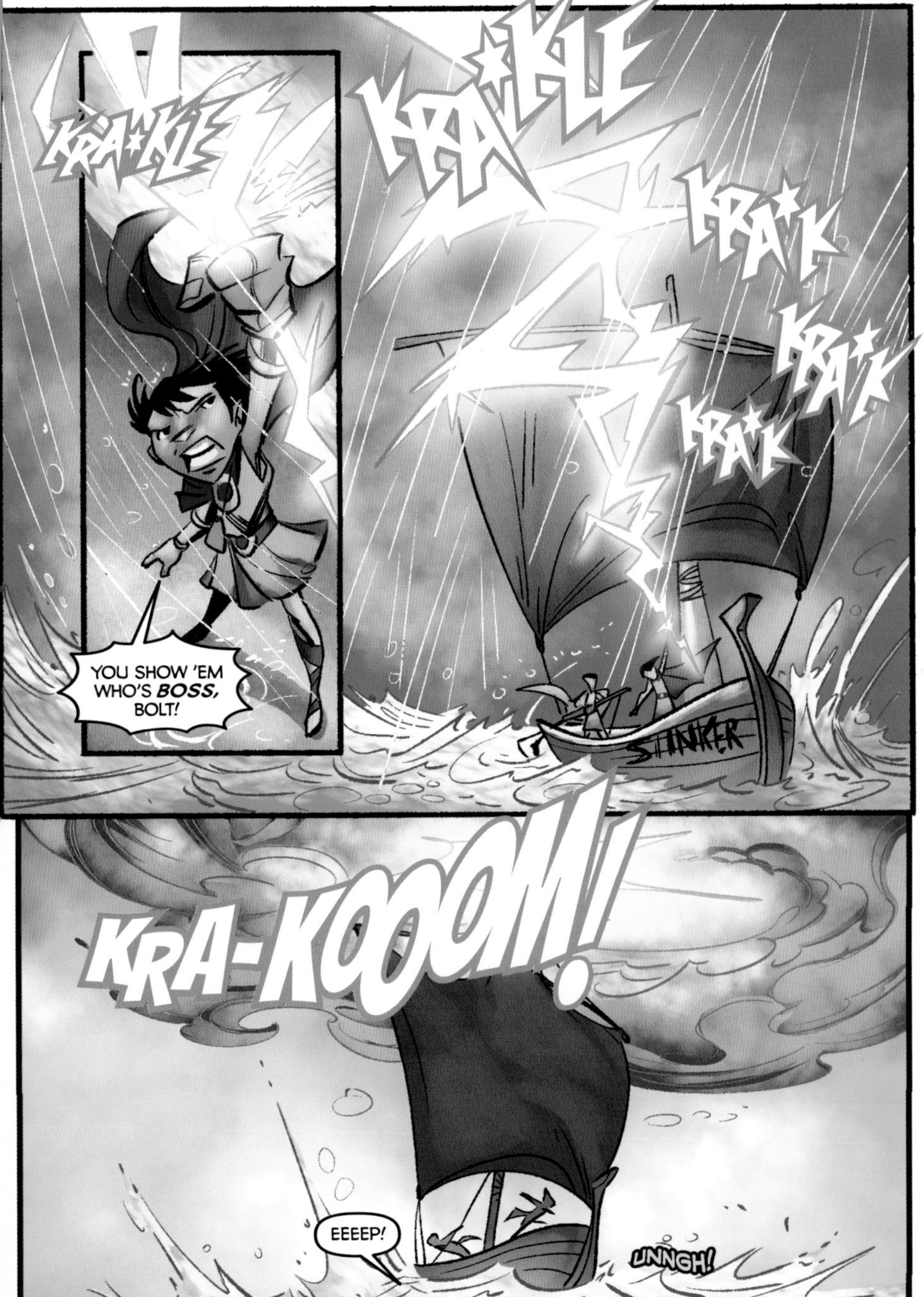
KRA*KLE
YOU SHOW 'EM WHO'S **BOSS,** BOLT!
KRA*KLE
KRA*K
KRA*K
KRA*K
STINKER
KRA-KOOOM!
EEEEP!
UNNGH!

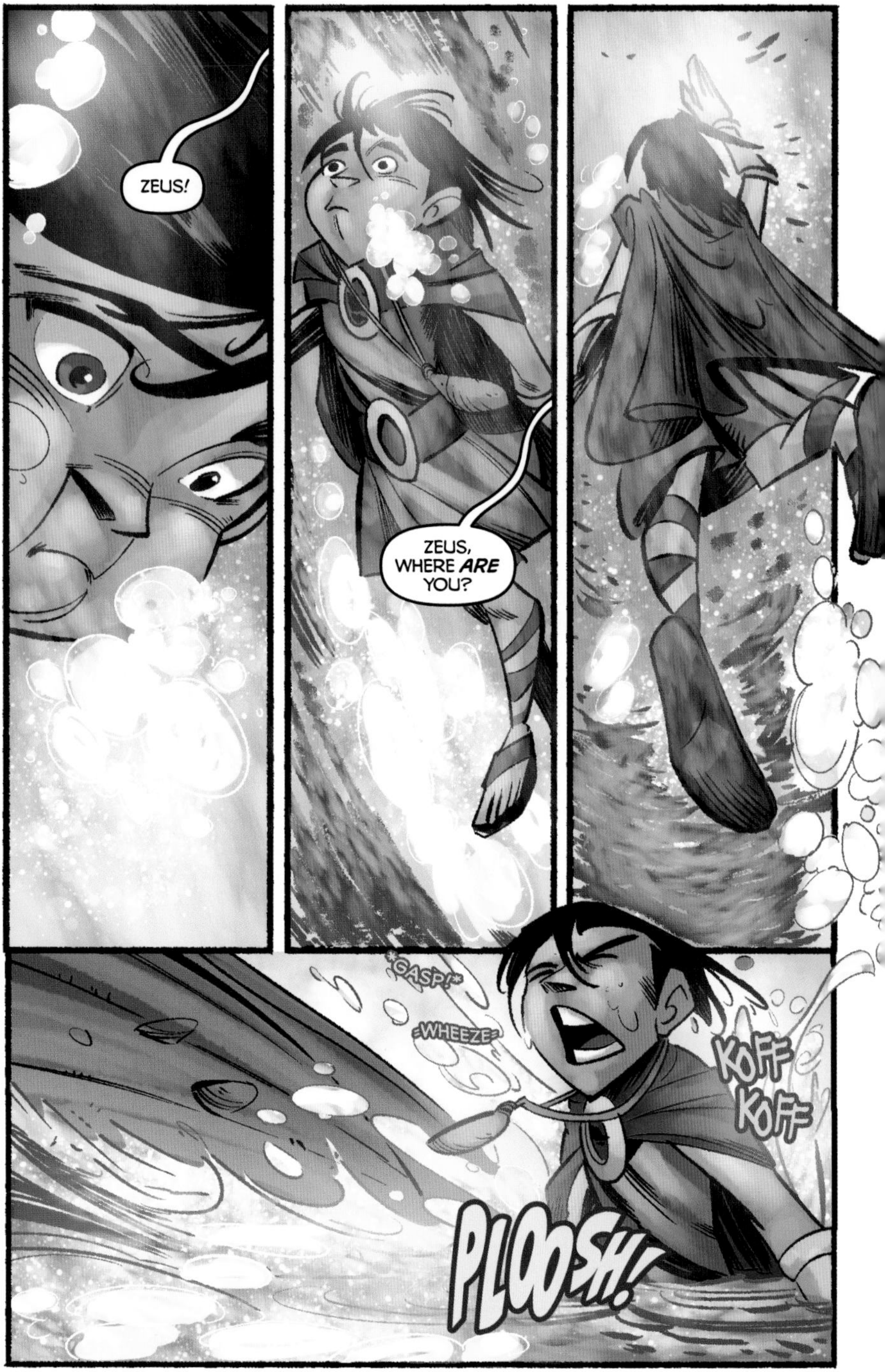
ZEUS!
ZEUS, WHERE ARE YOU?
GASP!
=WHEEZE=
KOFF KOFF
PLOOSH!

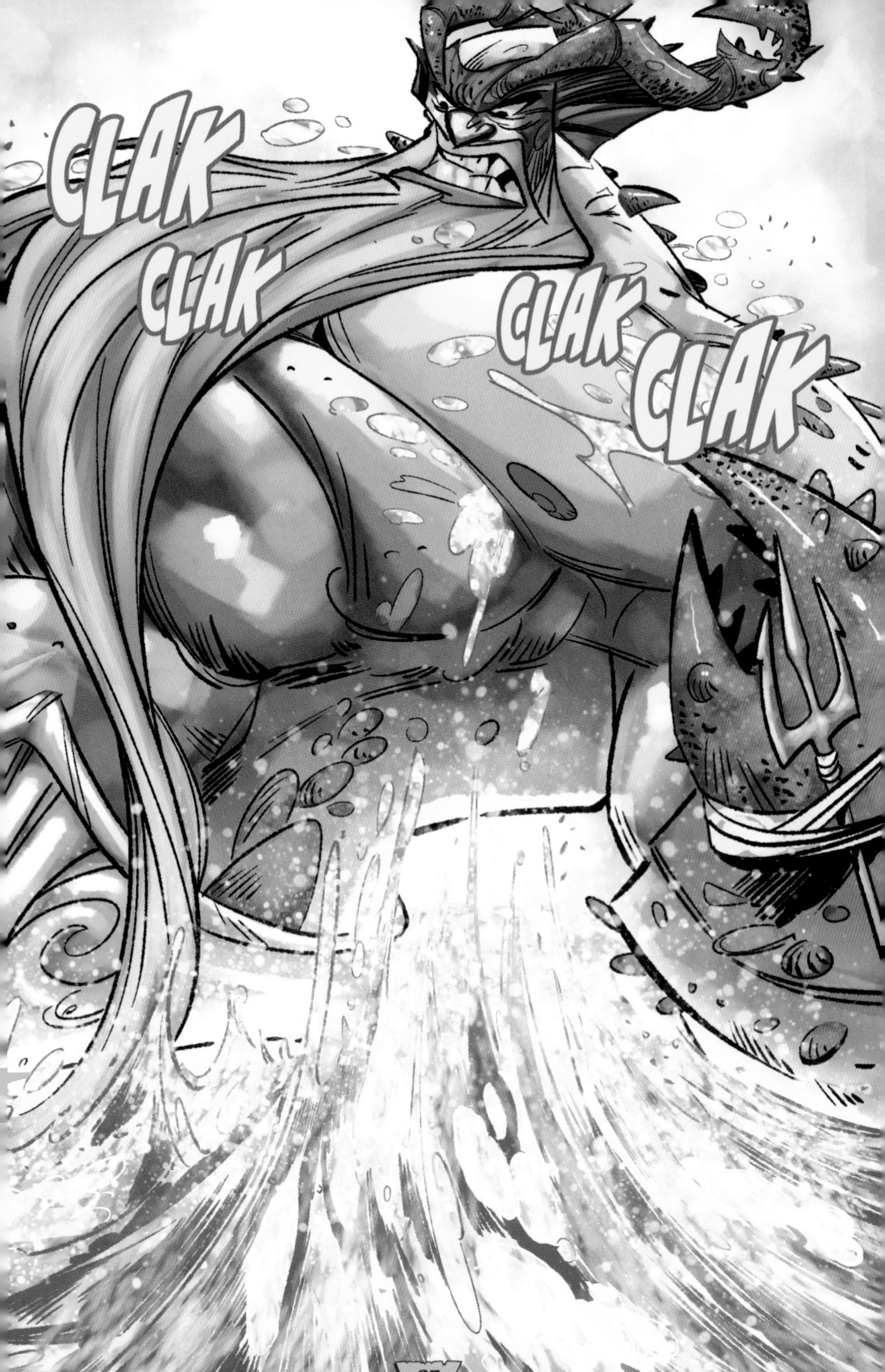
CLAK
CLAK
CLAK
CLAK

WELL? STATE YOUR BUSINESS!

...POSEIDON?

ALL RIGHT. *YOU* TELL HIM, POSEIDON...

CLAK CLAK CLAK CLAK

THAT *COWARD!* IS HE HIDING UNDER THE BOAT?

IF ZEUS CAN GET TO THE ISLAND AND FIND BOLT, AT LEAST HE'LL HAVE A *WEAPON!*

WELL?

AND ACCORDING TO HER *PROPHECY,* I'M SUPPOSED TO FIND A MAGICAL *TRIDENT!*

PYTHIA SENT US. SHE'S THIS *ORACLE* AT *DELPHI.*

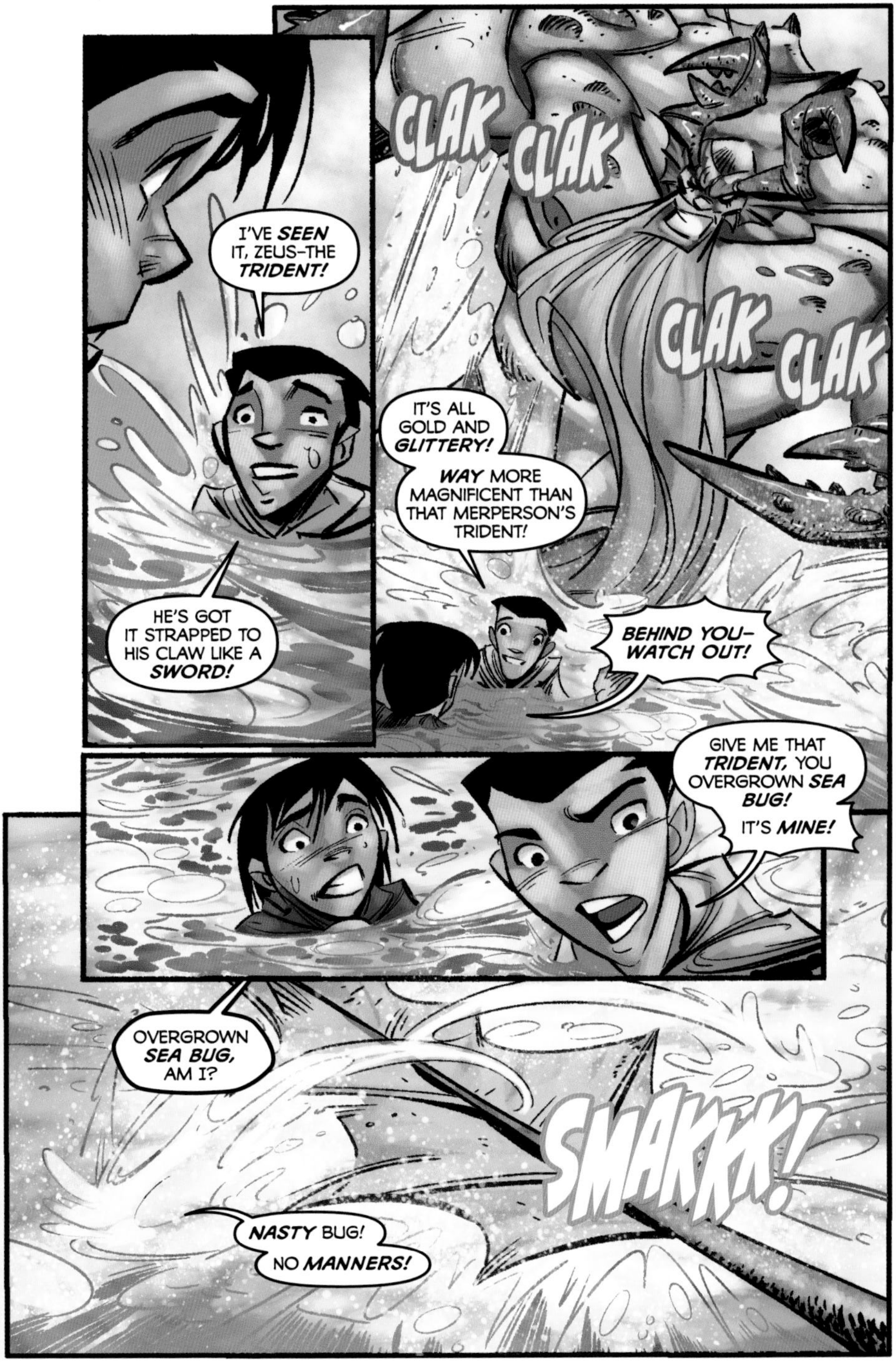
I'VE SEEN IT, ZEUS–THE TRIDENT!
HE'S GOT IT STRAPPED TO HIS CLAW LIKE A SWORD!
CLAK CLAK
CLAK CLAK
IT'S ALL GOLD AND GLITTERY!
WAY MORE MAGNIFICENT THAN THAT MERPERSON'S TRIDENT!
BEHIND YOU–WATCH OUT!
GIVE ME THAT TRIDENT, YOU OVERGROWN SEA BUG!
IT'S MINE!
OVERGROWN SEA BUG, AM I?
SMAKKK!
NASTY BUG!
NO MANNERS!

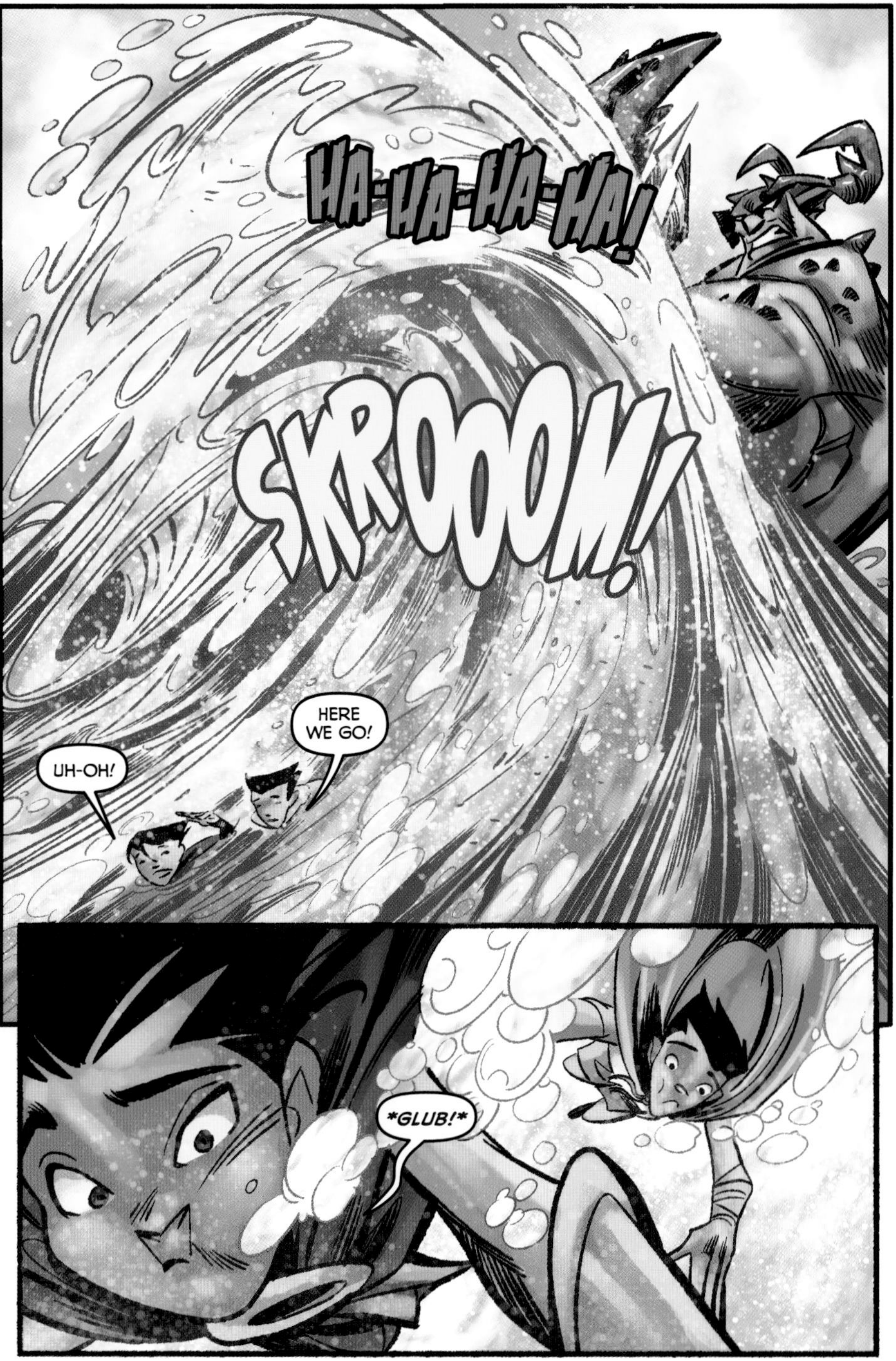
HA-HA-HA-HA!
SKROOOM!
UH-OH!
HERE WE GO!
GLUB!

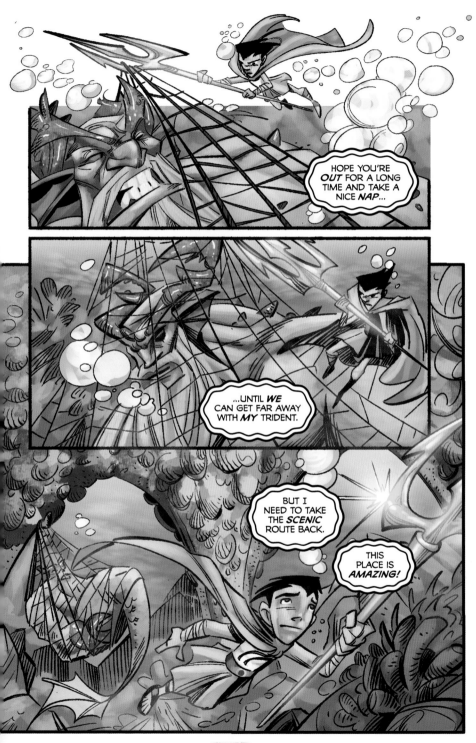

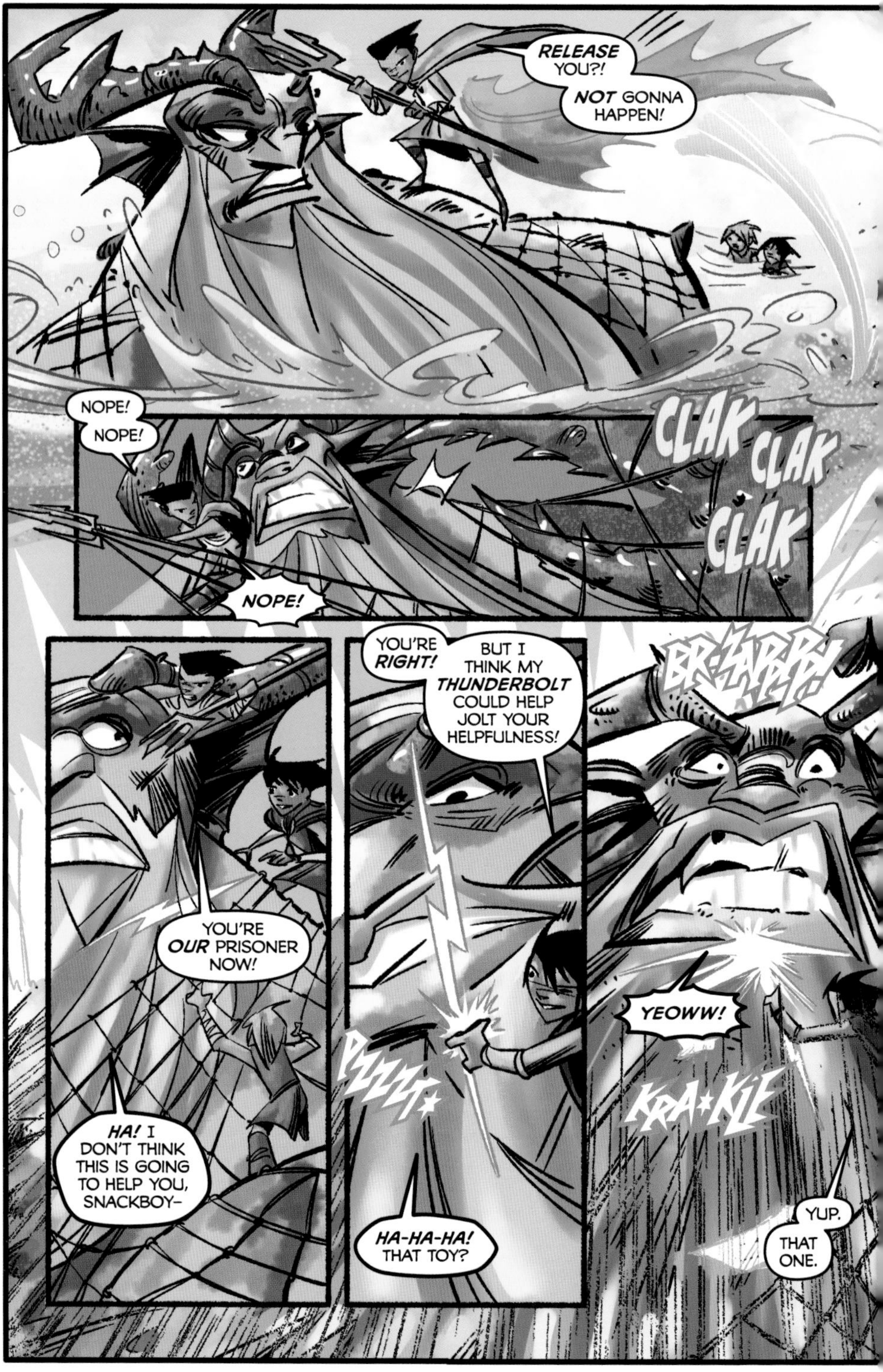
RELEASE YOU?! NOT GONNA HAPPEN!
NOPE! NOPE!
CLAK CLAK CLAK
NOPE!
YOU'RE OUR PRISONER NOW!
HA! I DON'T THINK THIS IS GOING TO HELP YOU, SNACKBOY–
YOU'RE RIGHT!
BUT I THINK MY THUNDERBOLT COULD HELP JOLT YOUR HELPFULNESS!
HA-HA-HA! THAT TOY?
BR-ZAP-P!
YEOWW!
KRA★KLE
YUP. THAT ONE.

"...INDEED, THE GODS ARE *GOOD.*"

WE HAVE ONE OF YOUR THREE MISSING FRIENDS *AND* THE TRIDENT NOW.

SO WHAT WAS THE BIG *SECRET* HERA WAS GOING TO TELL ME, ONCE WE GOT IT?

I PROMISED NOT TO *SAY.*

YOU'LL HAVE TO ASK *HER...*

...IF WE EVER SEE HER AGAIN.

HUSH! THINGS ARE *MOVING* UP THERE.

HE'S *RIGHT.*

UNFORTUNATELY *NOT.* CRONIES WEAR *ARMOR.* I *LIKE* CRONIES.

THEN *WHAT?*

MAYBE WE SHOULD *HIDE* AND–

WHAT WAS THAT–A *CRONY?*

CHAPTER TEN:
THE ANDROPHAGOI

YAAAH!

ZEUS RECALLS KING CRONUS, IN HIS FOREST MEETING OF TITANS, PLANNING TO *UNLEASH* THE CREATURES OF CHAOS.

PYTHIA MENTIONED THEM IN HER *PROPHECY.*

CRONUS HAS LET LOOSE THE FIRST *CREATURES OF CHAOS!*

WE'RE *DOOMED!*

DIDN'T SHE SAY THE *TRIDENT* COULD *DEFEAT* THEM?

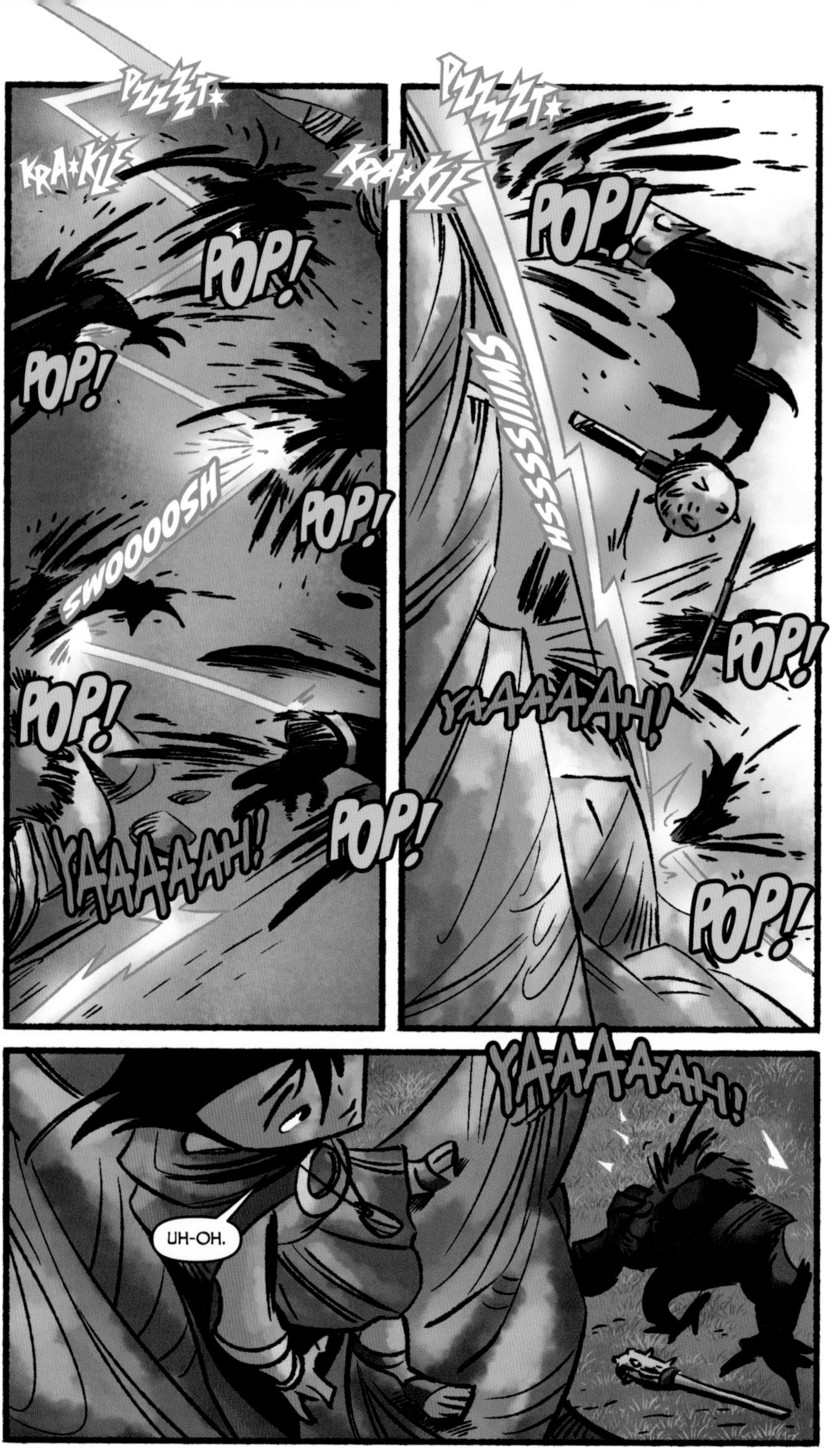
PZZZZT★
KRA★KLE
POP!
POP!
SWOOOOSH
POP!
POP!
YAAAAAAH!
POP!
PZZZZZT★
KRA★KLE
POP!
SWIIISSSSSH
POP!
YAAAAAAH!
POP!
YAAAAAAH!
UH-OH.

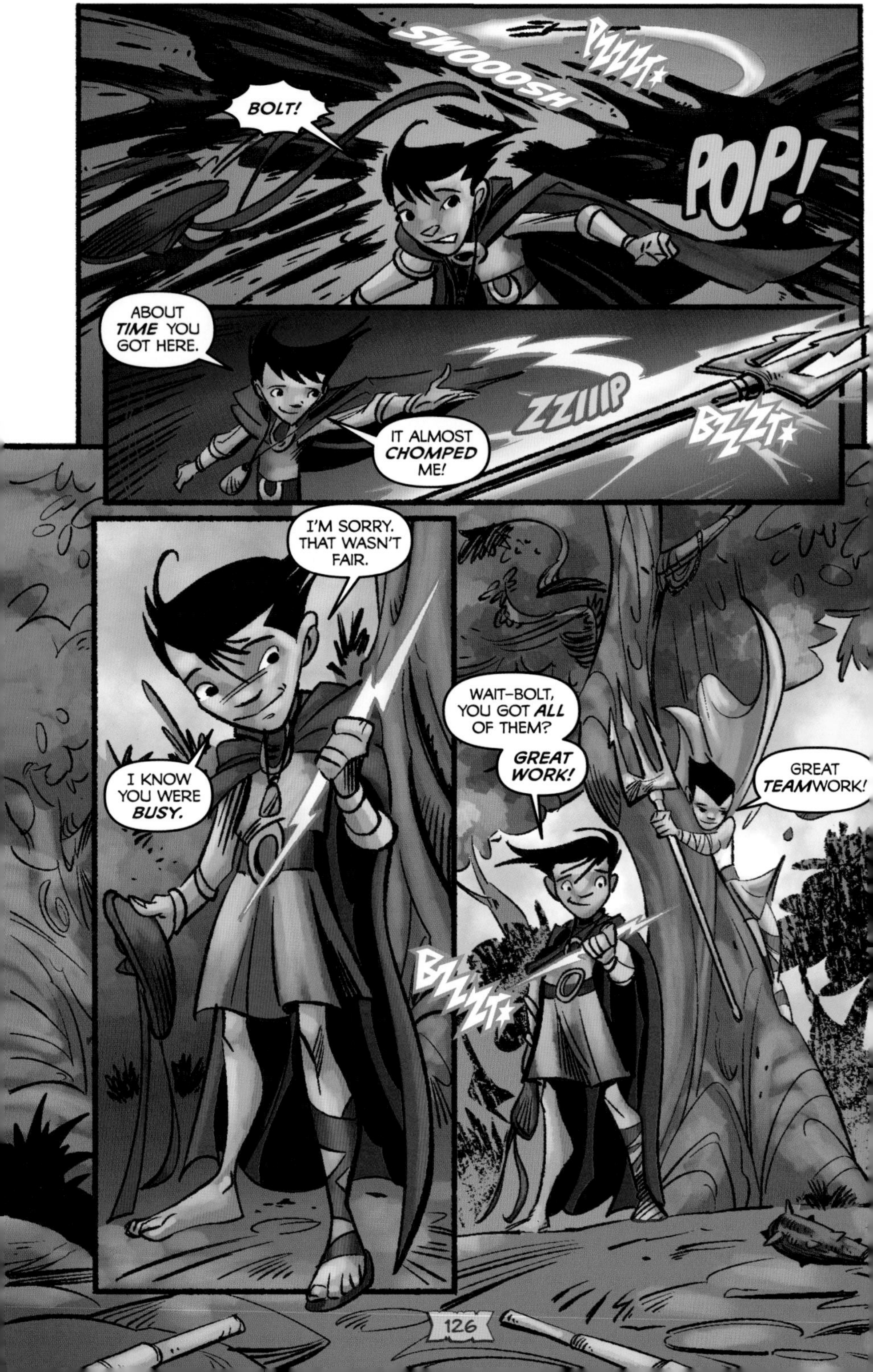
SWOOOSH
PZZZT★
BOLT!
POP!
ABOUT *TIME* YOU GOT HERE.
ZZIIIIP
BZZZT★
IT ALMOST *CHOMPED* ME!
I'M SORRY. THAT WASN'T FAIR.
I KNOW YOU WERE *BUSY.*
WAIT–BOLT, YOU GOT *ALL* OF THEM?
GREAT WORK!
GREAT *TEAM*WORK!
BZZZT★

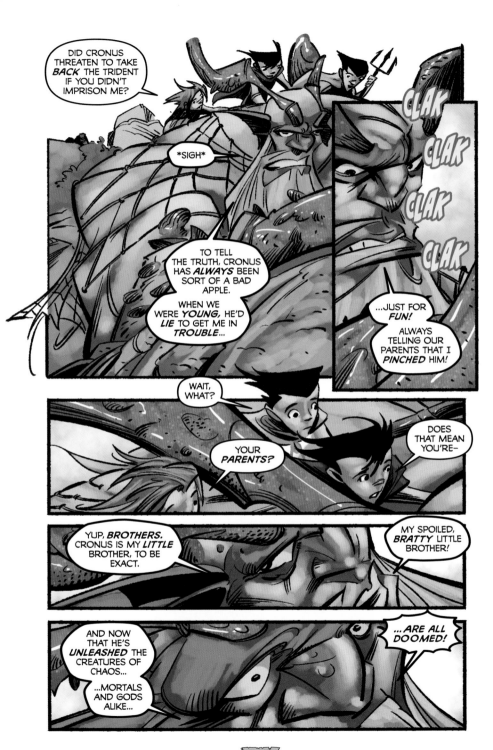

CRONUS IS SCHEMING TO RULE OVER *EVERYONE* WHO SURVIVES...

...AND THE *ONLY* THREATS TO HIS PLAN ARE *OLYMPIANS!*

BUT *WHY* ARE THEY A THREAT?

HOW? SOME KIND OF MAGICAL *POWERS?*

YOU MEAN YOU *DON'T KNOW?*

BECAUSE OF THE *PROPHECY!*

WHAT PROPHECY?

KRACKKK!

"AN OLYMPIAN SHALL RISE UP AND LEAD OTHER OLYMPIANS TO DEFEAT CRONUS."

BUT–

WHAT *NOW?*

RUMMMBLE

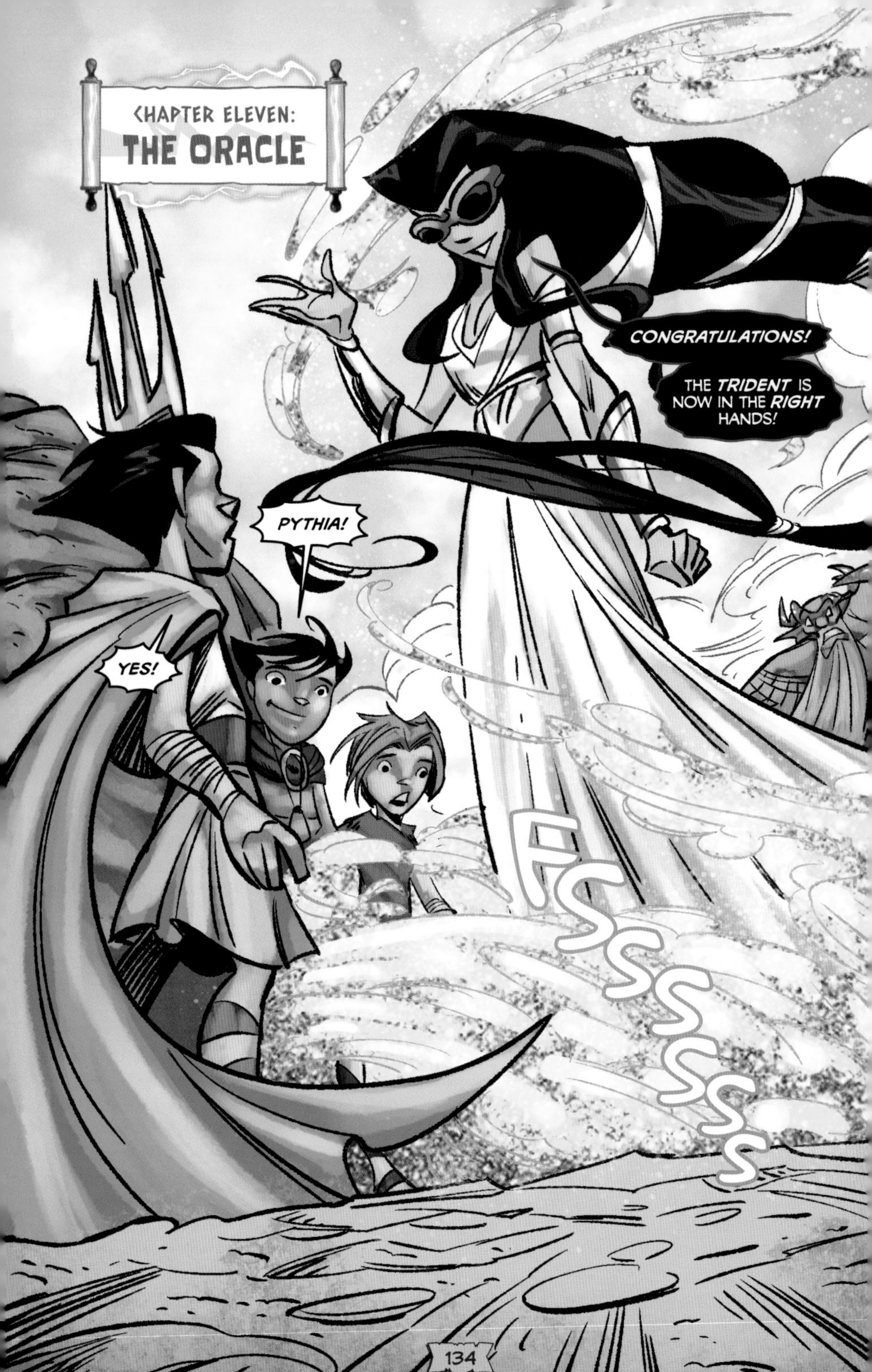
CHAPTER ELEVEN:
THE ORACLE
CONGRATULATIONS!
THE TRIDENT IS NOW IN THE RIGHT HANDS!
PYTHIA!
YES!
FSSSSSSS

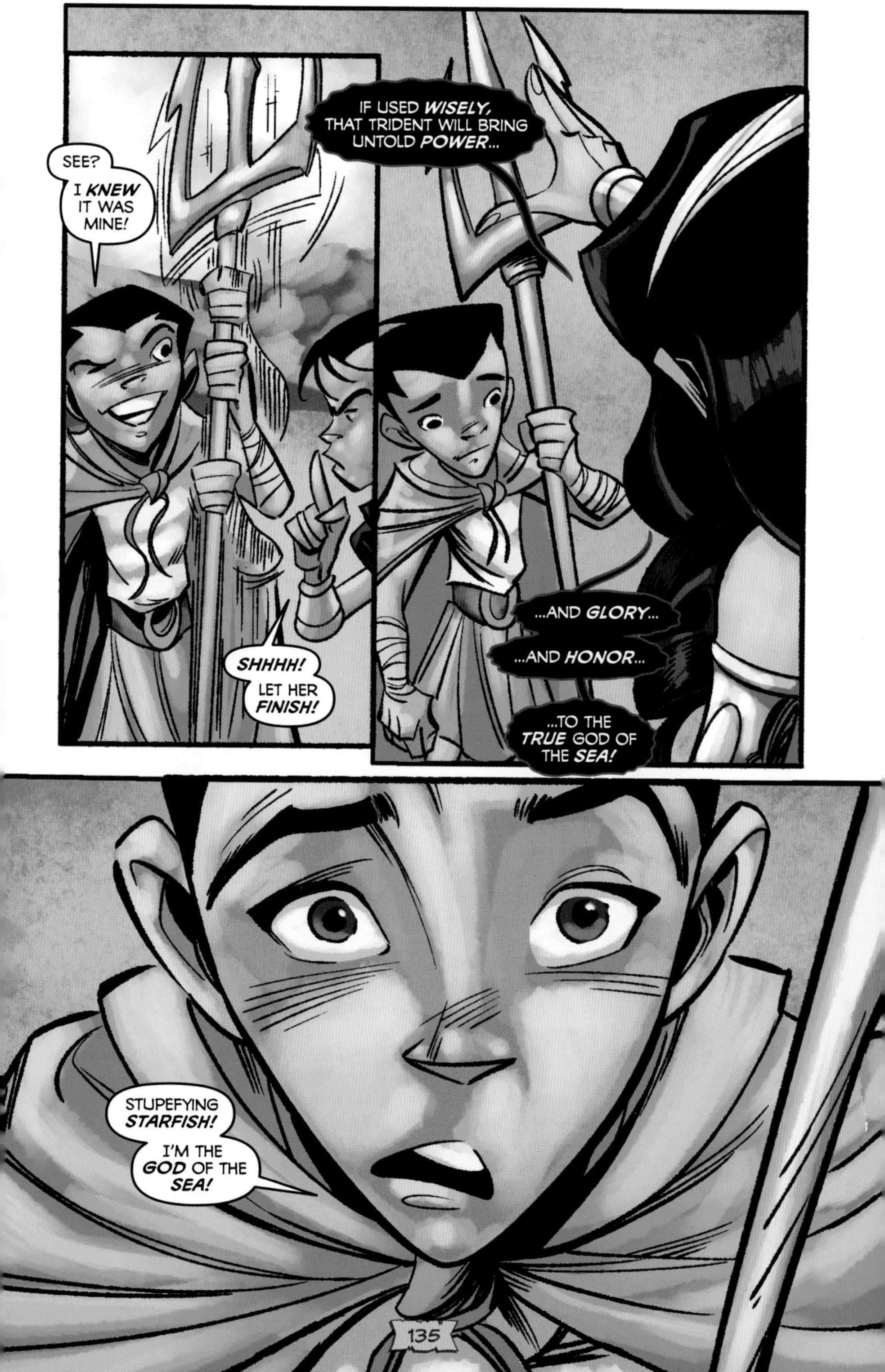

SEE? I KNEW IT WAS MINE!
SHHHH! LET HER FINISH!
IF USED WISELY, THAT TRIDENT WILL BRING UNTOLD POWER...
...AND GLORY...
...AND HONOR...
...TO THE TRUE GOD OF THE SEA!
STUPEFYING STARFISH!
I'M THE GOD OF THE SEA!

THE *HELM OF DARKNESS* RIGHTFULLY BELONGS TO THE ONE WHO IS *LORD* OF THE *UNDERWORLD!*

FIND IT— AND YOU WILL ALSO FIND *MORE* OF THE PERSONS YOU SEEK!

BUT BEWARE OF THE *SECOND* OF CRONUS'S *CREATURES OF CHAOS!*

FOR THEY ARE FAR, *FAR* MORE DANGEROUS THAN THE *ANDROPHAGO!!*

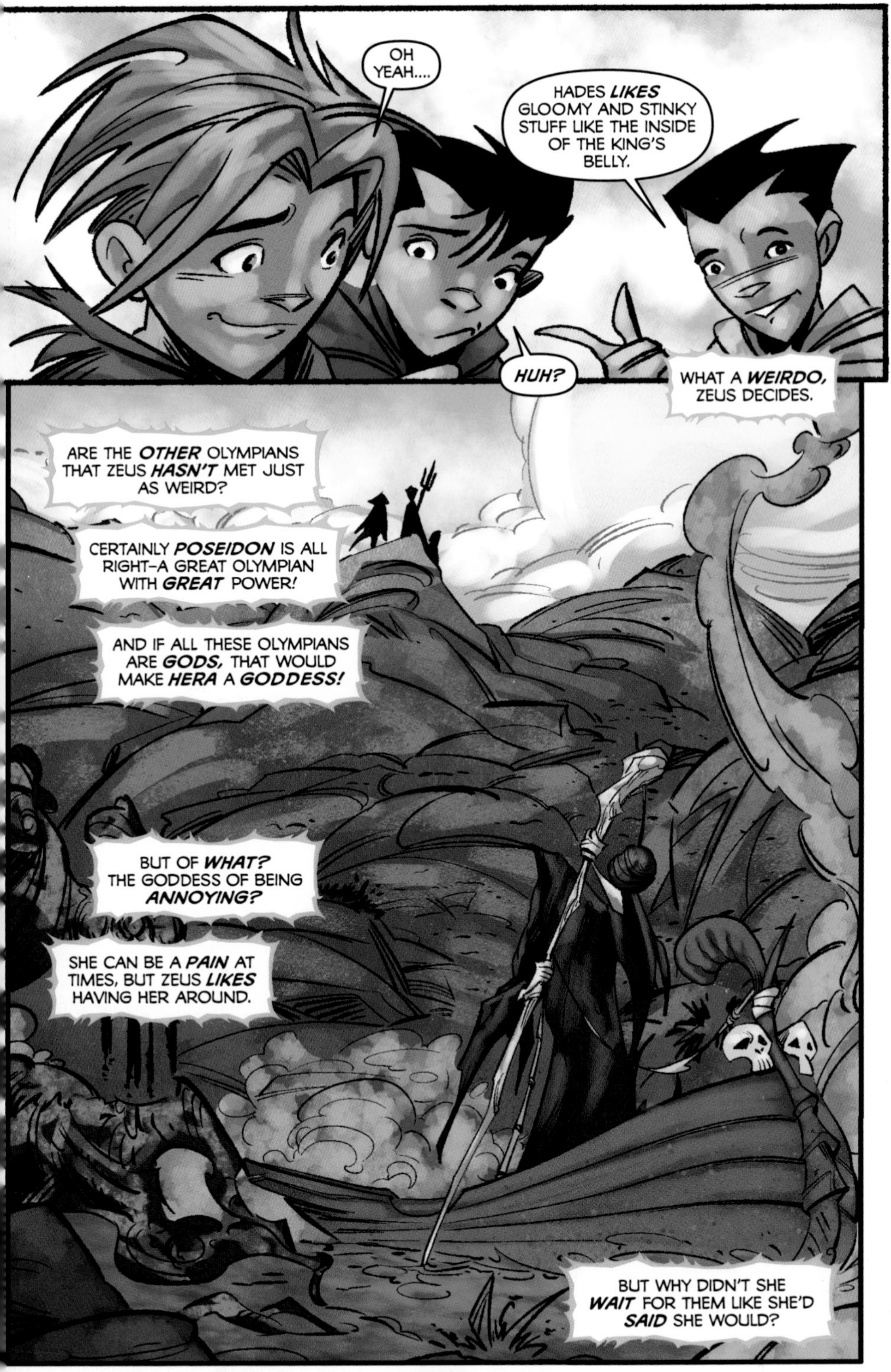

OH YEAH....
HADES LIKES GLOOMY AND STINKY STUFF LIKE THE INSIDE OF THE KING'S BELLY.
HUH?
WHAT A WEIRDO, ZEUS DECIDES.
ARE THE OTHER OLYMPIANS THAT ZEUS HASN'T MET JUST AS WEIRD?
CERTAINLY POSEIDON IS ALL RIGHT–A GREAT OLYMPIAN WITH GREAT POWER!
AND IF ALL THESE OLYMPIANS ARE GODS, THAT WOULD MAKE HERA A GODDESS!
BUT OF WHAT? THE GODDESS OF BEING ANNOYING?
SHE CAN BE A PAIN AT TIMES, BUT ZEUS LIKES HAVING HER AROUND.
BUT WHY DIDN'T SHE WAIT FOR THEM LIKE SHE'D SAID SHE WOULD?